Haunted
House
Stories

This edition is published in 2023 by Flame Tree 451

Flame Tree 451
6 Melbray Mews,
Fulham, London SW3 3NS
United Kingdom
www.flametree451.com

Flame Tree 451 is an imprint of Flame Tree Publishing Ltd
www.flametreepublishing.com

A CIP record for this book is available from the British Library

Print ISBN: 978-1-80417-593-4
ebook ISBN: 978-1-80417-597-2

23 25 27 28 26 24
1 3 5 7 8 6 4 2

Printed and bound in China

Haunted House Stories

With an introduction by
Hester Fox

Contents

A Taste for the Fantastic

From mystery to crime, the supernatural and fantasy to science fiction, the terrific range of paperbacks and ebooks from Flame Tree 451 offers a healthy diet of werewolves and mechanicals, vampires and villains, mad scientists, secret worlds, lost civilizations, escapist fantasies and dystopian visions. Discover a storehouse of tales gathered specifically for the reader of the fantastic.

Great works by H.G. Wells and Bram Stoker stand shoulder to shoulder with gripping reads by titans of the gothic novel (Charles Brockden Brown, Nathaniel Hawthorne), and individual novels by literary giants (Jane Austen, Charles Dickens, Emily Brontë) mingle with the intensity of H.P. Lovecraft and the psychological magic of Edgar Allan Poe.

Of course there are classic Conan Doyle adventures, Wilkie Collins mysteries and the pioneering fantasies of Mary Shelley, but there are so many other tales to tell: *The White Worm, Black Magic, The Murder Monster, The Awakening, Darkwater* and more.

Check our website for regular updates and new additions to our curated range of speculative fiction at *flametreepublishing.com*

Introduction

Every house, in its own way, is haunted.

A haunting is simply an unfinished story, and houses collect these as easily as they do dust. When we move on, we leave behind not just old furniture and peeling wallpaper, nail holes and faded photographs, but all sorts of earthly business that we cannot take with us. "Piled up like dead leaves...layers and layers of them, to preserve something forever budding underneath," muses Lady Jane of her ancestors, the previous tenants of her inherited estate, in Edith Wharton's 'Mr. Jones'. It is the people who have inhabited the walls before us, the mysterious and unknown lives that have been fueling our imaginations for as long as humans have been telling stories. The earliest known recorded haunted house story is believed to have been penned by Pliny the Younger in the first century CE, and, much like the plot of 'A Night of Horror' by James Edward Preston Muddock (writing as Dick Donovan), featured a spirit appealing to the home's occupant to help find its mortal remains so that it could have closure. In the present day, haunted houses continue to be a lucrative industry, whether in movies, or as a vacation destination (the infamous Lizzie Borden house, which now operates as a bed and breakfast, offers visitors the chance to participate in ghost hunts and haunted tours).

Perhaps it is because, as humans, we lack any sort of natural protection, and so our homes become our refuge, a calcified shell we build up around ourselves. They are an extension of us, reflective of our personalities and priorities. Yet homes are not inherently safe, are they? All sorts of horrors can happen behind closed doors, made all the more terrible because they are perpetrated by those closest to us. Ghost stories are a vehicle to repackage some of these traumas, a more palatable allegory that allows us to probe our deepest fears. In other cases, such as Mary E. Wilkins Freeman's story 'The Lost Ghost', the result of a traumatic event is responsible for creating a ghost looking for closure. Freeman rewards us with a bittersweet glimmer of hope that some of these injustices can be remedied in the next life. Likewise, in E.F. Benson's story 'How Fear Departed from the Long Gallery', a curse is broken by facing a long-forgotten trauma with love, an unspeakable tragedy in life finally made right by compassion in death.

I live in New England, where the past is ever present, houses of the first European settlers sitting shoulder-to-shoulder with painted Victorians, crooked old graveyards wedged in between brick row houses. These are homes that have seen generations of inhabitants come and go, and have witnessed countless joys and tragedies within their walls. Though certainly romantic, a house doesn't have to look the part in order to be haunted. In 'The Water Witch' by Henrietta Dorothy Everett (writing as H.D. Everett), the house in which our narrator is visiting is described as "A new-built place, raw, with no history behind it later than yesterday [...]" Yet that does not preclude it from being haunted by an unhappy spirit. Every house, once upon a time, was a new place, but there is always someone who has come before us, if not in the house itself, then the land. In the Western canon, these stories thus become a powerful lens through which to view events such as colonialism, slavery, and other horrors. They force us to hold up a mirror, to reconcile how we got here, and who called this place home before us.

There's a reason that the appeal of haunted house stories has not dwindled over the centuries. They promise us that the places that mean the most to us in this life will bear some vestige of us, that we are capable of leaving an echo, a shadow, long after we are gone. They give us hope that if some great tragedy befalls us before our natural time, that perhaps if we are lucky, we can find justice in the next world. They indulge our curiosity about lives we'll never live, people we will never know.

Outside the pages of a book, we can tell ourselves that there is a logical explanation, a scientific reason behind the strange occurrences in a supposedly haunted house, but who is to say? The student who takes lodgings in a house rumored to be haunted by the spirit of a merciless judge in Bram Stoker's 'The Judge's House' is not just skeptical about the warnings he receives about his new quarters, but finds them downright laughable. Too late, he learns that he is not immune to the fate of those who trespass in a place beset with evil. Science and reason may provide the illusion of safety, but they are no match for the primal human emotions that have seeped into the floorboards over centuries, woven themselves into the very fabric of the house. For those of us who don't believe in ghosts and haunted houses, these stories allow us to live vicariously and feel the thrill of fear. Perhaps, even deep down, they will open something inside of us, make believers of us after all.

The writers in this volume understood the power houses hold and the stories that unfold within them. They understood the fascination and morbid curiosity that manifests in us when we imagine who came before us. They were able to harness the anxiety that we feel as we shed one shell and scuttle into another, and the subsequent vulnerability as we step across the threshold and find that our new home is not quite as vacant as we'd expected.

Wherever you read these stories, take a moment to turn off your music, set aside your phone, and let yourself be still – really still. Can you hear it? Can you feel your neck prickle under unseen eyes? For that is the spirits of the past watching us, the weight of history pressing in around us.

Hester Fox
Concord, Massachusetts (Nipmuc land), 2023

Haunted
House
Stories

How Fear Departed from the Long Gallery

E.F. Benson

Church-Peveril is a house so beset and frequented by spectres, both visible and audible, that none of the family which it shelters under its acre and a half of green copper roofs takes psychical phenomena with any seriousness. For to the Peverils the appearance of a ghost is a matter of hardly greater significance than is the appearance of the post to those who live in more ordinary houses. It arrives, that is to say, practically every day, it knocks (or makes other noises), it is observed coming up the drive (or in other places). I myself, when staying there, have seen the present Mrs. Peveril, who is rather short-sighted, peer into the dusk, while we were taking our coffee on the terrace after dinner, and say to her daughter:

"My dear, was not that the Blue Lady who has just gone into the shrubbery. I hope she won't frighten Flo. Whistle for Flo, dear."

(Flo, it may be remarked, is the youngest and most precious of many dachshunds.)

Blanche Peveril gave a cursory whistle, and crunched the sugar left unmelted at the bottom of her coffee-cup between her very white teeth.

"Oh, darling, Flo isn't so silly as to mind," she said. "Poor blue Aunt Barbara is such a bore!"

"Whenever I meet her she always looks as if she wanted to speak to me, but when I say, 'What is it, Aunt Barbara?' she never utters, but only points somewhere towards the house, which is so vague. I believe there was something she wanted to confess about two hundred years ago, but she has forgotten what it is."

Here Flo gave two or three short pleased barks, and came out of the shrubbery wagging her tail, and capering round what appeared to me to be a perfectly empty space on the lawn.

"There! Flo has made friends with her," said Mrs. Peveril. "I wonder why she dresses in that very stupid shade of blue."

From this it may be gathered that even with regard to psychical phenomena there is some truth in the proverb that speaks of familiarity. But the Peverils do not exactly treat their ghosts with contempt, since most of that delightful family never despised anybody except such people as avowedly did not care for hunting or shooting, or golf or skating. And as all of their ghosts are of their family, it seems reasonable to suppose that they all, even the poor Blue Lady, excelled at one time in field-sports. So far, then, they harbour no such unkindness or contempt, but only pity. Of one Peveril, indeed, who broke his neck in vainly attempting to ride up the main staircase on a thoroughbred mare after some monstrous and violent deed in the back-garden, they are very fond, and Blanche comes downstairs in the morning with an eye unusually bright when she can announce that Master Anthony was "very loud" last night. He (apart from the fact of his having been so foul a ruffian) was a tremendous fellow across country, and they like these indications of the continuance of his superb vitality. In fact, it is supposed to be a compliment, when you go to stay at Church-Peveril, to be assigned a bedroom which is frequented by defunct members of the family. It means that you are worthy to look on the august and villainous dead, and you will find yourself shown into some vaulted or tapestried chamber, without benefit of electric light, and are told that great-great-grandmamma Bridget occasionally has vague business by the fireplace, but it is better not to talk to her, and that you will hear Master Anthony 'awfully well' if he attempts the front staircase any time before morning. There you are left for your night's repose, and, having quakingly undressed, begin reluctantly to put out your candles. It is draughty in these great chambers, and the solemn tapestry swings and bellows and subsides, and the firelight dances on the forms of huntsmen and warriors and stern pursuits. Then you climb into your bed, a bed so huge that you feel as if the desert of Sahara was spread for you, and pray, like the mariners who sailed with St. Paul, for day. And, all the time, you are aware that Freddy and Harry and Blanche and possibly even Mrs. Peveril are quite capable of dressing up and making disquieting tappings outside your door, so that when you open it some inconjecturable horror fronts you. For myself, I stick steadily to the assertion that I have an obscure valvular disease of the heart, and so sleep undisturbed in the new wing of the house where Aunt Barbara, and great-great-grandmamma Bridget and Master Anthony never penetrate. I forget the details of great-great-grandmamma Bridget, but she certainly cut the throat of some distant relation before she disembowelled herself with the axe that had been used at Agincourt. Before that she had led a very sultry life, crammed with amazing incident.

But there is one ghost at Church-Peveril at which the family never laugh, in which they feel no friendly and amused interest, and of which they only speak just as much as is necessary for the safety of their guests. More properly it should be described as two ghosts, for the 'haunt' in question is that of two very young children, who were twins. These, not without reason, the family take very seriously indeed. The story of them, as told me by Mrs. Peveril, is as follows:

In the year 1602, the same being the last of Queen Elizabeth's reign, a certain Dick Peveril was greatly in favour at Court. He was brother to Master Joseph Peveril, then owner of the family house and lands, who two years previously, at the respectable age of seventy-four, became father of twin boys, first-born of his progeny. It is known that the royal and ancient virgin had said to handsome Dick, who was nearly forty years his brother's junior, "'Tis pity that you are not master of Church-Peveril," and these words probably suggested to him a sinister design. Be that as it may, handsome Dick, who very adequately sustained the family reputation for wickedness, set off to ride down to Yorkshire, and found that, very conveniently, his brother Joseph had just been seized with an apoplexy, which appeared to be the result of a continued spell of hot weather combined with the necessity of quenching his thirst with an augmented amount of sack, and had actually died while handsome Dick, with God knows what thoughts in his mind, was journeying northwards. Thus it came about that he arrived at Church-Peveril just in time for his brother's funeral. It was with great propriety that he attended the obsequies, and returned to spend a sympathetic day or two of mourning with his widowed sister-in-law, who was but a faint-hearted dame, little fit to be mated with such hawks as these. On the second night of his stay, he did that which the Peverils regret to this day. He entered the room where the twins slept with their nurse, and quietly strangled the latter as she slept. Then he took the twins and put them into the fire which warms the long gallery. The weather, which up to the day of Joseph's death had been so hot, had changed suddenly to bitter cold, and the fire was heaped high with burning logs and was exultant with flame. In the core of this conflagration he struck out a cremation-chamber, and into that he threw the two children, stamping them down with his riding-boots. They could just walk, but they could not walk out of that ardent place. It is said that he laughed as he added more logs. Thus he became master of Church-Peveril.

The crime was never brought home to him, but he lived no longer than a year in the enjoyment of his blood-stained inheritance. When he lay a-dying he made his confession to the priest who attended him, but his spirit struggled forth from its fleshly coil before Absolution could be given him. On that very night there began in Church-Peveril the haunting which to this day is but seldom spoken of by the family, and then only in low tones and with serious mien. For only an hour or two after handsome Dick's death, one of the servants passing the door of the long gallery heard from within peals of the loud laughter so jovial and yet so sinister which he had thought would never be heard in the house again. In a moment of that cold courage which is so nearly akin to mortal terror he opened the door and entered, expecting to see he knew not what manifestation of him who lay dead in the room below. Instead he saw two little white-robed figures toddling towards him hand in hand across the moon-lit floor.

The watchers in the room below ran upstairs startled by the crash of his fallen body, and found him lying in the grip of some dread convulsion. Just before morning he regained consciousness and told his tale. Then pointing with trembling and ash-grey finger towards the door, he screamed aloud, and so fell back dead.

During the next fifty years this strange and terrible legend of the twin-babies became fixed and consolidated. Their appearance, luckily for those who inhabit the house, was exceedingly rare, and during these years they seem to have been seen four or five times only. On each occasion they appeared at night, between sunset and sunrise, always in the same long gallery, and always as two toddling children scarcely able to walk. And on each occasion the luckless individual who saw them died either speedily or terribly, or with both speed and terror, after the accursed vision had appeared to him. Sometimes he might live for a few months: he was lucky if he died, as did the servant who first saw them, in a few hours. Vastly more awful was the fate of a certain Mrs. Canning, who had the ill-luck to see them in the middle of the next century, or to be quite accurate, in the year 1760. By this time the hours and the place of their appearance were well known, and, as up till a year ago, visitors were warned not to go between sunset and sunrise into the long gallery.

But Mrs. Canning, a brilliantly clever and beautiful woman, admirer also and friend of the notorious sceptic M. Voltaire, wilfully went and sat night after night, in spite of all protestations, in the haunted place. For four evenings she saw nothing, but on the fifth she had her will, for the door in the middle of the gallery opened, and there came toddling towards her the ill-omened innocent little pair. It seemed that even then she was not frightened, but she thought it good, poor wretch, to mock at them, telling them it was time for them to get back into the fire. They gave no word in answer, but turned away from her crying and sobbing. Immediately after they disappeared from her vision and she rustled downstairs to where the family and guests in the house were waiting for her, with the triumphant announcement that she has seen them both, and must needs write to M. Voltaire, saying that she had spoken to spirits made manifest. It would make him laugh. But when some months later the whole news reached him he did not laugh at all.

Mrs. Canning was one of the great beauties of her day, and in the year 1760 she was at the height and zenith of her blossoming. The chief beauty, if it is possible to single out one point where all was so exquisite, lay in the dazzling colour and incomparable brilliance of her complexion. She was now just thirty years of age, but, in spite of the excesses of her life, retained the snow and roses of girlhood, and she courted the bright light of day which other women shunned, for it but showed to great advantage the splendour of her skin. In consequence she was very considerably dismayed one morning, about a fortnight after her strange experience in the long gallery, to observe on her left cheek, an inch or two below her turquoise-coloured eyes, a little greyish patch of skin, about as big as a threepenny piece. It was in vain that she applied her accustomed washes and unguents: vain, too, were the arts of her fardeuse and of her medical adviser. For a week she kept herself secluded, martyring herself with solitude and unaccustomed physics, and for result at the end of the week she had no amelioration to comfort herself with: instead this woeful grey patch had doubled itself in size. Thereafter the nameless disease, whatever it was, developed in new and terrible ways. From the centre of the discoloured place there sprouted forth little lichen-like tendrils of greenish-grey, and another patch appeared on her lower lip. This, too, soon vegetated, and one morning, on opening her eyes to the horror of a new day, she found that her vision was strangely blurred. She sprang to her looking-glass, and what she saw caused her to shriek aloud with horror. From under her upper eye-lid a fresh growth had sprung up, mushroom-like, in the night, and its filaments extended downwards, screening the pupil of her eye. Soon after, her tongue and throat were attacked: the air passages became obstructed, and death by suffocation was merciful after such suffering.

More terrible yet was the case of a certain Colonel Blantyre who fired at the children with his revolver. What he went through is not to be recorded here.

It is this haunting, then, that the Peverils take quite seriously, and every guest on his arrival in the house is told that the long gallery must not be entered after nightfall on any pretext whatever. By day, however, it is a delightful room and intrinsically merits description, apart from the fact that the due understanding of its geography is necessary for the account that here follows. It is full eighty feet in length, and is lit by a row of six tall windows looking over the gardens at the back of the house. A door communicates with the landing at the top of the main staircase, and about half-way down the gallery in the wall facing the windows is another door communicating with the back staircase and servants' quarters, and thus the gallery forms a constant place of passage for them in going to the rooms on the first landing. It was through this door that the baby-figures came when they appeared to Mrs. Canning, and on several other occasions they have been known to make their entry here, for the room out of which handsome Dick took them lies just beyond at the top of the back stairs. Further on again in the gallery is the fireplace into which he thrust them, and at the far end a large bow-window looks straight down the avenue. Above this fireplace there hangs with grim significance a portrait of handsome Dick, in the insolent beauty of early manhood, attributed to Holbein, and a dozen other portraits of great merit face the windows. During the day this is the most frequented sitting-room in the house, for its other visitors never appear there then, nor does it then ever resound with the harsh jovial laugh of handsome Dick, which sometimes, after dark has fallen, is heard by passers-by on the landing outside. But Blanche does not grow bright-eyed when she hears it: she shuts her ears and hastens to put a greater distance between her and the sound of that atrocious mirth.

But during the day the long gallery is frequented by many occupants, and much laughter in no wise sinister or saturnine resounds there. When summer lies hot over the land, those occupants lounge in the deep window seats, and when winter spreads his icy fingers and blows shrilly between his frozen palms, congregate round the fireplace at the far end, and perch, in companies of cheerful chatterers, upon sofa and chair, and chair-back and floor. Often have I sat there on long August evenings up till dressing-time, but never have I been there when anyone has seemed disposed to linger over-late without hearing the warning: "It is close on sunset: shall we go?" Later on in the shorter autumn days they often have tea laid there, and sometimes it has happened that, even while merriment was most uproarious, Mrs. Peveril has suddenly looked out of the window and said, "My dears, it is getting so late: let us finish our nonsense downstairs in the hall." And then for a moment a curious hush always falls on loquacious family and guests alike, and as if some bad news had just been known, we all make our silent way out of the place.

But the spirits of the Peverils (of the living ones, that is to say) are the most mercurial imaginable, and the blight which the thought of handsome Dick and his doings casts over them passes away again with amazing rapidity.

A typical party, large, young, and peculiarly cheerful, was staying at Church-Peveril shortly after Christmas last year, and as usual on December 31, Mrs. Peveril was giving her annual New Year's Eve ball. The house was quite full, and she had commandeered as well the greater part of the Peveril Arms to provide sleeping-quarters for the overflow from the house. For some days past a black and windless frost had stopped all hunting, but it is an ill windlessness that blows no good (if so mixed a metaphor may be forgiven), and the lake below the house had for the last day or two been covered with an adequate and admirable sheet of ice. Everyone in the house had been occupied all the morning of that day in performing swift and violent manoeuvres on the elusive surface, and as soon as lunch was over we all, with one exception, hurried out again. This one exception was Madge Dalrymple, who had had the misfortune to fall rather badly earlier in the day, but hoped, by resting her injured knee, instead of joining the skaters again, to be able to dance that evening. The hope, it is true, was the most sanguine sort, for she could but hobble ignobly back to the house, but with the breezy optimism which characterises the Peverils (she is Blanche's first cousin), she remarked that it would be but tepid enjoyment that she could, in her present state, derive from further skating, and thus she sacrificed little, but might gain much.

Accordingly, after a rapid cup of coffee which was served in the long gallery, we left Madge comfortably reclined on the big sofa at right-angles to the fireplace, with an attractive book to beguile the tedium till tea. Being of the family, she knew all about handsome Dick and the babies, and the fate of Mrs. Canning and Colonel Blantyre, but as we went out I heard Blanche say to her, "Don't run it too fine, dear," and Madge had replied, "No; I'll go away well before sunset." And so we left her alone in the long gallery.

Madge read her attractive book for some minutes, but failing to get absorbed in it, put it down and limped across to the window. Though it was still but little after two, it was but a dim and uncertain light that entered, for the crystalline brightness of the morning had given place to a veiled obscurity produced by flocks of thick clouds which were coming sluggishly up from the north-east. Already the whole sky was overcast with them, and occasionally a few snowflakes fluttered waveringly down past the long windows. From the darkness and bitter cold of the afternoon, it seemed to her that there was like to be a heavy snowfall before long, and these outward signs were echoed inwardly in her by that muffled drowsiness of the brain, which to those who are sensitive to the pressures and lightness of weather portends storm. Madge was peculiarly the prey of such external influences: to her a brisk morning gave an ineffable brightness and briskness of spirit, and correspondingly the approach of heavy weather produced a somnolence in sensation that both drowsed and depressed her.

It was in such mood as this that she limped back again to the sofa beside the log-fire. The whole house was comfortably heated by water-pipes, and though the fire of logs and peat, an adorable mixture, had been allowed to burn low, the room was very warm. Idly she watched the dwindling flames, not opening her book again, but lying on the sofa with face towards the fireplace, intending drowsily and not immediately to go to her own room and spend the hours, until the return of the skaters made gaiety in the house again, in writing one or two neglected letters. Still drowsily she began thinking over what she had to communicate: one letter several days overdue should go to her mother, who was immensely interested in the psychical affairs of the family. She would tell her how Master Anthony had been prodigiously active on the staircase a night or two ago, and how the Blue Lady, regardless of the severity of the weather, had been seen by Mrs. Peveril that morning, strolling about. It was rather interesting: the Blue Lady had gone down the laurel walk and had been seen by her to enter the stables, where, at the moment, Freddy Peveril was inspecting the frost-bound hunters. Identically then, a sudden panic had spread through the stables, and the horses had whinnied and kicked, and shied, and sweated. Of the fatal twins nothing had been seen for many years past, but, as her mother knew, the Peverils never used the long gallery after dark.

Then for a moment she sat up, remembering that she was in the long gallery now. But it was still but a little after half-past two, and if she went to her room in half an hour, she would have ample time to write this and another letter before tea. Till then she would read her book. But she found she had left it on the windowsill, and it seemed scarcely worthwhile to get it. She felt exceedingly drowsy.

The sofa where she lay had been lately recovered, in a greyish green shade of velvet, somewhat the colour of lichen. It was of very thick soft texture, and she luxuriously stretched her arms out, one on each side of her body, and pressed her fingers into the nap. How horrible that story of Mrs. Canning was: the growth on her face was of the colour of lichen. And then without further transition or blurring of thought Madge fell asleep.

She dreamed. She dreamed that she awoke and found herself exactly where she had gone to sleep, and in exactly the same attitude. The flames from the logs had burned up again, and leaped on the walls, fitfully illuminating the picture of handsome Dick above the fireplace. In her dream she knew exactly what she had done today, and for what reason she was lying here now instead of being out with the rest of the skaters. She remembered also (still dreaming), that she was going to write a letter or two before tea, and prepared to get up in order to go to her room. As she half-rose she caught sight of her own arms lying out on each side of her on the grey velvet sofa.

But she could not see where her hands ended, and where the grey velvet began: her fingers seemed to have melted into the stuff. She could see her wrists quite clearly, and a blue vein on the backs of her hands, and here and there a knuckle. Then, in her dream, she remembered the last thought which had been in her mind before she fell asleep, namely the growth of the lichen-coloured vegetation on the face and the eyes and the throat of Mrs. Canning. At that thought the strangling terror of real nightmare began: she knew that she was being transformed into this grey stuff, and she was absolutely unable to move. Soon the grey would spread up her arms, and over her feet; when they came in from skating they would find here nothing but a huge misshapen cushion of lichen-coloured velvet, and that would be she. The horror grew more acute, and then by a violent effort she shook herself free of the clutches of this very evil dream, and she awoke.

For a minute or two she lay there, conscious only of the tremendous relief at finding herself awake. She felt again with her fingers the pleasant touch of the velvet, and drew them backwards and forwards, assuring herself that she was not, as her dream had suggested, melting into greyness and softness. But she was still, in spite of the violence of her awakening, very sleepy, and lay there till, looking down, she was aware that she could not see her hands at all. It was very nearly dark.

At that moment a sudden flicker of flame came from the dying fire, and a flare of burning gas from the peat flooded the room. The portrait of handsome Dick looked evilly down on her, and her hands were visible again. And then a panic worse than the panic of her dreams seized her.

Daylight had altogether faded, and she knew that she was alone in the dark in the terrible gallery.

This panic was of the nature of nightmare, for she felt unable to move for terror. But it was worse than nightmare because she knew she was awake. And then the full cause of this frozen fear dawned on her; she knew with the certainty of absolute conviction that she was about to see the twin-babies.

She felt a sudden moisture break out on her face, and within her mouth her tongue and throat went suddenly dry, and she felt her tongue grate along the inner surface of her teeth. All power of movement had slipped from her limbs, leaving them dead and inert, and she stared with wide eyes into the blackness. The spurt of flame from the peat had burned itself out again, and darkness encompassed her.

Then on the wall opposite her, facing the windows, there grew a faint light of dusky crimson.

For a moment she thought it but heralded the approach of the awful vision, then hope revived in her heart, and she remembered that thick clouds had overcast the sky before she went to sleep, and guessed that this light came from the sun not yet quite sunk and set. This sudden revival of hope gave her the necessary stimulus, and she sprang off the sofa where she lay. She looked out of the window and saw the dull glow on the horizon. But before she could take a step forward it was obscured again. A tiny sparkle of light came from the hearth which did no more than illuminate the tiles of the fireplace, and snow falling heavily tapped at the window panes. There was neither light nor sound except these.

But the courage that had come to her, giving her the power of movement, had not quite deserted her, and she began feeling her way down the gallery. And then she found that she was lost. She stumbled against a chair, and, recovering herself, stumbled against another. Then a table barred her way, and, turning swiftly aside, she found herself up against the back of a sofa.

Once more she turned and saw the dim gleam of the firelight on the side opposite to that on which she expected it. In her blind gropings she must have reversed her direction. But which way was she to go now. She seemed blocked in by furniture. And all the time insistent and imminent was the fact that the two innocent terrible ghosts were about to appear to her.

Then she began to pray. "Lighten our darkness, O Lord," she said to herself. But she could not remember how the prayer continued, and she had sore need of it. There was something about the perils of the night. All this time she felt about her with groping, fluttering hands. The fire-glimmer which should have been on her left was on her right again; therefore she must turn herself round again. "Lighten our darkness," she whispered, and then aloud she repeated, "Lighten our darkness."

She stumbled up against a screen, and could not remember the existence of any such screen.

Hastily she felt beside it with blind hands, and touched something soft and velvety. Was it the sofa on which she had lain? If so, where was the head of it. It had a head and a back and feet – it was like a person, all covered with grey lichen. Then she lost her head completely. All that remained to her was to pray; she was lost, lost in this awful place, where no one came in the dark except the babies that cried. And she heard her voice rising from whisper to speech, and speech to scream. She shrieked out the holy words, she yelled them as if blaspheming as she groped among tables and chairs and the pleasant things of ordinary life which had become so terrible.

Then came a sudden and an awful answer to her screamed prayer. Once more a pocket of inflammable gas in the peat on the hearth was reached by the smouldering embers, and the room started into light. She saw the evil eyes of handsome Dick, she saw the little ghostly snowflakes falling thickly outside. And she saw where she was, just opposite the door through which the terrible twins made their entrance. Then the flame went out again, and left her in blackness once more. But she had gained something, for she had her geography now. The centre of the room was bare of furniture, and one swift dart would take her to the door of the landing above the main staircase and into safety. In that gleam she had been able to see the handle of the door, bright-brassed, luminous like a star. She would go straight for it; it was but a matter of a few seconds now.

She took a long breath, partly of relief, partly to satisfy the demands of her galloping heart.

But the breath was only half-taken when she was stricken once more into the immobility of nightmare.

There came a little whisper, it was no more than that, from the door opposite which she stood, and through which the twin-babies entered. It was not quite dark outside it, for she could see that the door was opening. And there stood in the opening two little white figures, side by side. They came towards her slowly, shufflingly. She could not see face or form at all distinctly, but the two little white figures were advancing. She knew them to be the ghosts of terror, innocent of the awful doom they were bound to bring, even as she was innocent. With the inconceivable rapidity of thought, she made up her mind what to do. She had not hurt them or laughed at them, and they, they were but babies when the wicked and bloody deed had sent them to their burning death. Surely the spirits of these children would not be inaccessible to the cry of one who was of the same blood as they, who had committed no fault that merited the doom they brought. If she entreated them they might have mercy, they might forebear to bring the curse on her, they might allow her to pass out of the place without blight, without the sentence of death, or the shadow of things worse than death upon her.

It was but for the space of a moment that she hesitated, then she sank down on to her knees, and stretched out her hands towards them.

"Oh, my dears," she said, "I only fell asleep. I have done no more wrong than that—"

She paused a moment, and her tender girl's heart thought no more of herself, but only of them, those little innocent spirits on whom so awful a doom was laid, that they should bring death where other children bring laughter, and doom for delight. But all those who had seen them before had dreaded and feared them, or had mocked at them.

Then, as the enlightenment of pity dawned on her, her fear fell from her like the wrinkled sheath that holds the sweet folded buds of Spring.

"Dears, I am so sorry for you," she said. "It is not your fault that you must bring me what you must bring, but I am not afraid any longer. I am only sorry for you. God bless you, you poor darlings."

She raised her head and looked at them. Though it was so dark, she could now see their faces, though all was dim and wavering, like the light of pale flames shaken by a draught. But the faces were not miserable or fierce – they smiled at her with shy little baby smiles. And as she looked they grew faint, fading slowly away like wreaths of vapour in frosty air.

Madge did not at once move when they had vanished, for instead of fear there was wrapped round her a wonderful sense of peace, so happy and serene that she would not willingly stir, and so perhaps disturb it. But before long she got up, and feeling her way, but without any sense of nightmare pressing her on, or frenzy of fear to spur her, she went out of the long gallery, to find Blanche just coming upstairs whistling and swinging her skates.

"How's the leg, dear," she asked. "You're not limping any more."

Till that moment Madge had not thought of it.

"I think it must be all right," she said; "I had forgotten it, anyhow. Blanche, dear, you won't be frightened for me, will you, but – but I have seen the twins."

For a moment Blanche's face whitened with terror.

"What?" she said in a whisper.

"Yes, I saw them just now. But they were kind, they smiled at me, and I was so sorry for them. And somehow I am sure I have nothing to fear."

It seems that Madge was right, for nothing has come to touch her. Something, her attitude to them, we must suppose, her pity, her sympathy, touched and dissolved and annihilated the curse.

Indeed, I was at Church-Peveril only last week, arriving there after dark. Just as I passed the gallery door, Blanche came out.

"Ah, there you are," she said: "I've just been seeing the twins. They looked too sweet and stopped nearly ten minutes. Let us have tea at once."

The Decoy

Algernon Blackwood

It belonged to the category of unlovely houses about which an ugly superstition clings, one reason being, perhaps, its inability to inspire interest in itself without assistance. It seemed too ordinary to possess individuality, much less to exert an influence. Solid and ungainly, its huge bulk dwarfing the park timber, its best claim to notice was a negative one – it was unpretentious.

From the little hill its expressionless windows stared across the Kentish Weald, indifferent to weather, dreary in winter, bleak in spring, unblessed in summer. Some colossal hand had tossed it down, then let it starve to death, a country mansion that might well strain the adjectives of advertisers and find inheritors with difficulty. Its soul had fled, said some; it had committed suicide, thought others; and it was an inheritor, before he killed himself in the library, who thought this latter, yielding, apparently, to an hereditary taint in the family. For two other inheritors followed suit, with an interval of twenty years between them, and there was no clear reason to explain the three disasters. Only the first owner, indeed, lived permanently in the house, the others using it in the summer months and then deserting it with relief. Hence, when John Burley, present inheritor, assumed possession, he entered a house about which clung an ugly superstition, based, nevertheless, upon a series of undeniably ugly facts.

This century deals harshly with superstitious folk, deeming them fools or charlatans; but John Burley, robust, contemptuous of half lights, did not deal harshly with them, because he did not deal with them at all. He was hardly aware of their existence. He ignored them as he ignored, say, the Esquimaux, poets, and other human aspects that did not touch his scheme of life. A successful business man, he concentrated on what was real; he dealt with business people. His philanthropy, on a big scale, was also real; yet, though he would have denied it vehemently, he had his superstition as well. No man exists without some taint of superstition in his blood; the racial heritage is too rich to be escaped entirely. Burley's took this form – that unless he gave his tithe to the poor he would not prosper. This ugly mansion, he decided, would make an ideal Convalescent Home.

"Only cowards or lunatics kill themselves," he declared flatly, when his use of the house was criticised. "I'm neither one nor t'other." He let out his gusty, boisterous laugh. In his invigorating atmosphere such weakness seemed contemptible, just as superstition in his presence seemed feeblest ignorance. Even its picturesqueness faded. "I can't conceive," he boomed, "can't even imagine to myself," he added emphatically, "the state of mind in which a man can think of suicide, much less do it." He threw his chest out with a challenging air. "I tell you, Nancy, it's either cowardice or mania. And I've no use for either."

Yet he was easy-going and good-humoured in his denunciation. He admitted his limitations with a hearty laugh his wife called noisy. Thus he made allowances for the fairy fears of sailorfolk, and had even been known to mention haunted ships his companies owned. But he did so in the terms of tonnage and £ s. d. His scope was big; details were made for clerks.

His consent to pass a night in the mansion was the consent of a practical business man and philanthropist who dealt condescendingly with foolish human nature. It was based on the common-sense of tonnage and £ s. d. The local newspapers had revived the silly story of the suicides, calling attention to the effect of the superstition upon the fortunes of the house, and so, possibly, upon the fortunes of its present owner. But the mansion, otherwise a white elephant, was precisely ideal for his purpose, and so trivial a matter as spending a night in it should not stand in the way. "We must take people as we find them, Nancy."

His young wife had her motive, of course, in making the proposal, and, if she was amused by what she called 'spook-hunting', he saw no reason to refuse her the indulgence. He loved her, and took her as he found her – late in life. To allay the superstitions of prospective staff and patients and supporters, all, in fact, whose goodwill was necessary to success, he faced this boredom of a night in the building before its opening was announced. "You see, John, if you, the owner, do this, it will nip damaging talk in the bud. If anything went wrong later it would only be put down to this suicide idea, this haunting influence. The Home will have a bad name from the start. There'll be endless trouble. It will be a failure."

"You think my spending a night there will stop the nonsense?" he inquired.

"According to the old legend it breaks the spell," she replied. "That's the condition, anyhow."

"But somebody's sure to die there sooner or later," he objected. "We can't prevent that."

"We can prevent people whispering that they died unnaturally." She explained the working of the public mind.

"I see," he replied, his lip curling, yet quick to gauge the truth of what she told him about collective instinct.

"Unless *you* take poison in the hall," she added laughingly, "or elect to hang yourself with your braces from the hat peg."

"I'll do it," he agreed, after a moment's thought. "I'll sit up with you. It will be like a honeymoon over again, you and I on the spree – eh?" He was even interested now; the boyish side of him was touched perhaps; but his enthusiasm was less when she explained that three was a better number than two on such an expedition.

"I've often done it before, John. We were always three."

"Who?" he asked bluntly. He looked wonderingly at her, but she answered that if anything went wrong a party of three provided a better margin for help. It was sufficiently obvious. He listened and agreed. "I'll get young Mortimer," he suggested. "Will he do?"

She hesitated. "Well – he's cheery; he'll be interested, too. Yes, he's as good as another." She seemed indifferent.

"And he'll make the time pass with his stories," added her husband.

So Captain Mortimer, late officer on a T.B.D., a 'cheery lad', afraid of nothing, cousin of Mrs. Burley, and now filling a good post in the company's London offices, was engaged as third hand in the expedition. But Captain Mortimer was young and ardent, and Mrs. Burley was young and pretty and ill-mated, and John Burley was a neglectful, and self-satisfied husband.

Fate laid the trap with cunning, and John Burley, blind-eyed, careless of detail, floundered into it. He also floundered out again, though in a fashion none could have expected of him.

The night agreed upon eventually was as near to the shortest in the year as John Burley could contrive – June 18th – when the sun set at 8:18 and rose about a quarter to four. There would be barely three hours of true darkness. "You're the expert," he admitted, as she explained that sitting through the actual darkness only was required, not necessarily from sunset to sunrise. "We'll do the thing properly. Mortimer's not very keen, he had a dance or something," he added, noticing the look of annoyance that flashed swiftly in her eyes; "but he got out of it. He's coming." The pouting expression of the spoilt woman amused him. "Oh, no, he didn't need much persuading really," he assured her. "Some girl or other, of course. He's young, remember." To which no comment was forthcoming, though the implied comparison made her flush.

They motored from South Audley Street after an early tea, in due course passing Sevenoaks and entering the Kentish Weald; and, in order that the necessary advertisement should be given, the chauffeur, warned strictly to keep their purpose quiet, was to put up at the country inn and fetch them an hour after sunrise; they would breakfast in London. "He'll tell everybody," said his practical and cynical master; "the local newspaper will have it all next day. A few hours' discomfort is worth while if it ends the nonsense. We'll read and smoke, and Mortimer shall tell us yarns about the sea." He went with the driver into the house to superintend the arrangement of the room, the lights, the hampers of food, and so forth, leaving the pair upon the lawn.

"Four hours isn't much, but it's something," whispered Mortimer, alone with her for the first time since they started. "It's simply ripping of you to have got me in. You look divine tonight. You're the most wonderful woman in the world." His blue eyes shone with the hungry desire he mistook for love. He looked as if he had blown in from the sea, for his skin was tanned and his light hair bleached a little by the sun. He took her hand, drawing her out of the slanting sunlight towards the rhododendrons.

"I didn't, you silly boy. It was John suggested your coming." She released her hand with an affected effort. "Besides, you overdid it – pretending you had a dance."

"You could have objected," he said eagerly, "and didn't. Oh, you're too lovely, you're delicious!" He kissed her suddenly with passion. There was a tiny struggle, in which she yielded too easily, he thought.

"Harry, you're an idiot!" she cried breathlessly, when he let her go. "I really don't know how you dare! And John's your friend. Besides, you know" – she glanced round quickly – "it isn't safe here." Her eyes shone happily, her cheeks were flaming. She looked what she was, a pretty, young, lustful animal, false to ideals, true to selfish passion only. "Luckily," she added, "he trusts me too fully to think anything."

The young man, worship in his eyes, laughed gaily. "There's no harm in a kiss," he said. "You're a child to him, he never thinks of you as a woman. Anyhow, his head's full of ships and kings and sealing-wax," he comforted her, while respecting her sudden instinct which warned him not to touch her again, "and he never sees anything. Why, even at ten yards—"

From twenty yards away a big voice interrupted him, as John Burley came round a corner of the house and across the lawn towards them. The chauffeur, he announced, had left the hampers in the room on the first floor and gone back to the inn. "Let's take a walk round," he added, joining them, "and see the garden. Five minutes before sunset we'll go in and feed." He laughed. "We must do the thing faithfully, you know, mustn't we, Nancy? Dark to dark, remember. Come on,

Mortimer" – he took the young man's arm – "a last look round before we go in and hang ourselves from adjoining hooks in the matron's room!" He reached out his free hand towards his wife.

"Oh, hush, John!" she said quickly. "I don't like – especially now the dusk is coming." She shivered, as though it were a genuine little shiver, pursing her lips deliciously as she did so; whereupon he drew her forcibly to him, saying he was sorry, and kissed her exactly where she had been kissed two minutes before, while young Mortimer looked on. "We'll take care of you between us," he said. Behind a broad back the pair exchanged a swift but meaning glance, for there was that in his tone which enjoined wariness, and perhaps after all he was not so blind as he appeared. They had their code, these two. "All's well," was signalled; "but another time be more careful!"

There still remained some minutes' sunlight before the huge red ball of fire would sink behind the wooded hills, and the trio, talking idly, a flutter of excitement in two hearts certainly, walked among the roses. It was a perfect evening, windless, perfumed, warm. Headless shadows preceded them gigantically across the lawn as they moved, and one side of the great building lay already dark; bats were flitting, moths darted to and fro above the azalea and rhododendron clumps. The talk turned chiefly on the uses of the mansion as a Convalescent Home, its probable running cost, suitable staff, and so forth.

"Come along," John Burley said presently, breaking off and turning abruptly, "we must be inside, actually inside, before the sun's gone. We must fulfil the conditions faithfully," he repeated, as though fond of the phrase. He was in earnest over everything in life, big or little, once he set his hand to it.

They entered, this incongruous trio of ghost-hunters, no one of them really intent upon the business in hand, and went slowly upstairs to the great room where the hampers lay. Already in the hall it was dark enough for three electric torches to flash usefully and help their steps as they moved with caution, lighting one corner after another. The air inside was chill and damp. "Like an unused museum," said Mortimer. "I can smell the specimens." They looked about them, sniffing. "That's humanity," declared his host, employer, friend, "with cement and whitewash to flavour it"; and all three laughed as Mrs. Burley said she wished they had picked some roses and brought them in. Her husband was again in front on the broad staircase, Mortimer just behind him, when she called out. "I don't like being last," she exclaimed. "It's so black behind me in the hall. I'll come between you two," and the sailor took her outstretched hand, squeezing it, as he passed her up. "There's a figure, remember," she said hurriedly, turning to gain her husband's attention, as when she touched wood at home. "A figure is seen; that's part of the story. The figure of a man." She gave a tiny shiver of pleasurable, half-imagined alarm as she took his arm.

"I hope we shall see it," he mentioned prosaically.

"I hope we shan't," she replied with emphasis. "It's only seen before – something happens." Her husband said nothing, while Mortimer remarked facetiously that it would be a pity if they had their trouble for nothing. "Something can hardly happen to all three of us," he said lightly, as they entered a large room where the paper-hangers had conveniently left a rough table of bare planks. Mrs. Burley, busy with her own thoughts, began to unpack the sandwiches and wine. Her husband strolled over to the window. He seemed restless.

"So this," his deep voice startled her, "is where one of us" – he looked round him – "is to—"

"John!" She stopped him sharply, with impatience. "Several times already I've begged you." Her voice rang rather shrill and querulous in the empty room, a new note in it. She was beginning to feel the atmosphere of the place, perhaps. On the sunny lawn it had not touched her, but now, with the fall of night, she was aware of it, as shadow called to shadow and the kingdom of darkness gathered power. Like a great whispering gallery, the whole house listened.

"Upon my word, Nancy," he said with contrition, as he came and sat down beside her, "I quite forgot again. Only I cannot take it seriously. It's so utterly unthinkable to me that a man—"

"But why evoke the idea at all?" she insisted in a lowered voice, that snapped despite its faintness. "Men, after all, don't do such things for nothing."

"We don't know everything in the universe, do we?" Mortimer put in, trying clumsily to support her. "All I know just now is that I'm famished and this veal and ham pie is delicious." He was very busy with his knife and fork. His foot rested lightly on her own beneath the table; he could not keep his eyes off her face; he was continually passing new edibles to her.

"No," agreed John Burley, "not everything. You're right there."

She kicked the younger man gently, flashing a warning with her eyes as well, while her husband, emptying his glass, his head thrown back, looked straight at them over the rim, apparently seeing nothing. They smoked their cigarettes round the table, Burley lighting a big cigar. "Tell us about the figure, Nancy?" he inquired. "At least there's no harm in that. It's new to me. I hadn't heard about a figure." And she did so willingly, turning her chair sideways from the dangerous, reckless feet. Mortimer could now no longer touch her. "I know very little," she confessed; "only what the paper said. It's a man.... And he changes."

"How changes?" asked her husband. "Clothes, you mean, or what?"

Mrs. Burley laughed, as though she was glad to laugh. Then she answered: "According to the story, he shows himself each time to the man—"

"The man who—?"

"Yes, yes, of course. He appears to the man who dies – as himself."

"H'm," grunted her husband, naturally puzzled. He stared at her.

"Each time the chap saw his own double" – Mortimer came this time usefully to the rescue – "before he did it."

Considerable explanation followed, involving much psychic jargon from Mrs. Burley, which fascinated and impressed the sailor, who thought her as wonderful as she was lovely, showing it in his eyes for all to see. John Burley's attention wandered. He moved over to the window, leaving them to finish the discussion between them; he took no part in it, made no comment even, merely listening idly and watching them with an air of absent-mindedness through the cloud of cigar smoke round his head. He moved from window to window, ensconcing himself in turn in each deep embrasure, examining the fastenings, measuring the thickness of the stonework with his handkerchief. He seemed restless, bored, obviously out of place in this ridiculous expedition. On his big massive face lay a quiet, resigned expression his wife had never seen before. She noticed it now as, the discussion ended, the pair tidied away the *débris* of dinner, lit the spirit lamp for coffee and laid out a supper which would be very welcome with the dawn. A draught passed through the room, making the papers flutter on the table. Mortimer turned down the smoking lamps with care.

"Wind's getting up a bit – from the south," observed Burley from his niche, closing one half of the casement window as he said it. To do this, he turned his back a moment, fumbling for several seconds with the latch, while Mortimer, noting it, seized his sudden opportunity with the foolish abandon of his age and temperament. Neither he nor his victim perceived that, against the outside darkness, the interior of the room was plainly reflected in the window-pane. One reckless, the other terrified, they snatched the fearful joy, which might, after all, have been lengthened by another full half-minute, for the head they feared, followed by the shoulders, pushed through the side of the casement still open, and remained outside, taking in the night.

"A grand air," said his deep voice, as the head drew in again, "I'd like to be at sea a night like this." He left the casement open and came across the room towards them. "Now," he said cheerfully, arranging a seat for himself, "let's get comfortable for the night. Mortimer, we expect stories from you without ceasing, until dawn or the ghost arrives. Horrible stories of chains and headless men, remember. Make it a night we shan't forget in a hurry." He produced his gust of laughter.

They arranged their chairs, with other chairs to put their feet on, and Mortimer contrived a footstool by means of a hamper for the smallest feet; the air grew thick with tobacco smoke; eyes flashed and answered, watched perhaps as well; ears listened and perhaps grew wise; occasionally, as a window shook, they started and looked round; there were sounds about the house from time to time, when the entering wind, using broken or open windows, set loose objects rattling.

But Mrs. Burley vetoed horrible stories with decision. A big, empty mansion, lonely in the country, and even with the comfort of John Burley and a lover in it, has its atmosphere. Furnished rooms are far less ghostly. This atmosphere now came creeping everywhere, through spacious halls and sighing corridors, silent, invisible, but all-pervading, John Burley alone impervious to it, unaware of its soft attack upon the nerves. It entered possibly with the summer night wind, but possibly it was always there.... And Mrs. Burley looked often at her husband, sitting near her at an angle; the light fell on his fine strong face; she felt that, though apparently so calm and quiet, he was really very restless; something about him was a little different; she could not define it; his mouth seemed set as with an effort; he looked, she thought curiously to herself, patient and very dignified; he was rather a dear after all. Why did she think the face inscrutable? Her thoughts wandered vaguely, unease, discomfort among them somewhere, while the heated blood – she had taken her share of wine – seethed in her.

Burley turned to the sailor for more stories. "Sea and wind in them," he asked. "No horrors, remember!" and Mortimer told a tale about the shortage of rooms at a Welsh seaside place where spare rooms fetched fabulous prices, and one man alone refused to let – a retired captain of a South Seas trader, very poor, a bit crazy apparently. He had two furnished rooms in his house worth twenty guineas a week. The rooms faced south; he kept them full of flowers; but he would not let. An explanation of his unworldly obstinacy was not forthcoming until Mortimer – they fished together – gained his confidence. "The South Wind lives in them," the old fellow told him. "I keep them free for her."

"For *her*?"

"It was on the South Wind my love came to me," said the other softly; "and it was on the South Wind that she left—"

It was an odd tale to tell in such company, but he told it well.

"Beautiful," thought Mrs. Burley. Aloud she said a quiet, "Thank you. By 'left', I suppose he meant she died or ran away?"

John Burley looked up with a certain surprise. "We ask for a story," he said, "and you give us a poem." He laughed. "You're in love, Mortimer," he informed him, "and with my wife probably."

"Of course I am, sir," replied the young man gallantly. "A sailor's heart, you know," while the face of the woman turned pink, then white. She knew her husband more intimately than Mortimer did, and there was something in his tone, his eyes, his words, she did not like. Harry was an idiot to choose such a tale. An irritated annoyance stirred in her, close upon dislike. "Anyhow, it's better than horrors," she said hurriedly.

"Well," put in her husband, letting forth a minor gust of laughter, "it's possible, at any rate. Though one's as crazy as the other." His meaning was not wholly clear. "If a man really loved," he added in his blunt fashion, "and was tricked by her, I could almost conceive his—"

"Oh, don't preach, John, for Heaven's sake. You're so dull in the pulpit." But the interruption only served to emphasise the sentence which, otherwise, might have been passed over.

"Could conceive his finding life so worthless," persisted the other, "that—" He hesitated. "But there, now, I promised I wouldn't," he went on, laughing good-humouredly. Then, suddenly, as though in spite of himself, driven it seemed: "Still, under such conditions, he might show his contempt for human nature and for life by—"

It was a tiny stifled scream that stopped him this time.

"John, I hate, I loathe you, when you talk like that. And you've broken your word again." She was more than petulant; a nervous anger sounded in her voice. It was the way he had said it, looking from them towards the window, that made her quiver. She felt him suddenly as a man; she felt afraid of him.

Her husband made no reply; he rose and looked at his watch, leaning sideways towards the lamp, so that the expression of his face was shaded. "Two o'clock," he remarked. "I think I'll take a turn through the house. I may find a workman asleep or something. Anyhow, the light will soon come now." He laughed; the expression of his face, his tone of voice, relieved her momentarily. He went out. They heard his heavy tread echoing down the carpetless long corridor.

Mortimer began at once. "Did he mean anything?" he asked breathlessly. "He doesn't love you the least little bit, anyhow. He never did. I do. You're wasted on him. You belong to me." The words poured out. He covered her face with kisses. "Oh, I didn't mean *that*," he caught between the kisses.

The sailor released her, staring. "What then?" he whispered. "Do you think he saw us on the lawn?" He paused a moment, as she made no reply. The steps were audible in the distance still. "I know!" he exclaimed suddenly. "It's the blessed house he feels. That's what it is. He doesn't like it."

A wind sighed through the room, making the papers flutter; something rattled; and Mrs. Burley started. A loose end of rope swinging from the paperhanger's ladder caught her eye. She shivered slightly.

"He's different," she replied in a low voice, nestling very close again, "and so restless. Didn't you notice what he said just now – that under certain conditions he could understand a man" – she hesitated – "doing it," she concluded, a sudden drop in her voice. "Harry," she looked full into his eyes, "that's not like him. He didn't say that for nothing."

"Nonsense! He's bored to tears, that's all. And the house is getting on your nerves, too." He kissed her tenderly. Then, as she responded, he drew her nearer still and held her passionately, mumbling incoherent words, among which "nothing to be afraid of" was distinguishable. Meanwhile, the steps were coming nearer. She pushed him away. "You must behave yourself. I insist. You shall, Harry," then buried herself in his arms, her face hidden against his neck – only to disentangle herself the next instant and stand clear of him. "I hate you, Harry," she exclaimed sharply, a look of angry annoyance flashing across her face. "And I *hate* myself. Why do you treat me—?" She broke off as the steps came closer, patted her hair straight, and stalked over to the open window.

"I believe after all you're only playing with me," he said viciously. He stared in surprised disappointment, watching her. "It's him you really love," he added jealously. He looked and spoke like a petulant spoilt boy.

She did not turn her head. "He's always been fair to me, kind and generous. He never blames me for anything. Give me a cigarette and don't play the stage hero. My nerves are on edge, to tell you the truth." Her voice jarred harshly, and as he lit her cigarette he noticed that her lips were trembling; his own hand trembled too. He was still holding the match, standing beside her at the window-sill, when the steps crossed the threshold and John Burley came into the room. He went straight up to the table and turned the lamp down. "It was smoking," he remarked. "Didn't you see?"

"I'm sorry, sir," and Mortimer sprang forward, too late to help him. "It was the draught as you pushed the door open." The big man said, "Ah!" and drew a chair over, facing them. "It's just *the* very house," he told them. "I've been through every room on this floor. It will make a splendid Home, with very little alteration, too." He turned round in his creaking wicker chair and looked up at his wife, who sat swinging her legs and smoking in the window embrasure. "Lives will be saved inside these old walls. It's a good investment," he went on, talking rather to himself it seemed. "People will die here, too—"

"Hark!" Mrs. Burley interrupted him. "That noise – what is it?" A faint thudding sound in the corridor or in the adjoining room was audible, making all three look round quickly, listening for a repetition, which did not come. The papers fluttered on the table, the lamps smoked an instant.

"Wind," observed Burley calmly, "our little friend, the South Wind. Something blown over again, that's all." But, curiously, the three of them stood up. "I'll go and see," he continued. "Doors and windows are all open to let the paint dry." Yet he did not move; he stood there watching a white moth that dashed round and round the lamp, flopping heavily now and again upon the bare deal table.

"Let me go, sir," put in Mortimer eagerly. He was glad of the chance; for the first time he, too, felt uncomfortable. But there was another who, apparently, suffered a discomfort greater than his own and was accordingly even more glad to get away. "I'll go," Mrs. Burley announced, with decision. "I'd like to. I haven't been out of this room since we came. I'm not an atom afraid."

It was strange that for a moment she did not make a move either; it seemed as if she waited for something. For perhaps fifteen seconds no one stirred or spoke. She knew by the look in her lover's eyes that he had now become aware of the slight, indefinite change in her husband's manner, and was alarmed by it. The fear in him woke her contempt; she suddenly despised the youth, and was conscious of a new, strange yearning towards her husband; against her worked nameless pressures, troubling her being. There was an alteration in the room, she thought; something had come in. The trio stood listening to the gentle wind outside, waiting for the sound to be repeated; two careless, passionate young lovers and a man stood waiting, listening, watching in that room; yet it seemed there were five persons altogether and not three, for two guilty consciences stood apart and separate from their owners. John Burley broke the silence.

"Yes, you go, Nancy. Nothing to be afraid of – there. It's only wind." He spoke as though he meant it.

Mortimer bit his lips. "I'll come with you," he said instantly. He was confused. "Let's all three go. I don't think we ought to be separated." But Mrs. Burley was already at the door. "I insist," she said, with a forced laugh. "I'll call if I'm frightened," while her husband, saying nothing, watched her from the table.

"Take this," said the sailor, flashing his electric torch as he went over to her. "Two are better than one." He saw her figure exquisitely silhouetted against the black corridor beyond; it was clear she wanted to go; any nervousness in her was mastered by a stronger emotion still; she was glad to be out of their presence for a bit. He had hoped to snatch a word of explanation in the corridor, but her manner stopped him. Something else stopped him, too.

"First door on the left," he called out, his voice echoing down the empty length. "That's the room where the noise came from. Shout if you want us."

He watched her moving away, the light held steadily in front of her, but she made no answer, and he turned back to see John Burley lighting his cigar at the lamp chimney, his face thrust forward as he did so. He stood a second, watching him, as the lips sucked hard at the cigar to make it draw; the strength of the features was emphasised to sternness. He had meant to stand by the door and listen for the least sound from the adjoining room, but now found his whole attention focused on the face above the lamp. In that minute he realised that Burley had wished – had meant – his wife to go. In that minute also he forgot his love, his shameless, selfish little mistress, his worthless, caddish little self. For John Burley looked up. He straightened slowly, puffing hard and quickly to make sure his cigar was lit, and faced him. Mortimer moved forward into the room, self-conscious, embarrassed, cold.

"Of course it was only wind," he said lightly, his one desire being to fill the interval while they were alone with commonplaces. He did not wish the other to speak, "Dawn wind, probably." He glanced at his wrist-watch. "It's half-past two already, and the sun gets up at a quarter to four. It's light by now, I expect. The shortest night is never quite dark." He rambled on confusedly, for the other's steady, silent stare embarrassed him. A faint sound of Mrs. Burley moving in the next room made him stop a moment. He turned instinctively to the door, eager for an excuse to go.

"That's nothing," said Burley, speaking at last and in a firm quiet voice. "Only my wife, glad to be alone – my young and pretty wife. She's all right. I know her better than you do. Come in and shut the door."

Mortimer obeyed. He closed the door and came close to the table, facing the other, who at once continued.

"If I thought," he said, in that quiet deep voice, "that you two were serious" – he uttered his words very slowly, with emphasis, with intense severity – "do you know what I should do? I will tell you, Mortimer. I should like one of us two – you or myself – to remain in this house, dead."

His teeth gripped his cigar tightly; his hands were clenched; he went on through a half-closed mouth. His eyes blazed steadily.

"I trust her so absolutely – understand me? – that my belief in women, in human beings, would go. And with it the desire to live. Understand me?"

Each word to the young careless fool was a blow in the face, yet it was the softest blow, the flash of a big deep heart, that hurt the most. A dozen answers – denial, explanation, confession, taking all guilt upon himself – crowded his mind, only to be dismissed. He stood motionless and silent, staring hard into the other's eyes. No word passed his lips; there was no time in any case. It was in this position that Mrs. Burley, entering at that moment, found them. She saw her husband's face; the other man stood with his back to her. She came in with a little nervous laugh. "A bell-rope swinging in the wind and hitting a sheet of metal before the fireplace," she informed them. And all three laughed together then, though each laugh had a different sound. "But I hate this house," she added. "I wish we had never come."

"The moment there's light in the sky," remarked her husband quietly, "we can leave. That's the contract; let's see it through. Another half-hour will do it. Sit down, Nancy, and have a bite of something." He got up and placed a chair for her. "I think I'll take another look round." He moved slowly to the door. "I may go out on to the lawn a bit and see what the sky is doing."

It did not take half a minute to say the words, yet to Mortimer it seemed as though the voice would never end. His mind was confused and troubled. He loathed himself, he loathed the woman through whom he had got into this awkward mess.

The situation had suddenly become extremely painful; he had never imagined such a thing; the man he had thought blind had after all seen everything – known it all along, watched them, waited. And the woman, he was now certain, loved her husband; she had fooled him, Mortimer, all along, amusing herself.

"I'll come with you, sir. Do let me," he said suddenly. Mrs. Burley stood pale and uncertain between them. She looked scared. What has happened, she was clearly wondering.

"No, no, Harry" – he called him 'Harry' for the first time – "I'll be back in five minutes at most. My wife mustn't be alone either." And he went out.

The young man waited till the footsteps sounded some distance down the corridor, then turned, but he did not move forward; for the first time he let pass unused what he called 'an opportunity'. His passion had left him; his love, as he once thought it, was gone. He looked at the pretty woman near him, wondering blankly what he had ever seen there to attract him so wildly. He wished to Heaven he was out of it all. He wished he were dead. John Burley's words suddenly appalled him.

One thing he saw plainly – she was frightened. This opened his lips.

"What's the matter?" he asked, and his hushed voice shirked the familiar Christian name. "Did you see anything?" He nodded his head in the direction of the adjoining room. It was the sound of his own voice addressing her coldly that made him abruptly see himself as he really was, but it was her reply, honestly given, in a faint even voice, that told him she saw her own self too with similar clarity. God, he thought, how revealing a tone, a single word can be!

"I saw – nothing. Only I feel uneasy – dear." That 'dear' was a call for help.

"Look here," he cried, so loud that she held up a warning finger, "I'm – I've been a damned fool, a cad! I'm most frightfully ashamed. I'll do anything – *anything* to get it right." He felt cold, naked, his worthlessness laid bare; she felt, he knew, the same. Each revolted suddenly from the other. Yet he knew not quite how or wherefore this great change had thus abruptly come about, especially on her side. He felt that a bigger, deeper emotion than he could understand was working on them, making mere physical relationships seem empty, trivial, cheap and vulgar. His cold increased in face of this utter ignorance.

"Uneasy?" he repeated, perhaps hardly knowing exactly why he said it. "Good Lord, but he can take care of himself—"

"Oh, *he* is a man," she interrupted; "yes."

Steps were heard, firm, heavy steps, coming back along the corridor. It seemed to Mortimer that he had listened to this sound of steps all night, and would listen to them till he died. He crossed to the lamp and lit a cigarette, carefully this time, turning the wick down afterwards. Mrs. Burley also rose, moving over towards the door, away from him. They listened a moment to these firm and heavy steps, the tread of a man, John Burley. A man... and a philanderer, flashed across Mortimer's brain like fire, contrasting the two with fierce contempt for himself. The tread became less audible. There was distance in it. It had turned in somewhere.

"There!" she exclaimed in a hushed tone. "He's gone in."

"Nonsense! It passed us. He's going out on to the lawn."

The pair listened breathlessly for a moment, when the sound of steps came distinctly from the adjoining room, walking across the boards, apparently towards the window.

"There!" she repeated. "He did go in." Silence of perhaps a minute followed, in which they heard each other's breathing. "I don't like his being alone – in there," Mrs. Burley said in a thin faltering voice, and moved as though to go out. Her hand was already on the knob of the door, when Mortimer stopped her with a violent gesture.

"Don't! For God's sake, don't!" he cried, before she could turn it. He darted forward. As he laid a hand upon her arm a thud was audible through the wall. It was a heavy sound, and this time there was no wind to cause it.

"It's only that loose swinging thing," he whispered thickly, a dreadful confusion blotting out clear thought and speech.

"There was no loose swaying thing at all," she said in a failing voice, then reeled and swayed against him. "I invented that. There was nothing." As he caught her, staring helplessly, it seemed to him that a face with lifted lids rushed up at him. He saw two terrified eyes in a patch of ghastly white. Her whisper followed, as she sank into his arms. "It's John. He's—"

At which instant, with terror at its climax, the sound of steps suddenly became audible once more – the firm and heavy tread of John Burley coming out again into the corridor. Such was their amazement and relief that they neither moved nor spoke. The steps drew nearer. The pair seemed petrified; Mortimer did not remove his arms, nor did Mrs. Burley attempt to release herself. They stared at the door and waited. It was pushed wider the next second, and John Burley stood beside them. He was so close he almost touched them – there in each other's arms.

"Jack, dear!" cried his wife, with a searching tenderness that made her voice seem strange.

He gazed a second at each in turn. "I'm going out on to the lawn for a moment," he said quietly. There was no expression on his face; he did not smile, he did not frown; he showed no feeling, no emotion – just looked into their eyes, and then withdrew round the edge of the door before either could utter a word in answer. The door swung to behind him. He was gone.

"He's going to the lawn. He said so." It was Mortimer speaking, but his voice shook and stammered. Mrs. Burley had released herself. She stood now by the table, silent, gazing with fixed eyes at nothing, her lips parted, her expression vacant. Again she was aware of an alteration in the room; something had gone out.... He watched her a second, uncertain what to say or do. It was the face of a drowned person, occurred to him. Something intangible, yet almost visible stood between them in that narrow space. Something had ended, there before his eyes, definitely ended. The barrier between them rose higher, denser. Through this barrier her words came to him with an odd whispering remoteness.

"Harry.... You saw? You noticed?"

"What d'you mean?" he said gruffly. He tried to feel angry, contemptuous, but his breath caught absurdly.

"Harry – he was different. The eyes, the hair, the" – her face grew like death – "the twist in his face—"

"What on earth are you saying? Pull yourself together." He saw that she was trembling down the whole length of her body, as she leaned against the table for support. His own legs shook. He stared hard at her.

"Altered, Harry... altered." Her horrified whisper came at him like a knife. For it was true. He, too, had noticed something about the husband's appearance that was not quite normal. Yet, even while they talked, they heard him going down the carpetless stairs; the sounds ceased as he crossed the hall; then came the noise of the front door banging, the reverberation even shaking the room a little where they stood.

Mortimer went over to her side. He walked unevenly.

"My dear! For God's sake – this is sheer nonsense. Don't let yourself go like this. I'll put it straight with him – it's all my fault." He saw by her face that she did not understand his words; he was saying the wrong thing altogether; her mind was utterly elsewhere. "He's all right," he went on hurriedly. "He's out on the lawn now—"

He broke off at the sight of her. The horror that fastened on her brain plastered her face with deathly whiteness.

"That was not John at all!" she cried, a wail of misery and terror in her voice. She rushed to the window and he followed. To his immense relief a figure moving below was plainly visible. It was John Burley. They saw him in the faint grey of the dawn, as he crossed the lawn, going away from the house. He disappeared.

"There you are! See?" whispered Mortimer reassuringly. "He'll be back in—" when a sound in the adjoining room, heavier, louder than before, cut appallingly across his words, and Mrs. Burley, with that wailing scream, fell back into his arms. He caught her only just in time, for she stiffened into ice, daft with the uncomprehended terror of it all, and helpless as a child.

"Darling, my darling – oh, God!" He bent, kissing her face wildly. He was utterly distraught.

"Harry! Jack – oh, oh!" she wailed in her anguish. "It took on his likeness. It deceived us… to give him time. He's done it."

She sat up suddenly. "Go," she said, pointing to the room beyond, then sank fainting, a dead weight in his arms.

He carried her unconscious body to a chair, then entering the adjoining room he flashed his torch upon the body of her husband hanging from a bracket in the wall. He cut it down five minutes too late.

A Night of Horror

Dick Donovan

Bleak Hill Castle

My dear old Chum, – *Before you leave England for the East I claim the redemption of a promise you made to me some time ago that you would give me the pleasure of a week or two of your company. Besides, as you may have already guessed, I have given up the folly of my bachelor days, and have taken unto myself the sweetest, dearest little woman that ever walked the face of the earth. We have been married just six months, and are as happy as the day is long. And then this place is entirely after your own heart. It will excite all your artistic fancies, and appeal with irresistible force to your romantic nature. To call the building a castle is somewhat pretentious, but I believe it has been known as the Castle ever since it was built, more than two hundred years ago. Hester – need I say that Hester is my better half! – is just delighted with it, and if either of us was in the least degree superstitious, we might see or hear ghosts every hour of the day. Of course, as becomes a castle, we have a haunted room, though my own impression is that it is haunted by nothing more fearsome* *than rats. Anyway, it is such a picturesque, curious sort of chamber that if it hasn't a ghost it ought to have. But I have no doubt, old chap, that you will make one of us, for, as I remember, you have always had a love for the eerie and creepy, and you cannot forget how angry you used to get with me sometimes for chaffing you about your avowed belief in the occult and supernatural, and what you were pleased to term the 'unexplainable phenomena of psychomancy.' However, it is possible you have got over some of the errors of your youth but whether or not, come down, dear boy, and rest assured that you will meet with the heartiest of welcomes.*

    Your old pal,

    DICK DIRCKMAN.

The above letter was from my old friend and college chum, who, having inherited a substantial fortune, and being passionately fond of the country and country pursuits, had thus the means of gratifying his tastes to their fullest bent. Although Dick and I were very differently constituted, we had always been greatly attached to each other. In the best sense of the term he was what is generally called a hard-headed, practical man. He was fond of saying he never believed in anything he couldn't see, and even that which he could see he was not prepared to accept as truth without due investigation. In short, Dick was neither romantic, poetical, nor, I am afraid, artistic, in the literal sense. He preferred facts to fancies, and was possessed of what the world generally calls 'an unimpressionable nature'. For nearly four years I had lost sight of my friend, as I had been wandering about Europe as tutor and companion to a delicate young nobleman. His death had set me free; but I had no sooner returned to England than I was offered and accepted a lucrative appointment in the service of his Highness the Nizam of Chundlepore, in Northern India, and there was every probability of my being absent for a number of years.

On returning home I had written to Dick to the chambers he had formerly occupied, telling him of my appointment, and expressing a fear that unless we could snatch a day or two in town I might not be able to see him, as I had so many things to do. It was true I had promised that when opportunity occurred I should do myself the pleasure of accepting his oft-proffered hospitality which I knew to be lavish and generous. I had not heard of his marriage; his letter gave me the first intimation of that fact, and I confess that when I got his missive I experienced some curiosity to know the kind of lady he had succeeded in captivating. I had always had an idea that Dick was cut out for a bachelor, for there was nothing of the ladies' man about him, and he used at one time to speak of the gentler sex with a certain levity and brusqueness of manner that by no means found favour with the majority of his friends. And now Dick was actually married, and living in a remote region, where most town-bred people would die of ennui.

It will be gathered from the foregoing remarks that I did not hesitate about accepting Dick's cordial invitation. I determined to spare a few days at least of my somewhat limited time, and duly noted Dick to that effect, giving him the date of my departure from London, and the hour at which I should arrive at the station nearest to his residence.

Bleak Hill Castle was situated in one of the most picturesque parts of Wales; consequently, on the day appointed I found myself comfortably ensconced in a smoking carriage of a London and North-Western train. And towards the close of the day – the time of the year was May – I was the sole passenger to alight at the wayside station, where Dick awaited me with a smart dog-cart. His greeting was hearty and robust, and when his man had packed in my traps he gave the handsome little mare that drew the cart the reins, and we spanked along the country roads in rare style. Dick always prided himself on his knowledge of horseflesh, and with a sense of keen satisfaction he drew my attention to the points of the skittish little mare which bowled along as if we had been merely featherweights.

A drive of eight miles through the bracing Welsh air so sharpened our appetites that the smell of dinner was peculiarly welcome; and telling me to make a hurried toilet, as his cook would not risk her reputation by keeping a dinner waiting, Dick handed me over to the guidance of a natty chambermaid. As it was dark when we arrived I had no opportunity of observing the external characteristics of Bleak Hill Castle; but there was nothing in the interior that suggested bleakness. Warmth, comfort, light, held forth promise of carnal delights.

Following my guide up a broad flight of stairs, and along a lofty and echoing corridor, I found myself in a large and comfortably furnished bedroom. A bright wood fire burned upon the hearthstone, for although it was May the temperature was still very low on the Welsh hills. Hastily changing my clothes, I made my way to the dining room, where Mrs. Dirckman emphasised the welcome her husband had already given me. She was an exceedingly pretty and rather delicate-looking little woman, in striking contrast to her great, bluff, busy husband. A few neighbours had been gathered together to meet me, and we sat down, a dozen all told, to a dinner that from a gastronomic point of view left nothing to be desired. The viands were appetising, the wines perfect, and all the appointments were in perfect consonance with the good things that were placed before us.

It was perhaps natural, when the coffee and cigar stage had arrived, that conversation should turn upon our host's residence, by way of affording me – a stranger to the district – some information. Of course, the information was conveyed to me in a scrappy way, but I gathered in substance that Bleak Hill Castle had originally belonged to a Welsh family, which was chiefly distinguished by the extravagance and gambling propensities of its male members. It had gone through some exciting times, and numerous strange and startling stories had come to centre round it. There were stories of wrong, and shame, and death, and more than a suggestion of dark crimes. One of these stories turned upon the mysterious disappearance of the wife and daughter of a young scion of the house, whose career had been somewhat shady. His wife was considerably older than he, and it was generally supposed that he had married her for money. His daughter, a girl of about twelve, was an epileptic patient, while the husband and father was a gloomy, disappointed man. Suddenly the wife and daughter disappeared. At first no surprise was felt; but, then some curiosity was expressed to know where they had gone to and curiosity led to wonderment, and wonderment to rumour – for people will gossip, especially in a country district. Of course, Mr. Greeta Jones, the husband, had to submit to much questioning as to where his wife and child were staying. But being sullen and morose of temperament he contented himself by brusquely and tersely saying, "They had gone to London." But as no one had seen them go, and no one had heard of their going, the statement was accepted as a perversion of fact. Nevertheless, incredible as it may seem, no one thought it worth his while to insist upon an investigation, and a few weeks later Greeta Jones himself went away – and to London, as was placed beyond doubt. For a long time Bleak Hill Castle was shut up, and throughout the countryside it began to be whispered that sights and sounds had been seen and heard at the castle which were suggestive of things unnatural, and soon it became a crystallised belief in men's minds that the place was haunted.

On the principle of giving a dog a bad name you have only to couple ghosts with the name of an old country residence like this castle for it to fall into disfavour, and to be generally shunned. As might have been expected in such a region, the castle was shunned; no tenant could be found for it. It was allowed to go to ruin, and for a long time was the haunt of smugglers. They were cleared out in the process of time, and at last hard-headed, practical Dick Dirckman heard of the place through a London agent, went down to see it, took a fancy to it, bought it for an old song, and, having taste and money, he soon converted the half-ruined building into a country gentleman's home, and thither he carried his bride.

Such was the history of Bleak Hill Castle as I gathered it in outline during the postprandial chat on that memorable evening.

On the following day I found the place all that my host had described it in his letter to me. Its situation was beautiful in the extreme; and there wasn't one of its windows that didn't command a magnificent view of landscape and sea. He and I rambled about the house, he evinced a keen delight in showing me every nook and corner, in expatiating on the beauties of the locality generally, and of the advantages of his dwelling-place in particular. Why he reserved taking me to the so-called haunted chamber until the last I never have known; but so it was; and as he threw open the heavy door and ushered me into the apartment he smiled ironically and remarked:

"Well, old man, this is the ghost's den; and as I consider that a country mansion of this kind should, in the interests of all tradition and of fiction writers, who, under the guise of truth, he like Ananias, have its haunted room, I have let this place go untouched, except that I have made it a sort of lumber closet for some antique and mouldering old furniture which I picked up a bargain in Wardour Street, London. But I needn't tell you that I regard the ghost stories as rot."

I did not reply to my friend at once, for the room absorbed my attention. It was unquestionably the largest of the bedrooms in the house, and, while in keeping with the rest of the house, had characteristics of its own. The walls were panelled with dark oak, the floor was oak, polished. There was a deep V-shaped bay, formed by an angle of the castle, and in each side of the bay was a diamond-paned window, and under each window an oak seat, which was also a chest with an ancient iron lock. A large wooden bedstead with massive hangings stood in one corner, and the rest of the furniture was of a very nondescript character, and calls for no special mention. In a word, the room was picturesque, and to me it at once suggested the mise-en-scène for all sorts of dramatic situations of a weird and eerie character. I ought to add that there was a very large fireplace with a most capacious hearthstone, on which stood a pair of ponderous and rusty steel dogs. Finally, the window commanded superb views, and altogether my fancy was pleased, and my artistic susceptibilities appealed to in an irresistible manner, so that I replied to my friend thus:

"I like this room, Dick, awfully. Let me occupy it, will you?"

He laughed.

"Well, upon my word, you are an eccentric fellow to want to give up the comfortable den which I have assigned to you for this mouldy, draughty, dingy old lumber room. However" – here he shrugged his shoulders – "there is no accounting for tastes, and as this is liberty hall, my friends do as they like; so I'll tell the servants to put the bed in order, light a fire, and cart your traps from the other room."

I was glad I had carried my point, for I frankly confess to having romantic tendencies. I was fond of old things, old stories and legends, old furniture, and anything that was removed above the dull level of commonplaceness. This room in a certain sense, was unique, and I was charmed with it.

When pretty little Mrs. Dirckman heard of the arrangements she said, with a laugh that did not conceal a certain nervousness, "I am sorry you are going to sleep in that wretched room. It always makes me shudder, for it seems so uncomfortable. Besides, you know, although Dick laughs at me and calls me a little goose, I am inclined to believe there may be some foundation for the current stories. Anyway, I wouldn't sleep in the room for a crown of gold. I hope you will be comfortable, and not be frightened to death or into insanity by gruesome apparitions."

I hastened to assure my hostess that I should be comfortable enough, while as for apparitions, I was not likely to be frightened by them.

The rest of the day was spent exploring the country round about, and after a recherché dinner Dick and I played billiards until one o'clock, and then having drained a final 'peg', I retired to rest. When I reached the haunted chamber I found that much had been done to give an air of cheerfulness and comfort to the place. Some rugs had been laid about the floor, a modern chair or two introduced, a wood fire blazed on the hearth. On a little 'occasional table' that stood near the fire was a silver jug, filled with hot water, and an antique decanter containing spirits, together with lemon and sugar, in case I wanted a final brew. I could not but feel grateful for my host and hostess's thoughtfulness, and, having donned my dressing gown and slippers, I drew a chair within the radius of the wood fire's glow, and proceeded to fill my pipe for a few whiffs previous to tumbling into bed. This was a habit of mine – a habit of years and years of growth, and, while perhaps an objectionable one in some respects, it afforded me solace and conduced to restful sleep. So I lit my pipe, and fell to pondering and trying to see if I could draw any suggestiveness as to my future from the glowing embers. Suddenly a remarkable thing happened. My pipe was drawn gently from my lips and laid upon the table, and at the same moment I heard what seemed to me to be a sigh. For a moment or two I felt confused, and wondered whether I was awake or dreaming. But there was the pipe on the table, and I could have taken the most solemn oath that to the best of my belief it had been placed there by unseen hands.

My feelings, as may be imagined, were peculiar. It was the first time in my life that I had ever been the subject of a phenomenon which was capable of being attributed to supernatural agency. After a little reflection, and some reasoning with myself, however, I tried to believe that my own senses had made a fool of me, and that in a half-somnolent and dreamy condition I had removed the pipe myself, and placed it on the table. Having come to this conclusion I divested myself of my clothing, extinguished the two tall candles, and jumped into bed. Although usually a good sleeper, I did not go to sleep at once, as was my wont, but lay thinking of many things, and mingling with my changing thoughts was a low, monotonous undertone – nature's symphony – of booming sea on the distant beach, and a bass piping – rising occasionally to a shrill and weird upper note – of the wind. From its situation the house was exposed to every wind that blew, hence its name 'Bleak Hill Castle', and probably a south-east gale would have made itself felt to an uncomfortable degree in this room, which was in the south-east angle of the building. But now the booming sea and wind had a lullaby effect, and my nerves sinking into restful repose I fell asleep. How long I slept I do not know, and never shall know; but I awoke suddenly, and with a start, for it seemed as if a stream of ice-cold water was pouring over my face. With an impulse of indefinable alarm I sprang up in bed, and then a strange, awful, ghastly sight met my view.

I don't know that I could be described as a nervous man in any sense of the word. Indeed, I think I may claim to be freer from nerves than the average man, nor would my worst enemy, if he had a regard for truth, accuse me of lacking courage. And yet I confess here, frankly, that the sight I gazed upon appalled me. Yet was I fascinated with a horrible fascination, that rendered it impossible for me to turn my eyes away. I seemed bound by some strange weird spell. My limbs appeared to have grown rigid; there was a sense of burning in my eyes; my mouth was parched and dry; my tongue swollen, so it seemed. Of course, these were mere sensations, but they were sensations I never wish to experience again. They were sensations that tested my sanity. And the sight that held me in the thrall was truly calculated to test the nerves of the strongest.

There, in mid-air, between floor and ceiling, surrounded or made visible by a trembling nebulous light, that was weird beyond the power of any words to describe, was the head and bust of a woman. The face was paralysed into an unutterably awful expression of stony horror; the long black hair was tangled and dishevelled, and the eyes appeared to be bulging from the head. But this was not all. Two ghostly hands were visible. The fingers of one were twined savagely in the black hair, and the other grasped a long-bladed knife, and with it hacked, and gashed, and tore, and stabbed at the bare white throat of the woman, and the blood gushed forth from the jagged wounds, reddening the spectre hand and flowing in one continuous stream to the oak floor, where I heard it drip, drip, drip until my brain seemed as if it would burst, and

66

I felt as if I was going raving mad. Then I saw with my strained eyes the unmistakable sign of death pass over the woman's face; and next, the devilish hands flung the mangled remnants away, and I heard a low chuckle of satisfaction – heard, I say, and swear it, as plainly as I have ever heard anything in this world. The light had faded; the vision of crime and death I had gone, and yet the spell held me. Although the night was cold, I believe I was bathed in perspiration. I think I tried to cry out – nay, I am sure I did – but no sound came from my burning, parched lips; my tongue refused utterance; it clove to the roof of my mouth. Could I have moved so much as a joint of my little finger, I could have broken the spell; at least, such was the idea that occupied my half-stunned brain. It was a nightmare of waking horror, and I shudder now, and shrink within myself as I recall it all. But the revelation – for revelation it was – had not yet reached its final stage. Out of the darkness was once more evolved a faint, phosphorescent glow, and in the midst of it appeared the dead body of a beautiful girl with the throat all gashed and bleeding, the red blood flowing in a crimson blood over her night robe, which only partially concealed her young limbs; and the cruel, spectral hands, dyed with her blood, appeared again, and grasped her, and lifted her, and bore her along. Then that vision faded, and a third appeared. This time I seemed to be looking into a gloomy, damp, arched cave or cellar, and the horror that froze me was intensified as I saw the hands busy preparing a hole in the wall at one end of the cave; and presently they lifted two bodies – the body of the woman, and the body of the young girl – all gory and besmirched; and the hands crushed them into the hole in the wall, and then proceeded to brick them up.

All these things I saw as I have described them, and this I solemnly swear to be the truth as I hope for mercy at the Supreme Judgment.

It was a vision of crime; a vision of merciless, pitiless, damnable murder. How long it all lasted I don't know. Science has told us that dreams which seem to embrace a long series of years, last but seconds; and in the few moments of consciousness that remain to the drowning man his life's scroll is unrolled before his eyes. This vision of mine, therefore, may only have lasted seconds, but it seemed to me hours, years, nay, an eternity. With that final stage in the ghostly drama of blood and death, the spell was broken, and flinging my arms wildly about, I know that I uttered a great cry as I sprang up in bed.

"Have I been in the throes of a ghastly nightmare?" I asked myself.

Every detail of the horrific vision I recalled, and yet somehow it seemed to me that I had been the victim of a hideous nightmare. I felt strangely ill. I was wet and clammy with perspiration, and nervous to a degree that I had never before experienced in my existence. Nevertheless, I noted everything distinctly. On the hearthstone there was still a mass of glowing red embers. I heard the distant booming of the sea, and round the house the wind moaned with a peculiar, eerie, creepy sound.

Suddenly I sprang from the bed, impelled thereto by an impulse I was bound to obey, and by the same impulse was drawn towards the door. I laid my hand on the handle. I turned it, opened the door, and gazed into the long dark corridor. A sigh fell upon my ears. An unmistakable human sigh, in which was expressed all intensity of suffering and sorrow that thrilled me to the heart. I shrank back, and was about to close the door, when out of the darkness was evolved the glowing figure of a woman clad in blood-stained garments and with dishevelled hair. She turned her white corpse-like face towards me, and her eyes pleaded with a pleading that was irresistible, while she pointed the index finger of her left hand downwards, and then beckoned me. Then I followed whither she led. I could no more resist than the unrestrained needle can resist the attracting magnet. Clad only in my night apparel, and with bare feet and legs, I followed the spectre along the corridor, down the broad oak stairs, traversing another passage to the rear of the building until I found myself standing before a heavy barred door. At that moment the spectre vanished, and I retraced my steps like one who walked in a dream. I got back to my bedroom, but how I don't quite know; nor have any recollection of getting into bed. Hours afterwards I awoke. It was broad daylight. The horror of the night came back to me with overwhelming force, and made me faint and ill. I managed, however, to struggle through with my toilet, and hurried from that haunted room. It was a beautifully fine morning. The sun was shining brightly, and the birds carolled blithely in every tree and bush. I strolled out on to the lawn, and paced up and down. I was strangely agitated, and asked myself over and over again if what I had seen or dreamed about had any significance.

Presently my host came out. He visibly started as he saw me.

"Hullo, old chap. What's the matter with you?" he exclaimed. "You look jolly queer; as though you had been having a bad night of it."

"I have had a bad night."

His manner became more serious and grave.

"What – seen anything?"

"Yes."

"The deuce! You don't mean it, really!"

"Indeed I do. I have gone through a night of horror such as I could not live through again. But let us have breakfast first, and then I will try and make you understand what I have suffered, and you shall judge for yourself whether any significance is to be attached to my dream, or whatever you like to call it."

We walked, without speaking, into the breakfast room, where my charming hostess greeted me cordially; but she, like her husband, noticed my changed appearance, and expressed alarm and anxiety. I reassured her by saying I had had a rather restless night, and didn't feel particularly well, but that it was a mere passing ailment. I was unable to partake of much breakfast, and both my good friend and his wife again showed some anxiety, and pressed me to state the cause of my distress. As I could not see any good cause that was to be gained by concealment, and even at the risk of being laughed at by my host, I recounted the experience I had gone through during the night of terror.

So far from my host showing any disposition to ridicule me, as I quite expected he would have done, he became unusually thoughtful, and presently said:

"Either this is a wild fantasy of your own brain, or there is something in it. The door that the ghost of the woman led you to is situated on the top of a flight of stone steps, leading to a vault below the building, which I have never used, and have never even had the curiosity to enter, though I did once go to the bottom of the steps; but the place was so exceedingly suggestive of a tomb that I mentally exclaimed, 'I've no use for this dungeon', and so I shut it up, bolted and barred the door, and have never opened it since."

I answered that the time had come when he must once more descend into that cellar or vault, whatever it was. He asked me if I would accompany him, and, of course, I said I would. So he summoned his head gardener, and after much searching about, the key of the door was found; but even then the door was only opened with difficulty, as lock and key alike were foul with rust.

As we descended the slimy, slippery stone steps, each of us carrying a candle, a rank, mouldy smell greeted us, and a cold noisome atmosphere pervaded the place. The steps led into a huge vault, that apparently extended under the greater part of the building. The roof was arched, and was supported by brick pillars. The floor was the natural earth, and was soft and oozy. The miasma was almost overpowering, notwithstanding that there were ventilating slits in the wall in various places.

We proceeded to explore this vast cellar, and found that there was an air shaft which apparently communicated with the roof of the house; but it was choked with rubbish, old boxes, and the like. The gardener cleared this away, and then looking up, we could see the blue sky overhead.

Continuing our exploration, we noted that in a recess formed by the angle of the walls was a quantity of bricks and mortar. Under other circumstances this would not, perhaps, have aroused our curiosity or suspicions. But in this instance it did; and we examined the wall thereabouts with painful interest, until the conviction was forced upon us that a space of over a yard in width, and extending from door to roof, had recently been filled in. I was drawn towards the new brickwork by some subtle magic, some weird fascination. I examined it with an eager, critical, curious interest, and the thoughts that passed through my brain were reflected in the faces of my companions. We looked at each other, and each knew by some unexplainable instinct what was passing in his fellow's mind.

"It seems to me we are face to face with some mystery," remarked Dick, solemnly. Indeed, throughout all the years I had known him I had never before seen him so serious. Usually his expression was that of good-humoured cynicism, but now he might have been a judge about to pass the doom of death on a red-handed sinner.

"Yes," I answered, "there is a mystery, unless I have been tricked by my own fancy."

"Umph! It is strange," muttered Dick to himself.

"Well, sir," chimed in the gardener, "you know there have been some precious queer stories going about for a long time. And before you come and took the place plenty of folks round about used to say they'd seen some uncanny sights. I never had no faith in them stories myself; but, after all, maybe there's truth in 'em."

Dick picked up half a brick and began to tap the wall with it where the new work was, and the taps gave forth a hollow sound, quite different from the sound produced when the other parts of the wall were struck.

"I say, old chap," exclaimed my host, with a sorry attempt at a smile, "upon my word, I begin to experience a sort of uncanny kind of feeling. I'll be hanged if I am not getting as superstitious as you are."

"You may call me superstitious if you like, but either I have seen what I have seen, or my senses have played the fool with me. Anyway, let us put it to the test."

"How?"

"By breaking away some of that new brickwork."

Dick laughed a laugh that wasn't a laugh, as he asked:

"What do you expect to find?" I hesitated what to say, and he added the answer himself – "Mouldering bones, if our ghostly visitor hasn't deceived you."

"Mouldering bones!" I echoed involuntarily.

"Gardener, have you got a crowbar amongst your tools?" Dick asked.

"Yes, sir."

"Go up and get it."

The man obeyed the command.

"This is a strange sort of business altogether," Dick continued, after glancing round the vast and gloomy cellar. "But, upon my word, to tell you the truth, I'm half ashamed of myself for yielding to anything like superstition. It strikes me that you'll find you are the victim of a trick of the imagination, and that these bogey fancies of yours have placed us in rather a ridiculous position."

In answer to this I could not possibly resist reminding Dick that even scientists admitted that there were certain phenomena – they called them 'natural phenomena' – that could not be accounted for by ordinary laws.

Dick shrugged his shoulders and remarked with assumed indifference:

"Perhaps – perhaps it is so." He proceeded to fill his pipe with tobacco, and having lit it he smoked with a nervous energy quite unusual with him.

The gardener was only away about ten minutes, but it seemed infinitely longer. He brought both a pickaxe and a crowbar with him, and in obedience to his master's orders he commenced to hack at the wall. A brick was soon dislodged. Then the crowbar was inserted in the hole, and a mass prized out. From the opening came forth a sickening odour, so that we all drew back instinctively, and I am sure we all shuddered, and I saw the pipe fall from Dick's lips; but he snatched it up quickly and puffed at it vigorously until a cloud of smoke hung in the fetid and stagnant air. Then picking up a candle from the ground, where it had been placed, he approached the hole, holding the candle in such a position that its rays were thrown into the opening. In a few moments he started back with an exclamation:

"My God! The ghost hasn't lied," he said, and I noticed that his face paled. I peered into the hole and so did the gardener, and we both

73

drew back with a start, for sure enough in that recess were decaying human remains.

"This awful business must be investigated," said Dick. "Come, let us go."

We needed no second bidding. We were only too glad to quit that place of horror, and get into the fresh air and bright sunlight. We verily felt that we had come up out of a tomb, and we knew that once more the adage, 'Murder will out', had proved true.

Half an hour later Dick and I were driving to the nearest town to lay information of the awful discovery we had made, and the subsequent search carried out by the police brought two skeletons to light. Critical medical examination left not the shadow of a doubt that they were the remains of a woman and a girl and each had been brutally murdered. Of course it became necessary to hold an inquest, and the police set to work to collect evidence as to the identity of the bodies hidden in the recess in the wall.

Naturally all the stories which had been current for so many years throughout the country were revived, and the gossips were busy in retelling all they had heard, with many additions of their own, of course. But the chief topic was that of the strange disappearance of the wife and daughter of the once-owner of the castle, Greeta Jones. This story had been touched upon the previous night, during the after-dinner chat in my host's smoking room. Morgan, as was remembered had gambled his fortune away, and married a lady much older than himself, who bore him a daughter who was subject to epileptic fits. When this girl was about twelve she and her mother disappeared from the neighbourhood, and, according to the husband's account, they had gone to London.

Then he left, and people troubled themselves no more about him and his belongings.

A quarter of a century had passed since that period, and Bleak Hill Castle had gone through many vicissitudes until it fell into the hands of my friend Dick Dirckman. The more the history of Greeta Jones was gone into the more it was made clear that the remains which had been bricked up in the cellar were those of his wife and daughter. That the unfortunate girl and woman had been brutally and barbarously murdered there wasn't a doubt. The question was, who murdered them? After leaving Wales Greeta Jones – as was brought to light – led a wild life in London. One night, while in a state of intoxication, he was knocked down by a cab, and so seriously injured that he died while being carried to the hospital; and with him his secret, for could there be any reasonable doubt that, even if he was not the actual murderer, he had connived at the crime. But there was reason to believe that he killed his wife and child with his own hand, and that with the aid of a navvy, whose services he bought, he bricked the bodies up in the cellar. It was remembered that a navvy named Howell Williams had been in the habit of going to the castle frequently, and that suddenly he became possessed of what was, for him, a considerable sum of money. For several weeks he drank hard; then being a single man, he packed up his few belongings and gave out that he was going to California, and all efforts to trace him failed.

So much for this ghastly crime. As to the circumstances that led to its discovery, it was curious that I should have been selected as the medium for bringing it to light. Why it should have been so I cannot and do not pretend to explain. I have recorded facts as they occurred; I leave others to solve the mystery.

A Water Witch

H.D. Everett

Chapter I

We were disappointed when Robert married. We had for long wanted him to marry, as he is our only brother and head of the family since my father died, as well as of the business firm; but we should have liked his wife to be a different sort of person. We, his sisters, could have chosen much better for him than he did for himself. Indeed we had our eye on just the right girl – bright-tempered and sensibly brought up, who would not have said No: of that I am assured, had Robert on his side shown signs of liking. But he took a holiday abroad the spring of 1912, and the next thing we heard was that he had made up his mind to marry Frederica. Frederica, indeed! We Larcombs have been plain Susans and Annes and Marys and Elizabeths for generations (I am Mary), and the fantastic name was an annoyance. The wedding took place at Mentone in a great hurry, because the stepmother was marrying again, and Frederica was unhappy. Was not that weak of Robert? – he did not give himself time to think. We may perhaps take that as some excuse for a departure from Larcomb traditions: on consideration, the match would very likely have been broken off.

Frederica had some money of her own, though not much: all the Larcomb brides have had money up to now. And her dead father was a General and a K.C.B., which did not look amiss in the announcement; but there our satisfaction ended. He brought her to make our acquaintance three weeks after the marriage, a delicate little shrinking thing well matched to her fanciful name, and desperately afraid of mother and of us girls, so the introductory visit was hardly a success. Then Robert took her off to London, and when the baby was born – a son, but too weakly to live beyond a day or two – she had a severe illness, and was slow in recovering strength. And there is little doubt that by this time he was conscious of having made a mistake.

I used to be his favourite sister, being next to him in age, and when he found himself in a difficulty at Roscawen he appealed to me. Roscawen was a moor Robert had lately rented on the Scotch side of the Border, and we were given to understand that a bracing air, and the complete change of scene, were expected to benefit Frederica, who was pleased by the arrangement. So his letter took me by surprise.

"Dear Mary," he wrote, and, characteristically, he did not beat about the bush. "Pack up your things as soon as you get this, and come off here the day after tomorrow. You will have to travel via York, and I will meet you at Draycott Halt, where the afternoon train stops by signal. Freda is a bit nervous, and doesn't like staying alone here, so I am in a fix. I want you to keep her company the weeks I am at Shepstow. I know you'll do as much as this for – Your affectionate brother, Robert Larcomb."

This abrupt call upon me, making sure of response and help, recalled bygone times when we were much to each other, and

Frederica still in the unknown. A bit nervous, was she, and Robert in a fix because of it: here again was evidence of the mistake. It was not very easy then to break off from work, and for an indefinite time; but I resolved to satisfy the family curiosity, to say nothing of my own, by doing as I was bid.

When I got out of the train at Draycott Halt, Robert was waiting for me with his car. My luggage was put in at the back, and I mounted to the seat beside him; and again it reminded me of old times, for he seemed genuinely pleased to see me.

"Good girl," he said, "to make no fuss, and come at once."

"We Larcombs are not apt to fuss, are we?" – and as I said this, it occurred to me that probably he was in these days well acquainted with fuss – Frederica's fuss. Then I asked: "What is the matter?"

I only had a sideways glimpse of him as he answered, for he was busy with the driving-gear.

"Why, I told you, didn't I, that it was arranged for me to be here and at Shepstow week and week about, Falkner and I together, for it is better than taking either moor with a single gun. And I can't take Freda there, for the Shepstow cottage has no accommodation for a lady – only the one room that Falkner and I share. Freda is nervous, poor girl, since her illness, and somehow she has taken a dislike to Roscawen. It is nothing but a fancy, of course, but something had to be done."

"Why, you wrote to mother that you had both fallen in love with the place, and thought it quite ideal."

"Oh, the place is right enough, it is just my poor girl's fancy. She'll tell you I daresay, but don't let her dwell on it more than you can help. You will have Falkner's room, and the week he is over here I've arranged for Vickers to put him up, though I daresay he will come in to meals. Vickers? – oh, he's a neighbour on the opposite side of the water, Roscawen Water, the stream that overflows from the lake in the hills. He's a doctor of science as well as medicine, and has written some awfully clever books. I understand he's at work on another, and comes here for the sake of quiet. But he's a very good sort though not a sportsman, does not mind taking in Falkner, and he is by way of being a friend of Freda's – they read Italian together. No, he isn't married, neither is the parson, worse luck; and there isn't another woman of her own sort within miles. It's desperately lonely for her, I allow, when I'm not here. So there was no help for it. I was bound to send for you or for the mater, and I thought you would be best!"

We were passing through wild scenery of barren broken hills, following the course of the river up-stream. It came racing down a rocky course, full and turbulent from recent rains. Presently the road divided, crossing a narrow bridge; and there we came in sight of the leap the water makes over a shelf of rock, plunging into a deep pool below with a swirl of foam and spray. I would have liked to linger and look, but the car carried us forward quickly, allowing only a glimpse in passing. And, directly after, Robert called my attention to a stone-built small house high up on the hill-side – a bare place it looked, flanked by a clump of firs, but with no surrounding garden-ground; the wild moor and the heather came close under the windows.

"That's Roscawen," he said. "Just a shooting-box, you see. A new-built place, raw, with no history behind it later than yesterday. I was in treaty for Corby, seventeenth century that was, with a ghost in the gallery, but the arrangement fell through. And I'm jolly glad it did" – and here he laughed; an uncomfortable laugh, not of the Larcomb sort, or like himself. And in another minute we were at the door.

Freda welcomed me, and I thought her improved; she was indeed pretty – as pretty as such a frail little thing could be, who looked as if a puff of wind would blow her away. She was very well dressed – of course Robert would take care of that – and her one thought appeared to be of him. She was constantly turning to him with appeal of one sort or another, and seemed nervous and ill at ease when he was out of her sight. "Must you really go tomorrow?" I caught her whisper later, and heard his answer: "Needs must, but you will not mind now you have Mary." I could plainly see that she did mind, and that my companionship was no fair exchange for the loss of his. But was not all this exaction the very way to tire out love?

The ground-floor of the house was divided into a sitting-hall, upon which the front door opened without division, and to the right you entered a fair-sized dining-room. Each of these apartments had the offshoot of a smaller room, one being Freda's snuggery, and the other the gun-room where the gentlemen smoked. Above there were two good bedrooms, a dressing-room and a bathroom, but no higher floor: the gable-space was not utilised, and the servants slept over the kitchen at the back. The room allotted to me, from which Captain Falkner had been ejected, had a wide window and a pleasant aspect. As I was hurriedly dressing for dinner, I could hear the murmur of the river close at hand, but the actual water was not visible, as it flowed too far below the overhanging bank.

I could not see the flowing water, but as I glanced from the window, a wreath of white mist or spray floated up from it, stretched itself out before the wind, and disappeared after the fashion of a puff of steam. Probably there was at that point another fall (so I thought) churning the river into foam. But I had no time to waste in speculation, for we

Larcombs adhere to the good ways of punctuality. I fastened a final hook and eye, and ran downstairs.

Captain Falkner came to dinner and made a fourth at table, but the fifth place which had been laid remained vacant. The two men were full of plans for the morrow, and there was to be an early setting out: Shepstow, the other moor, was some thirty miles away.

"I am afraid you will be dull, Mary," Robert said to me in a sort of apology. "I am forced to keep the car at Shepstow, as I am my own chauffeur. But you and Freda will have her cart to jog about in, so you will be able to look round the nearer country while I am away. You will have to put up with the old mare. I know you like spirit in a horse, but this quiet gee suits Freda, as she can drive her going alone. Then Vickers will look in on you most days. I do not know what is keeping him away tonight."

Freda was in low spirits next morning, and she hung about Robert up to the time of his departure, in a way that I should have found supremely irritating had I been her husband. And I will not be sure that she did not beg him again not to leave her – to my tender mercies I supposed – though I did not hear the request. When the two men had set out with their guns and baggage, the cart was ordered round, and my sister-in-law took me for a drive.

Robert had done well to prepare me for the 'quiet gee': a meek old creature named Grey Madam, that had whitened in the snows of many winters, and expected to progress at a walk whenever the road inclined uphill. And all the roads inclined uphill or down about Roscawen; I do not remember anywhere a level quarter of a mile. It was truly a dull progress, and Freda did not find much to say; perhaps she still was fretting after Robert. But the moors and the swelling hills were beautiful to look at in their crimson flush of heather. "I think Roscawen is lovely," I was prompted to exclaim; and when she agreed in my admiration I added: "You liked it when you first came here, did you not?"

"Yes, I liked it when first I came," she assented, repeating my words, but did not go on to say why she disliked Roscawen now.

She had an errand to discharge at one of the upland farms which supplied them with milk and butter. She drew rein at the gate, and was about to alight, but the woman of the house came forward, and so I heard what passed. Freda gave her order, and then made an inquiry.

"I hope you have found your young cow, Mrs. Elliott? I was sorry to hear it had strayed."

"We've found her, ma'am, but she was dead in the river, and a sad loss it has been to us. A fine young beast as ever we reared, and coming on with her second calf. My husband has been rarely put about, and I'll own I was fit to cry over her myself. This is the fifth loss we have had within the year – a sheep and two lambs in March, and the cart-foal in July."

Freda expressed sympathy.

"You need better fences, is that it, to keep your cattle from the river?"

Mrs. Elliott pursed up her lips and shook her head.

"I won't say, ma'am, but that our fences might be bettered if the landlord would give us material; as it is, we do our best. But when the creatures take that madness for the water, nought but deer-palings would keep them in. I've seen enough in my time here to be sure of that. What makes it come over them I don't take upon myself to say. They make up fine tales in the district about the white woman, but I know nothing of any white women. I only know that when the madness takes them they make for the river, and then they get swept into the deeps."

When we were driving away, I asked Freda what the farmer's wife meant about a white woman and the drowning of her stock.

"I believe there is some story about a woman who was drowned, whose spirit calls the creatures to the river. If you ask Dr. Vickers he will tell you. He makes a study of folklore and local superstitions, and – and that sort of thing. Robert thinks it is all nonsense, and no doubt you will think it nonsense too."

What her own opinion was, Freda did not say. She had a transparent complexion, and a trifling matter made her change colour; a blush rose unaccountably as she answered me, and for a full minute her cheek burned. Why should she blush about Roscawen superstitions and a drowned cow? Then the attention of both of us was suddenly diverted, because Grey Madam took it into her head to shy.

She had mended her pace appreciably since Freda turned her head towards home, trotting now without needing to be urged. We were close upon a cross-roads where three ways met, a triangular green centred by a finger-post. There was in our direction a bank and hedge (hedges here and there replaced the stone walls of the district) and the right wheel went up that bank, giving the cart a dangerous tilt; it recovered balance, however, and went on. Freda, a timid driver, was holding on desperately to the reins.

"Does she often do this sort of thing?" I asked. "I thought Robert said she was quiet."

"So she is – so we thought her. I never knew her do it before," gasped my sister-in-law, still out of breath with her fright.

"And I cannot think what made her shy. There was nothing – absolutely nothing; not even a heap of stones."

Freda did not answer, but I was to hear more about that cross-roads in the course of the day.

Chapter II

After lunch Freda did not seem willing to go out again, so, as I was there to companion her, we both settled down to needlework and a book for alternate reading aloud. The reading, however, languished; when it came to Freda's turn she tired quickly, lost her place twice and again, and seemed unable to fix her attention on the printed page. Was she listening, I wondered later. When silence fell between us, I became aware of a sound recurring at irregular intervals, the sound of water dropping. I looked up at the ceiling expecting to see a stain of wet, for the drop seemed to fall within the room, and close beside me.

"Do you hear that?" I asked. "Has anything gone wrong in the bathroom, do you think?" For we were in Freda's snuggery, and the bathroom was overhead.

But my suggestion of overflowing taps and broken water-pipes left her cold.

"I don't think it is from the bathroom," she replied. "I hear it often. We cannot find out what it is."

Directly she ceased speaking the drop fell again, apparently between us as we sat, and plump upon the carpet. I looked up at the ceiling again, but Freda did not raise her eyes from her embroidery.

"It is very odd," I remarked, and this time she assented, repeating my words, and I saw a shiver pass over her. "I shall go upstairs to the bathroom," I said decidedly, putting down my work. "I am sure those taps must be wrong."

She did not object, or offer to accompany me, she only shivered again.

"Don't be long away, Mary," she said, and I noticed she had grown pale.

There was nothing wrong with the bathroom, or with any part of the water supply; and when I returned to the snuggery the drip had ceased. The next event was a ring at the door bell, and again Freda changed colour, much as she had done when we were driving. In that quiet place, where comers and goers are few, a visitor is an event. But I think this visitor must have been expected. The servant announced Dr. Vickers.

Freda gave him her hand, and made the necessary introduction. This was the friend Robert said would come often to see us, but he was not at all the snuffy, old scientist my fancy had pictured. He was old certainly, if it is a sign of age to be grey-haired, and I daresay there were crowsfeet about those piercing eyes of his; but when you met the eyes, the wrinkles were forgotten. They, at least, were full of youth and fire, and his figure was still upright and flat-shouldered.

We exchanged a few remarks; he asked me if I was familiar with that part of Scotland; and when I answered that I was making its acquaintance for the first time, he praised Roscawen and its neighbourhood. It suited him well, he said, when his object was to seek quiet; and I should find, as he did, that it possessed many attractions. Then he asked me if I was an Italian scholar, and showed a book in his hand, the *Vita Nuova*. Mrs. Larcomb was forgetting her Italian, and he had promised to brush it up for her. So, if I did not find it too great a bore to sit by, he proposed to read aloud. And, should I not know the book, he would give me a sketch of its purport, so that I could follow.

I had, of course, heard of the *Vita Nuova*, who has not! but my knowledge of the language in which it was written went no further than a few modern phrases, of use to a traveller. I disclaimed my ability to follow, and I imagine Dr. Vickers was not ill-pleased to find me ignorant. He took his seat at one end of the Chesterfield sofa, Freda occupying the other, still with that flush on her cheek; and after an observation or two in Italian, he opened his book and began to read.

I imagine he read well. The crisp, flowing syllables sounded very foreign to my ear, and he gave his author the advantage of dramatic expression and emphasis. Now and then he remarked in English on some difficulty in the text, or slipped in a question in Italian which Freda answered, usually by a monosyllable. She kept her eyes fixed upon her work. It was as if she would not look at him, even when he was most impassioned; but I was watching them both, although I never thought – but of course I never thought!

Presently I remembered how time was passing, and the place where letters should be laid ready for the post-bag going out. I had left an unfinished one upstairs, so I slipped away to complete and seal. This done, I re-entered softly (the entrance was behind a screen) and found the Italian lesson over, and a conversation going on in English. Freda was speaking with some animation.

"It cannot any more be called my fancy, for Mary heard it too."

"And you had not told her beforehand? There was no suggestion?"

"I had not said a word to her. Had I, Mary?" – appealing to me as I advanced into sight.

"About what?" I asked, for I had forgotten the water incident.

"About the drops falling. You remarked on them first: I had told you nothing. And you went to look at the taps."

"No, certainly you had not told me. What is the matter? Is there any mystery?"

Dr. Vickers answered:

"The mystery is that Mrs. Larcomb heard these droppings when everyone else was deaf to them. It was supposed to be auto-suggestion on her part. You have disproved that, Miss Larcomb, as your ears are open to them too. That will go far to convince your brother; and now we must seriously seek for cause. This Roscawen district has many legends of strange happenings. We do not want to add one more to the list, and give this modern shooting-box the reputation of a haunted house."

"And it would be an odd sort of ghost, would it not – the sound of dropping water! But – you speak of legends of the district; do you know anything of a white woman who is said to drown cattle? Mrs. Elliott mentioned her this morning at the farm, when she told us she had lost her cow in the river."

"Ay, I heard a cow had been found floating dead in the Pool. I am sorry it belonged to the Elliotts. Nobody lives here for long without hearing that story, and, though the wrath of Roscawen is roused against her, I cannot help being sorry for the white woman. She was young and beautiful once, and well-to-do, for she owned land in her own right, and flocks and herds. But she became very unhappy—"

He was speaking to me, but he looked at Freda. She had taken up her work again, but with inexpert hands, dropping first cotton, and then her thimble.

"She was unhappy, because her husband neglected her. He had – other things to attend to, and the charm she once possessed for him was lost and gone. He left her too much alone. She lost her health, they say, through fretting, and so fell into a melancholy way, spending her time in weeping, and in wandering up and down on the banks of Roscawen Water. She may have fallen in by accident, it was not exactly known; but her death was thought to be suicide, and she was buried at the cross-roads."

"That was where Grey Madam shied this morning," Freda put in.

"And – people suppose – that on the other side of death, finding herself lonely (too guilty, perhaps, for Heaven, but at the same time too innocent for Hell) she wants companions to join her; wants sheep and cows and horses such as used to stock her farms. So she puts madness upon the creatures, and also upon some humans, so that they go down to the river. They see her, so it is said, or they receive a sign which in some way points to the manner of her death. If they see her, she comes for them once, twice, thrice, and the third time they are bound to follow."

This was a gruesome story, I thought as I listened, though not of the sort I could believe. I hoped Freda did not believe it, but of this I was not sure.

"What does she look like?" I asked. "If human beings see her as you say, do they give any account?"

"The story goes that they see foam rising from the water, floating away and dissolving, vaguely in form at first, but afterwards more like the woman she was once; and some say there is a hand that beckons. But I have never seen her. Miss Larcomb, nor spoken to one who has: first hand evidence of this sort is rare, as I daresay you know. So I can tell you no more."

And I was glad there was no more for me to hear, for the story was too tragic for my liking. The happenings of that afternoon left me discomforted – annoyed with Dr. Vickers, which perhaps was unreasonable – with poor Freda, whose fancies had thus proved contagious – annoyed, and here more justly, with myself. Somehow, with such tales going about, Roscawen seemed a far from desirable residence for a nervous invalid; and I was also vaguely conscious of an undercurrent I did not understand. It gave me the feeling you have when you stumble against something unexpected blind-fold, or in the dark, and cannot define its shape.

Dr. Vickers accepted a cup of tea when the tray was brought to us, and then he took his departure, which was as well, seeing we had no gentleman at home to entertain him.

"So Larcomb is away again for a whole week? Is that so?" he said to Freda as he made his adieux.

There was no need for the question, I thought impatiently, as he must very well have known when he was required again to put up Captain Falkner.

"Yes, for a whole week," Freda answered, with again that flush on her cheek; and as soon as we were alone she put up her hand, as if the hot colour burned.

Chapter III

I did not like Dr. Vickers and his Italian lessons, and I had the impression Freda would have been better pleased by their intermission. On the third day she had a headache and charged me to make her excuses, so it fell to me to receive this friend of Robert's, who seemed quite unruffled by her absence. He took advantage of the opportunity to cross-examine me about the water-dropping: had I heard it again since that first occasion, and what explanation of the sounds appeared satisfactory to myself?

The fact was, I had heard it again, twice when I was alone in my room, and once more when sitting with Freda. Then we both sat listening – listening, such small nothings as we had to say to each other dying away, waiting to see which of us would first admit it to the other, and this went on for more than an hour. At last Freda broke out into hysterical crying, the result of over-strained nerves, and with her outburst the sounds ceased. I had been inclined to entertain a notion of the spiritist order, that they might be connected with her presence as medium; but I suppose that must be held disproved, as I also heard them when alone in my own room.

I admitted as little as possible to Dr. Vickers, and was stout in asserting that a natural cause would and must be found, if the explanation were diligently sought for. But I confess I was posed when confronted with the fact that these sounds heard by Freda were inaudible to her husband, also present – to Robert, who has excellent hearing, in common with all our family. Until I came, and was also an auditor, no one in the house but Freda had noticed the dropping, so there was reason for assuming it to be hallucination. Yes, I was sorry for her trouble (answering a question pressed on me), but I maintained that, pending discovery, the best course was to take no notice of drops that wet nothing and left no stain, and did not proceed from overflowing cisterns or faulty pipes.

"They will leave off doing it if not noticed; is that what you think, Miss Larcomb?" And when I rashly assented – "Now perhaps you will define for me what you mean by *they*? Is it the 'natural cause'?"

Here again was a poser: I had formulated no idea that I cared to define. Probably the visitor divined the subject was unwelcome, for he turned to others, conversing agreeably enough for another quarter of an hour. Then he departed, leaving a message of concern for Freda's headache. He hoped it would have amended by next day, when he would call to inquire.

He did call on the following day, when the Italian lesson was mainly conversational, and I had again a feeling Freda was distressed by what was said, though I could only guess at what passed between them under the disguise of a foreign tongue. But at the end I recognised the words "not tomorrow" as spoken by her, and when some protest appeared to follow, she dumbly shook her head.

Dr. Vickers did not stay on for tea as before. Did Freda think she had offended him, for some time later I noticed she had been crying?

That night I had an odd dream that the Roscawen house was sliding down from its foundations into the river at the call of the white woman, and I woke suddenly with the fright.

The next day was the last of Robert's stay at Shepstow. In the evening he and Captain Falkner returned, and at once a different atmosphere seemed to pervade the house. Freda recovered cheerfulness, I heard no more dropping water, and except at dinner on the second evening we saw nothing of Dr. Vickers. But he sent an Italian book with many scored passages, and a note in it, also in Italian, which I saw her open and read, and then immediately tear up into the minutest pieces. I supposed he wished her to keep up her studies, though the lessons were for a while suspended; I heard him say at dinner that he was busy correcting proofs.

So passed four days out of the seven Robert should have spent at Roscawen. But on the fourth evening came a telegraphic summons: his presence was needed in London, at the office, and he was bound to go up to town by the early express next day. And the arrangement was that in returning he should go straight to Shepstow and join

Captain Falkner there; this distant moor was to be reached from a station on another line.

Freda must have known that Robert could not help himself, but it was easy to see how her temporarily restored spirits fell again to zero. I hope I shall never be so dependent on another person's society as she seemed to be on Robert's. I got up to give him his early breakfast, but Freda did not appear; she had a headache, he said, and had passed a restless night. She would not rise till later: perhaps I would go up and see her by-and-bye.

I did go later in the morning, to find her lying like a child that had sobbed itself to sleep, her eyelashes still wet, and a tear sliding down her cheek. So I took a book, and drew a chair to the bedside, waiting for her to wake.

It was a long waiting; she slept on, and slept heavily. And as I sat and watched, there began again the dropping of water, and, for the first time in my experience of them, the drops were wet.

I could find traces now on the carpet of where they fell, and on the spread linen of the sheet; were they made, I wondered fantastically, out of Freda's tears? But they had ceased before she woke, and I did not remark on them to her. Yes, she had a headache, she said, answering my question: it was better, but not gone: she would lie quietly where she was for the present. The servants might bring her a cup of tea when I had luncheon, and she would get up later in the afternoon.

So, as I was not needed, I went out after lunch for a solitary walk. Not being governed by Freda's choice of direction, I determined to explore the course of the river, and especially how it flowed under the steep bank below the house, where I saw the wreath of foam rise in the air on my first evening at Roscawen. I expected to find a fall at this spot, but there was only broken water and rapids, alternating with smoother reaches and deep pools, one of which, I concluded, had been the death-trap of the Elliotts' cow. It was a still, perfect autumn day, warm, but not with the oppression of summer heat, and I walked with enjoyment, following the stream upward to where it issued from the miniature lake among the hills, in which it slept for a while in mid-course. Then I turned homewards, and was within sight of our dwelling when I again beheld the phenomenon of the pillar of foam.

It rose above the rapids, as nearly as I could guess in the same spot as before; and as there was now little or no wind, it did not so quickly spread out and dissipate. I could imagine that at early morning, or in the dimness of evening, it might be taken for a figure of the ghostly sort, especially as, in dissolving, it seemed to move and beckon. I smiled to myself to think that, according to local superstition, I too had seen the white woman; but I felt no least inclination to rush to the river and precipitate myself into its depths. Nor would I gratify Dr. Vickers by telling him what had been my experience, or confide in Freda lest she should tell again.

On reaching home, I turned into the snuggery to see if Freda was downstairs; it must, I thought, be nearly tea-time. She was there; and, as I pushed the door open and was still behind the screen, I heard Dr. Vickers' voice. "Mind," he was saying in English, "I do not press you to decide at once. Wait till you are convinced he does not care. To my thinking he has already made it plain."

I stood arrested, not intending to play eavesdropper, but stricken with surprise. As I moved into sight, the two were standing face to face, and the doctor's figure hid Freda from me. I think his hands were on her shoulders, holding her before him, but of this I am not sure. He was quick of hearing as a cat, and he turned on me at once.

"Ah, how do you do, Miss Larcomb? I was just bidding adieu to your sister-in-law, for I do not think she is well enough today to take her lesson. In fact, I think she is very far from well. These headaches spell slow progress with our study, but we must put up with delay."

He took up the slim book from the table and bestowed it in his pocket, bowed over my hand and was gone.

If Freda had been agitated she concealed any disturbance, and we talked as usual over tea, of my walk, and even of Robert's journey. But she surprised me later in the evening by an unexpected proposition:

"Do you think Mrs. Larcomb would have me to stay at Aston Bury? It would be very kind of her if she would take me in while Robert has these shootings. I do not like Roscawen, and I am not well here. Will you ask her, Mary?"

I answered that I was sure mother would have her if she wished to come to us; but what would Robert say when he had asked me to companion her here? If Robert was willing, I would write – of course. Did he know what she proposed?

No, she said, and there would be no time to consult him. She would like to go as soon as tomorrow. Could we send a telegram, and set out in the morning, staying the night in York, to receive an answer there? That she was very much in earnest about this wish of hers there could be no doubt. She was trembling visibly, and a red fever-spot burned on her cheek.

I wish I had done as she asked. But my Larcomb common-sense was up in arms, and I required to know the reason why. Mother would think it strange if we rushed off to her so, and Robert might not like it; but, given time to make the arrangement, she could certainly pay the visit, and would be received as a welcome guest. I would write to mother and post on the morrow, and she could write to Robert and send the letter by Captain Falkner. Then I said: "Are you nervous here, Freda? Is it because these water-droppings are unexplained?" And when she made a sort of dumb assent, I went on: "You ought not to dwell on anything so trivial; it isn't fair to Robert. It cannot be only this. Surely there is something more?"

The question seemed to increase her distress.

"I want to be a good wife to Robert; oh, I want that, Mary. I can do my duty if I go away; if you will keep me safe at Aston Bury for only a little while. Robert does not understand; he thinks me crazed with delusions. I tried to tell him – I did indeed; hard as it was to tell." While this was spoken she was torn with sobs. "I am terrified to be alone. What is compelling me is too strong. Oh Mary, take me away."

I could get no fuller explanation than this of what was at the root of the trouble. We agreed at last that the two letters should be written and sent on the morrow, and we would hold ourselves in readiness to set out as soon as answers were received. It might be no more than an hysterical fancy on Freda's part, but I was not without suspicion of another sort. But she never mentioned their neighbour's name, and I could not insult her by the suggestion.

The letters were written early on that Thursday morrow, and then Grey Madam was brought round for Freda's drive. The direction chosen took us past the cross-roads in the outward going, and also in return. I remember Freda talked more cheerfully and freely than usual, asking questions about Aston Bury, as if relieved at the prospect of taking refuge there with us. As we went, Grey Madam shied badly at the same spot as before, though there was no visible cause for her terror. I suggested we had better go home a different way; but this appeared impracticable, as the other direction involved an added distance of several miles, and the crossing of a bridge which was thought to be unsafe. In returning, the mare went unwillingly, and, though our pace had been a sober one and the day was not warm, I could see she had broken out into a lather of sweat. As we came to the cross-roads for the second time, the poor creature again shied away from the invisible object which terrified her, and then, seizing the bit between her teeth, she set off at a furious gallop.

Freda was tugging at the reins, but it was beyond her power to stop that mad career, or even guide it; but the mare kept by instinct to the middle of the road. The home gate was open, and I expected she would turn in stablewards; but instead she dashed on to the open moor, making for the river.

We might possibly have jumped out, but there was no time even for thought before we were swaying on the edge of the steep bank. The next moment there was a plunge, a crash, and I remember no more.

The accident was witnessed from the further side – so I heard later. A man left his digging and ran, and it was he who dragged me out, stunned, but not suffocated by the immersion. I came to myself quickly on the bank, and my instant thought was of Freda, but she, entangled with the reins, had been swept down with the mare into the deeper pool. When I staggered up, dizzy and half-blind, begging she might be sought for, he ran on down stream, and there he and Dr. Vickers and another man drew her from the water – lifeless it seemed at first, and it was long before any spark of animation repaid their utmost efforts.

That was a strange return to Roscawen house, she tenderly carried, I able to walk thither; both of us dripping water, real drops, of which the ghostly ones may have been some mysterious forecast, if that's not too fantastic for belief!

It was impossible to shut Dr. Vickers out, and of course he accompanied us; for all my doubt of him, I welcomed the service of his skill when Freda's life was hanging in the balance, and she herself was too remote from this world to recognise who was beside her. But I would have preferred to owe that debt of service to any other; and the feeling I had against him deepened as I witnessed his anguished concern, and caught some unguarded expressions he let fall.

I wired to Robert to acquaint him with what had happened, and he replied "I am coming." And upon that I resolved to speak out, and tell him what I had guessed as the true cause of Freda's trouble, and why she must be removed, not so much from a haunted house, as from an overmastering influence which she dreaded.

Did the risk of loss – the peril barely surmounted, restore the old tenderness between these two? I think it did, at any rate for the time, when Robert found her lying white as a broken lily, and when her weak hands clung about his neck. Perhaps this made him more patient than he would have been otherwise with what I had to say.

He could hardly tax me with being fancy-ridden, but he was aghast – angry – incredulous, all in one. Vickers, of all people in the world; and Freda so worked upon as to be afraid to tell him – afraid to claim the protection that was hers by right. And now the situation was complicated by the fact that Vickers had saved her life, so that thanks were due to him as well as a kicking out of doors. And there was dignity to be thought of too: Freda's dignity as well as his own. Any open scandal must be avoided; she must neither be shamed nor pained.

I do not know what passed between him and Dr. Vickers when they met, but the latter came no more to Roscawen, and after a while I heard incidentally that he had gone abroad. As soon as Freda could be moved, her wish was fulfilled, and I took her to Aston Bury.

Mother was very gentle with her, and I think before the end a genuine affection grew up between the two.

The end was not long delayed; a few months passed, and then she faded out of life in a sort of decline; the shock to the system, so they said, had been greater than her vitality could repair. Robert was a free man again, war had been declared, and he was one of the earliest volunteers for service.

That service won distinction, as everybody knows; and now he is convalescent from his second wound, and here at Aston Bury on leave. And I think the wiser choice his sisters made for him in the first place is now likely to be his own. A much more suitable person than Frederica, and her name is quite a plain one – a real Larcomb name: it is Mary, like my own. I am glad; but in spite of all, poor Freda has a soft place in my memory and my heart. Whatever were her faults and failings, I believe she strove hard to be loyal. And I am sure that she loved Robert well.

The Lost Ghost
Mary E. Wilkins Freeman

Mrs. John Emerson, sitting with her needlework beside the window, looked out and saw Mrs. Rhoda Meserve coming down the street, and knew at once by the trend of her steps and the cant of her head that she meditated turning in at her gate. She also knew by a certain something about her general carriage – a thrusting forward of the neck, a bustling hitch of the shoulders – that she had important news. Rhoda Meserve always had the news as soon as the news was in being, and generally Mrs. John Emerson was the first to whom she imparted it. The two women had been friends ever since Mrs. Meserve had married Simon Meserve and come to the village to live.

Mrs. Meserve was a pretty woman, moving with graceful flirts of ruffling skirts; her clear-cut, nervous face, as delicately tinted as a shell, looked brightly from the plumy brim of a black hat at Mrs. Emerson in the window. Mrs. Emerson was glad to see her coming. She returned the greeting with enthusiasm, then rose hurriedly, ran into the cold parlour and brought out one of the best rocking-chairs. She was just in time, after drawing it up beside the opposite window, to greet her friend at the door.

"Good afternoon," said she. "I declare, I'm real glad to see you. I've been alone all day. John went to the city this morning. I thought of coming over to your house this afternoon, but I couldn't bring my sewing very well. I am putting the ruffles on my new black dress skirt."

"Well, I didn't have a thing on hand except my crochet work," responded Mrs. Meserve, "and I thought I'd just run over a few minutes."

"I'm real glad you did," repeated Mrs. Emerson. "Take your things right off. Here, I'll put them on my bed in the bedroom. Take the rocking-chair."

Mrs. Meserve settled herself in the parlour rocking-chair, while Mrs. Emerson carried her shawl and hat into the little adjoining bedroom. When she returned Mrs. Meserve was rocking peacefully and was already at work hooking blue wool in and out.

"That's real pretty," said Mrs. Emerson.

"Yes, I think it's pretty," replied Mrs. Meserve.

"I suppose it's for the church fair?"

"Yes. I don't suppose it'll bring enough to pay for the worsted, let alone the work, but I suppose I've got to make something."

"How much did that one you made for the fair last year bring?"

"Twenty-five cents."

"It's wicked, ain't it?"

"I rather guess it is. It takes me a week every minute I can get to make one. I wish those that bought such things for twenty-five cents had to make them. Guess they'd sing another song. Well, I suppose I oughtn't to complain as long as it is for the Lord, but sometimes it does seem as if the Lord didn't get much out of it."

"Well, it's pretty work," said Mrs. Emerson, sitting down at the opposite window and taking up her dress skirt.

"Yes, it is real pretty work. I just *love* to crochet."

The two women rocked and sewed and crocheted in silence for two or three minutes. They were both waiting. Mrs. Meserve waited for the other's curiosity to develop in order that her news might have, as it were, a befitting stage entrance. Mrs. Emerson waited for the news. Finally she could wait no longer.

"Well, what's the news?" said she.

"Well, I don't know as there's anything very particular," hedged the other woman, prolonging the situation.

"Yes, there is; you can't cheat me," replied Mrs. Emerson.

"Now, how do you know?"

"By the way you look."

Mrs. Meserve laughed consciously and rather vainly.

"Well, Simon says my face is so expressive I can't hide anything more than five minutes no matter how hard I try," said she. "Well, there is some news. Simon came home with it this noon. He heard it in South Dayton. He had some business over there this morning. The old Sargent place is let."

Mrs. Emerson dropped her sewing and stared.

"You don't say so!"

"Yes, it is."

"Who to?"

"Why, some folks from Boston that moved to South Dayton last year. They haven't been satisfied with the house they had there – it wasn't large enough. The man has got considerable property and can afford to live pretty well. He's got a wife and his unmarried sister in the family. The sister's got money, too. He does business in Boston and it's just as easy to get to Boston from here as from South Dayton, and so they're coming here. You know the old Sargent house is a splendid place."

"Yes, it's the handsomest house in town, but—"

"Oh, Simon said they told him about that and he just laughed. Said he wasn't afraid and neither was his wife and sister. Said he'd risk ghosts rather than little tucked-up sleeping-rooms without any sun, like they've had in the Dayton house. Said he'd rather risk *seeing* ghosts, than risk being ghosts themselves. Simon said they said he was a great hand to joke."

"Oh, well," said Mrs. Emerson, "it is a beautiful house, and maybe there isn't anything in those stories. It never seemed to me they came very straight anyway. I never took much stock in them. All I thought was – if his wife was nervous."

"Nothing in creation would hire me to go into a house that I'd ever heard a word against of that kind," declared Mrs. Meserve with emphasis. "I wouldn't go into that house if they would give me the rent. I've seen enough of haunted houses to last me as long as I live."

Mrs. Emerson's face acquired the expression of a hunting hound.

"Have you?" she asked in an intense whisper.

"Yes, I have. I don't want any more of it."

"Before you came here?"

"Yes; before I was married – when I was quite a girl."

Mrs. Meserve had not married young. Mrs. Emerson had mental calculations when she heard that.

"Did you really live in a house that was—" she whispered fearfully.

Mrs. Meserve nodded solemnly.

"Did you really ever – see – anything—"

Mrs. Meserve nodded.

"You didn't see anything that did you any harm?"

"No, I didn't see anything that did me harm looking at it in one way, but it don't do anybody in this world any good to see things that haven't any business to be seen in it. You never get over it."

There was a moment's silence. Mrs. Emerson's features seemed to sharpen.

"Well, of course I don't want to urge you," said she, "if you don't feel like talking about it; but maybe it might do you good to tell it out, if it's on your mind, worrying you."

"I try to put it out of my mind," said Mrs. Meserve.

"Well, it's just as you feel."

"I never told anybody but Simon," said Mrs. Meserve. "I never felt as if it was wise perhaps. I didn't know what folks might think. So many don't believe in anything they can't understand, that they might think my mind wasn't right. Simon advised me not to talk about it. He said he didn't believe it was anything supernatural, but he had to own up that he couldn't give any explanation for it to save his life. He had to own up that he didn't believe anybody could. Then he said he wouldn't talk about it. He said lots of folks would sooner tell folks my head wasn't right than to own up they couldn't see through it."

"I'm sure I wouldn't say so," returned Mrs. Emerson reproachfully. "You know better than that, I hope."

"Yes, I do," replied Mrs. Meserve. "I know you wouldn't say so."

"And I wouldn't tell it to a soul if you didn't want me to."

"Well, I'd rather you wouldn't."

"I won't speak of it even to Mr. Emerson."

"I'd rather you wouldn't even to him."

"I won't."

Mrs. Emerson took up her dress skirt again; Mrs. Meserve hooked up another loop of blue wool. Then she begun:

"Of course," said she, "I ain't going to say positively that I believe or disbelieve in ghosts, but all I tell you is what I saw. I can't explain it. I don't pretend I can, for I can't. If you can, well and good; I shall be glad, for it will stop tormenting me as it has done and always will otherwise. There hasn't been a day nor a night since it happened that I haven't thought of it, and always I have felt the shivers go down my back when I did."

"That's an awful feeling," Mrs. Emerson said.

"Ain't it? Well, it happened before I was married, when I was a girl and lived in East Wilmington. It was the first year I lived there. You know my family all died five years before that. I told you."

Mrs. Emerson nodded.

"Well, I went there to teach school, and I went to board with a Mrs. Amelia Dennison and her sister, Mrs. Bird. Abby, her name was – Abby Bird. She was a widow; she had never had any children. She had a little money – Mrs. Dennison didn't have any – and she had come to East Wilmington and bought the house they lived in. It was a real pretty house, though it was very old and run down. It had cost Mrs. Bird a good deal to put it in order. I guess that was the reason they took me to board. I guess they thought it would help along a little. I guess what I paid for my board about kept us all in victuals. Mrs. Bird had enough to live on if they were careful, but she had spent so much fixing up the old house that they must have been a little pinched for awhile.

"Anyhow, they took me to board, and I thought I was pretty lucky to get in there. I had a nice room, big and sunny and furnished pretty, the paper and paint all new, and everything as neat as wax. Mrs. Dennison was one of the best cooks I ever saw, and I had a little stove in my room, and there was always a nice fire there when I got home from school. I thought I hadn't been in such a nice place since I lost my own home, until I had been there about three weeks.

"I had been there about three weeks before I found it out, though I guess it had been going on ever since they had been in the house, and that was most four months. They hadn't said anything about it, and I didn't wonder, for there they had just bought the house and been to so much expense and trouble fixing it up.

"Well, I went there in September. I begun my school the first Monday. I remember it was a real cold fall, there was a frost the middle of September, and I had to put on my winter coat. I remember when I came home that night (let me see, I began school on a Monday, and that was two weeks from the next Thursday), I took off my coat downstairs and laid it on the table in the front entry. It was a real nice coat – heavy black broadcloth trimmed with fur; I had had it the winter before. Mrs. Bird called after me as I went upstairs that I ought not to leave it in the front entry for fear somebody might come in and take it, but I only laughed and called back to her that I wasn't afraid. I never was much afraid of burglars.

"Well, though it was hardly the middle of September, it was a real cold night. I remember my room faced west, and the sun was getting low, and the sky was a pale yellow and purple, just as you see it sometimes in the winter when there is going to be a cold snap. I rather think that was the night the frost came the first time. I know Mrs. Dennison covered up some flowers she had in the front yard, anyhow. I remember looking out and seeing an old green plaid shawl of hers over the verbena bed. There was a fire in my little wood-stove. Mrs. Bird made it, I know. She was a real motherly sort of woman; she always seemed to be the happiest when she was doing something to make other folks happy and comfortable. Mrs. Dennison told me she had always been so. She said she had coddled her husband within an inch of his life. 'It's lucky Abby never had any children,' she said, 'for she would have spoilt them.'

"Well, that night I sat down beside my nice little fire and ate an apple. There was a plate of nice apples on my table. Mrs. Bird put them there. I was always very fond of apples. Well, I sat down and ate an apple, and was having a beautiful time, and thinking how lucky I was to have got board in such a place with such nice folks, when I heard a queer little sound at my door. It was such a little hesitating sort of sound that it sounded more like a fumble than a knock, as if someone very timid, with very little hands, was feeling along the door, not quite daring to knock. For a minute I thought it was a mouse. But I waited and it came again, and then I made up my mind it was a knock, but a very little scared one, so I said, 'Come in.'

"But nobody came in, and then presently I heard the knock again. Then I got up and opened the door, thinking it was very queer, and I had a frightened feeling without knowing why.

"Well, I opened the door, and the first thing I noticed was a draught of cold air, as if the front door downstairs was open, but there was a strange close smell about the cold draught. It smelled more like a cellar that had been shut up for years, than out-of-doors. Then I saw something. I saw my coat first. The thing that held it was so small that I couldn't see much of anything else. Then I saw a little white face with eyes so scared and wishful that they seemed as if they might eat a hole in anybody's heart. It was a dreadful little face, with something about it which made it different from any other face on earth, but it was so pitiful that somehow it did away a good deal with the dreadfulness. And there were two little hands spotted purple with the cold, holding up my winter coat, and a strange little far-away voice said: 'I can't find my mother.'

"'For Heaven's sake,' I said, 'who are you?'

"Then the little voice said again: 'I can't find my mother.'

"All the time I could smell the cold and I saw that it was about the child; that cold was clinging to her as if she had come out of some deadly cold place. Well, I took my coat, I did not know what else to do, and the cold was clinging to that. It was as cold as if it had come off ice. When I had the coat I could see the child more plainly. She was dressed in one little white garment made very simply. It was a nightgown, only very long, quite covering her feet, and I could see dimly through it her little thin body mottled purple with the cold. Her face did not look so cold; that was a clear waxen white. Her hair was dark, but it looked as if it might be dark only because it was so damp, almost wet, and might really be light hair. It clung very close to her forehead, which was round and white. She would have been very beautiful if she had not been so dreadful.

"'Who are you?' says I again, looking at her.

"She looked at me with her terrible pleading eyes and did not say anything.

"'What are you?' says I. Then she went away. She did not seem to run or walk like other children. She flitted, like one of those little filmy white butterflies, that don't seem like real ones they are so light, and move as if they had no weight. But she looked back from the head of the stairs. 'I can't find my mother,' said she, and I never heard such a voice.

"'Who is your mother?' says I, but she was gone.

"Well, I thought for a moment I should faint away. The room got dark and I heard a singing in my ears. Then I flung my coat onto the bed. My hands were as cold as ice from holding it, and I stood in my door, and called first Mrs. Bird and then Mrs. Dennison. I didn't dare go down over the stairs where that had gone. It seemed to me I should go mad if I didn't see somebody or something like other folks on the face of the earth. I thought I should never make anybody hear, but I could hear them stepping about downstairs, and I could smell biscuits baking for supper. Somehow the smell of those biscuits seemed the only natural thing left to keep me in my right mind. I didn't dare go over those stairs. I just stood there and called, and finally I heard the entry door open and Mrs. Bird called back:

"'What is it? Did you call, Miss Arms?'

"'Come up here; come up here as quick as you can, both of you,' I screamed out; 'quick, quick, quick!'

"I heard Mrs. Bird tell Mrs. Dennison: 'Come quick, Amelia, something is the matter in Miss Arms' room.' It struck me even then that she expressed herself rather queerly, and it struck me as very queer, indeed, when they both got upstairs and I saw that they knew what had happened, or that they knew of what nature the happening was.

"'What is it, dear?' asked Mrs. Bird, and her pretty, loving voice had a strained sound. I saw her look at Mrs. Dennison and I saw Mrs. Dennison look back at her.

"'For God's sake,' says I, and I never spoke so before – 'for God's sake, what was it brought my coat upstairs?'

"'What was it like?' asked Mrs. Dennison in a sort of failing voice, and she looked at her sister again and her sister looked back at her.

"'It was a child I have never seen here before. It looked like a child,' says I, 'but I never saw a child so dreadful, and it had on a nightgown, and said she couldn't find her mother. Who was it? What was it?'

"I thought for a minute Mrs. Dennison was going to faint, but Mrs. Bird hung onto her and rubbed her hands, and whispered in her ear (she had the cooingest kind of voice), and I ran and got her a glass of cold water. I tell you it took considerable courage to go downstairs alone, but they had set a lamp on the entry table so I could see. I don't believe I could have spunked up enough to have gone downstairs in the dark, thinking every second that child might be close to me. The lamp and the smell of the biscuits baking seemed to sort of keep my courage up, but I tell you I didn't waste much time going down those stairs and out into the kitchen for a glass of water. I pumped as if the house was afire, and I grabbed the first thing I came across in the shape of a tumbler: it was a painted one that Mrs. Dennison's Sunday school class gave her, and it was meant for a flower vase.

"Well, I filled it and then ran upstairs. I felt every minute as if something would catch my feet, and I held the glass to Mrs. Dennison's lips, while Mrs. Bird held her head up, and she took a good long swallow, then she looked hard at the tumbler.

"'Yes,' says I, 'I know I got this one, but I took the first I came across, and it isn't hurt a mite.'

"'Don't get the painted flowers wet,' says Mrs. Dennison very feebly, 'they'll wash off if you do.'

"'I'll be real careful,' says I. I knew she set a sight by that painted tumbler.

"The water seemed to do Mrs. Dennison good, for presently she pushed Mrs. Bird away and sat up. She had been laying down on my bed.

"'I'm all over it now,' says she, but she was terribly white, and her eyes looked as if they saw something outside things. Mrs. Bird wasn't much better, but she always had a sort of settled sweet, good look that nothing could disturb to any great extent. I knew I looked dreadful, for I caught a glimpse of myself in the glass, and I would hardly have known who it was.

"Mrs. Dennison, she slid off the bed and walked sort of tottery to a chair. 'I was silly to give way so,' says she.

"'No, you wasn't silly, sister,' says Mrs. Bird. 'I don't know what this means any more than you do, but whatever it is, no one ought to be called silly for being overcome by anything so different from other things which we have known all our lives.'

"Mrs. Dennison looked at her sister, then she looked at me, then back at her sister again, and Mrs. Bird spoke as if she had been asked a question.

"'Yes,' says she, 'I do think Miss Arms ought to be told – that is, I think she ought to be told all we know ourselves.'

"'That isn't much,' said Mrs. Dennison with a dying-away sort of sigh. She looked as if she might faint away again any minute. She was a real delicate-looking woman, but it turned out she was a good deal stronger than poor Mrs. Bird.

"'No, there isn't much we do know,' says Mrs. Bird, 'but what little there is she ought to know. I felt as if she ought to when she first came here.'

"'Well, I didn't feel quite right about it,' said Mrs. Dennison, 'but I kept hoping it might stop, and anyway, that it might never trouble her, and you had put so much in the house, and we needed the money, and I didn't know but she might be nervous and think she couldn't come, and I didn't want to take a man boarder.'

"'And aside from the money, we were very anxious to have you come, my dear,' says Mrs. Bird.

"'Yes,' says Mrs. Dennison, 'we wanted the young company in the house; we were lonesome, and we both of us took a great liking to you the minute we set eyes on you.'

"And I guess they meant what they said, both of them. They were beautiful women, and nobody could be any kinder to me than they were, and I never blamed them for not telling me before, and, as they said, there wasn't really much to tell.

"They hadn't any sooner fairly bought the house, and moved into it, than they began to see and hear things. Mrs. Bird said they were sitting together in the sitting-room one evening when they heard it the first time. She said her sister was knitting lace (Mrs. Dennison made beautiful knitted lace) and she was reading the Missionary Herald (Mrs. Bird was very much interested in mission work), when all of a sudden they heard something. She heard it first and she laid down her Missionary Herald and listened, and then Mrs. Dennison she saw her listening and she drops her lace. 'What is it you are listening to, Abby?' says she. Then it came again and they both heard, and the cold shivers went down their backs to hear it, though they didn't know why. 'It's the cat, isn't it?' says Mrs. Bird.

"'It isn't any cat,' says Mrs. Dennison.

"'Oh, I guess it *must* be the cat; maybe she's got a mouse,' says Mrs. Bird, real cheerful, to calm down Mrs. Dennison, for she saw she was 'most scared to death, and she was always afraid of her fainting away. Then she opens the door and calls, 'Kitty, kitty, kitty!' They had brought their cat with them in a basket when they came to East Wilmington to live. It was a real handsome tiger cat, a tommy, and he knew a lot.

"Well, she called 'Kitty, kitty, kitty!' and sure enough the kitty came, and when he came in the door he gave a big yawl that didn't sound unlike what they had heard.

"'There, sister, here he is; you see it was the cat,' says Mrs. Bird. 'Poor kitty!'

"But Mrs. Dennison she eyed the cat, and she give a great screech.

"'What's that? What's that?' says she.

"'What's what?' says Mrs. Bird, pretending to herself that she didn't see what her sister meant.

"'Somethin's got hold of that cat's tail,' says Mrs. Dennison. 'Somethin's got hold of his tail. It's pulled straight out, an' he can't get away. Just hear him yawl!'

"'It isn't anything,' says Mrs. Bird, but even as she said that she could see a little hand holding fast to that cat's tail, and then the child seemed to sort of clear out of the dimness behind the hand, and the child was sort of laughing then, instead of looking sad, and she said that was a great deal worse. She said that laugh was the most awful and the saddest thing she ever heard.

"Well, she was so dumbfounded that she didn't know what to do, and she couldn't sense at first that it was anything supernatural. She thought it must be one of the neighbour's children who had run away and was making free of their house, and was teasing their cat, and that they must be just nervous to feel so upset by it. So she speaks up sort of sharp.

"'Don't you know that you mustn't pull the kitty's tail?' says she. 'Don't you know you hurt the poor kitty, and she'll scratch you if you don't take care. Poor kitty, you mustn't hurt her.'

"And with that she said the child stopped pulling that cat's tail and went to stroking her just as soft and pitiful, and the cat put his back up and rubbed and purred as if he liked it. The cat never seemed a mite afraid, and that seemed queer, for I had always heard that animals were dreadfully afraid of ghosts; but then, that was a pretty harmless little sort of ghost.

"Well, Mrs. Bird said the child stroked that cat, while she and Mrs. Dennison stood watching it, and holding onto each other, for, no matter how hard they tried to think it was all right, it didn't look right. Finally Mrs. Dennison she spoke.

"'What's your name, little girl?' says she.

"Then the child looks up and stops stroking the cat, and says she can't find her mother, just the way she said it to me. Then Mrs. Dennison she gave such a gasp that Mrs. Bird thought she was going to faint away, but she didn't. 'Well, who is your mother?' says she. But the child just says again 'I can't find my mother – I can't find my mother.'

"'Where do you live, dear?' says Mrs. Bird.

"'I can't find my mother,' says the child.

"Well, that was the way it was. Nothing happened. Those two women stood there hanging onto each other, and the child stood in front of them, and they asked her questions, and everything she would say was: 'I can't find my mother.'

"Then Mrs. Bird tried to catch hold of the child, for she thought in spite of what she saw that perhaps she was nervous and it was a real child, only perhaps not quite right in its head, that had run away in her little nightgown after she had been put to bed.

"She tried to catch the child. She had an idea of putting a shawl around it and going out – she was such a little thing she could have carried her easy enough – and trying to find out to which of the neighbours she belonged. But the minute she moved toward the child there wasn't any child there; there was only that little voice seeming to come from nothing, saying 'I can't find my mother,' and presently that died away.

"Well, that same thing kept happening, or something very much the same. Once in awhile Mrs. Bird would be washing dishes, and all at once the child would be standing beside her with the dish-towel, wiping them. Of course, that was terrible. Mrs. Bird would wash the dishes all over. Sometimes she didn't tell Mrs. Dennison, it made her so nervous. Sometimes when they were making cake they would find the raisins all picked over, and sometimes little sticks of kindling-wood would be found laying beside the kitchen stove. They never knew when they would come across that child, and always she kept saying over and over that she couldn't find her mother. They never tried talking to her, except once in awhile Mrs. Bird would get desperate and ask her something, but the child never seemed to hear it; she always kept right on saying that she couldn't find her mother.

"After they had told me all they had to tell about their experience with the child, they told me about the house and the people that had lived there before they did. It seemed something dreadful had happened in that house. And the land agent had never let on to them. I don't think they would have bought it if he had, no matter how cheap it was, for even if folks aren't really afraid of anything, they don't want to live in houses where such dreadful things have happened that you keep thinking about them. I know after they told me I should never have stayed there another night, if I hadn't thought so much of them, no matter how comfortable I was made; and I never was nervous, either. But I stayed. Of course, it didn't happen in my room. If it had I could not have stayed."

"What was it?" asked Mrs. Emerson in an awed voice.

"It was an awful thing. That child had lived in the house with her father and mother two years before. They had come – or the father had – from a real good family. He had a good situation: he was a drummer for a big leather house in the city, and they lived real pretty, with plenty to do with. But the mother was a real wicked woman. She was as handsome as a picture, and they said she came from good sort of people enough in Boston, but she was bad clean through, though she was real pretty spoken and most everybody liked her. She used to dress out and make a great show, and she never seemed to take much interest in the child, and folks began to say she wasn't treated right.

"The woman had a hard time keeping a girl. For some reason one wouldn't stay. They would leave and then talk about her awfully, telling all kinds of things. People didn't believe it at first; then they began to. They said that the woman made that little thing, though she wasn't much over five years old, and small and babyish for her age, do most of the work, what there was done; they said the house used to look like a pig-sty when she didn't have help. They said the little thing used to stand on a chair and wash dishes, and they'd seen her carrying in sticks of wood most as big as she was many a time, and they'd heard her mother scolding her. The woman was a fine singer, and had a voice like a screech-owl when she scolded.

"The father was away most of the time, and when that happened he had been away out West for some weeks. There had been a married man hanging about the mother for some time, and folks had talked some; but they weren't sure there was anything wrong, and he was a man very high up, with money, so they kept pretty still for fear he would hear of it and make trouble for them, and of course nobody was sure, though folks did say afterward that the father of the child had ought to have been told.

"But that was very easy to say; it wouldn't have been so easy to find anybody who would have been willing to tell him such a thing as that, especially when they weren't any too sure. He set his eyes by his wife, too. They said all he seemed to think of was to earn money to buy things to deck her out in. And he about worshiped the child, too. They said he was a real nice man. The men that are treated so bad mostly are real nice men. I've always noticed that.

"Well, one morning that man that there had been whispers about was missing. He had been gone quite a while, though, before they really knew that he was missing, because he had gone away and told his wife that he had to go to New York on business and might be gone a week, and not to worry if he didn't get home, and not to worry if he didn't write, because he should be thinking from day to day that he might take the next train home and there would be no use in writing. So the wife waited, and she tried not to worry until it was two days over the week, then she run into a neighbour's and fainted dead away on the floor; and then they made inquiries and found out that he had skipped – with some money that didn't belong to him, too.

"Then folks began to ask where was that woman, and they found out by comparing notes that nobody had seen her since the man went away; but three or four women remembered that she had told them that she thought of taking the child and going to Boston to visit her folks, so when they hadn't seen her around, and the house shut, they jumped to the conclusion that was where she was. They were the neighbours that lived right around her, but they didn't have much to do with her, and she'd gone out of her way to tell them about her Boston plan, and they didn't make much reply when she did.

"Well, there was this house shut up, and the man and woman missing and the child. Then all of a sudden one of the women that lived the nearest remembered something. She remembered that she had waked up three nights running, thinking she heard a child crying somewhere, and once she waked up her husband, but he said it must be the Bisbees' little girl, and she thought it must be. The child wasn't well and was always crying. It used to have colic spells, especially at night. So she didn't think any more about it until this came up, then all of a sudden she did think of it. She told what she had heard, and finally folks began to think they had better enter that house and see if there was anything wrong.

"Well, they did enter it, and they found that child dead, locked in one of the rooms. (Mrs. Dennison and Mrs. Bird never used that room; it was a back bedroom on the second floor.)

"Yes, they found that poor child there, starved to death, and frozen, though they weren't sure she had frozen to death, for she was in bed with clothes enough to keep her pretty warm when she was alive. But she had been there a week, and she was nothing but skin and bone. It looked as if the mother had locked her into the house when she went away, and told her not to make any noise for fear the neighbours would hear her and find out that she herself had gone.

"Mrs. Dennison said she couldn't really believe that the woman had meant to have her own child starved to death. Probably she thought the little thing would raise somebody, or folks would try to get in the house and find her. Well, whatever she thought, there the child was, dead.

"But that wasn't all. The father came home, right in the midst of it; the child was just buried, and he was beside himself. And – he went on the track of his wife, and he found her, and he shot her dead; it was in all the papers at the time; then he disappeared. Nothing had been seen of him since. Mrs. Dennison said that she thought he had either made way with himself or got out of the country, nobody knew, but they did know there was something wrong with the house.

"'I knew folks acted queer when they asked me how I liked it when we first came here,' says Mrs. Dennison, 'but I never dreamed why till we saw the child that night.'

"I never heard anything like it in my life," said Mrs. Emerson, staring at the other woman with awestruck eyes.

"I thought you'd say so," said Mrs. Meserve. "You don't wonder that I ain't disposed to speak light when I hear there is anything queer about a house, do you?"

"No, I don't, after that," Mrs. Emerson said.

"But that ain't all," said Mrs. Meserve.

"Did you see it again?" Mrs. Emerson asked.

"Yes, I saw it a number of times before the last time. It was lucky I wasn't nervous, or I never could have stayed there, much as I liked the place and much as I thought of those two women; they were beautiful women, and no mistake. I loved those women. I hope Mrs. Dennison will come and see me sometime.

"Well, I stayed, and I never knew when I'd see that child. I got so I was very careful to bring everything of mine upstairs, and not leave any little thing in my room that needed doing, for fear she would come lugging up my coat or hat or gloves or I'd find things done when there'd been no live being in the room to do them. I can't tell you how I dreaded seeing her; and worse than the seeing her was the hearing her say, 'I can't find my mother.' It was enough to make your blood run cold. I never heard a living child cry for its mother that was anything so pitiful as that dead one. It was enough to break your heart.

"She used to come and say that to Mrs. Bird oftener than to anyone else. Once I heard Mrs. Bird say she wondered if it was possible that the poor little thing couldn't really find her mother in the other world, she had been such a wicked woman.

"But Mrs. Dennison told her she didn't think she ought to speak so nor even think so, and Mrs. Bird said she shouldn't wonder if she was right. Mrs. Bird was always very easy to put in the wrong. She was a good woman, and one that couldn't do things enough for other folks. It seemed as if that was what she lived on. I don't think she was ever so scared by that poor little ghost, as much as she pitied it, and she was 'most heartbroken because she couldn't do anything for it, as she could have done for a live child.

"'It seems to me sometimes as if I should die if I can't get that awful little white robe off that child and get her in some clothes and feed her and stop her looking for her mother,' I heard her say once, and she was in earnest. She cried when she said it. That wasn't long before she died.

"Now I am coming to the strangest part of it all. Mrs. Bird died very sudden. One morning – it was Saturday, and there wasn't any school – I went downstairs to breakfast, and Mrs. Bird wasn't there; there was nobody but Mrs. Dennison. She was pouring out the coffee when I came in. 'Why, where's Mrs. Bird?' says I.

"'Abby ain't feeling very well this morning,' says she; 'there isn't much the matter, I guess, but she didn't sleep very well, and her head aches, and she's sort of chilly, and I told her I thought she'd better stay in bed till the house gets warm.' It was a very cold morning.

"'Maybe she's got cold,' says I.

"'Yes, I guess she has,' says Mrs. Dennison. 'I guess she's got cold. She'll be up before long. Abby ain't one to stay in bed a minute longer than she can help.'

"Well, we went on eating our breakfast, and all at once a shadow flickered across one wall of the room and over the ceiling the way a shadow will sometimes when somebody passes the window outside. Mrs. Dennison and I both looked up, then out of the window; then Mrs. Dennison she gives a scream.

"'Why, Abby's crazy!' says she. 'There she is out this bitter cold morning, and – and –' She didn't finish, but she meant the child.

For we were both looking out, and we saw, as plain as we ever saw anything in our lives, Mrs. Abby Bird walking off over the white snow-path with that child holding fast to her hand, nestling close to her as if she had found her own mother.

"'She's dead,' says Mrs. Dennison, clutching hold of me hard. 'She's dead; my sister is dead!'

"She was. We hurried upstairs as fast as we could go, and she was dead in her bed, and smiling as if she was dreaming, and one arm and hand was stretched out as if something had hold of it; and it couldn't be straightened even at the last – it lay out over her casket at the funeral."

"Was the child ever seen again?" asked Mrs. Emerson in a shaking voice.

"No," replied Mrs. Meserve; "that child was never seen again after she went out of the yard with Mrs. Bird."

The Whistling Room

William Hope Hodgson

Carnacki shook a friendly fist at me as I entered, late. Then he opened the door into the dining room, and ushered the four of us – Jessop, Arkright, Taylor and myself – in to dinner.

We dined well, as usual, and, equally as usual, Carnacki was pretty silent during the meal. At the end, we took our wine and cigars to our usual positions, and Carnacki – having got himself comfortable in his big chair – began without any preliminary:

"I have just got back from Ireland, again," he said. "And I thought you chaps would be interested to hear my news. Besides, I fancy I shall see the thing clearer, after I have told it all out straight. I must tell you this, though, at the beginning – up to the present moment, I have been utterly and completely 'stumped'. I have tumbled upon one of the most peculiar cases of 'haunting' – or devilment of some sort – that I have come against. Now listen.

"I have been spending the last few weeks at Iastrae Castle, about twenty miles northeast of Galway. I got a letter about a month ago from a Mr. Sid K. Tassoc, who it seemed had bought the place lately, and moved in, only to find that he had bought a very peculiar piece of property.

"When I got there, he met me at the station, driving a jaunting car, and drove me up to the castle, which, by the way, he called a 'house shanty'. I found that he was 'pigging it' there with his boy brother and another American, who seemed to be half-servant and half-companion. It seems that all the servants had left the place, in a body, as you might say, and now they were managing among themselves, assisted by some day-help.

"The three of them got together a scratch feed, and Tassoc told me all about the trouble whilst we were at table. It is most extraordinary, and different from anything that I have had to do with; though that Buzzing Case was very queer, too.

"Tassoc began right in the middle of his story. 'We've got a room in this shanty,' he said, 'which has got a most infernal whistling in it; sort of haunting it. The thing starts any time; you never know when, and it goes on until it frightens you. All the servants have gone, as you know. It's not ordinary whistling, and it isn't the wind. Wait till you hear it.'

"'We're all carrying guns,' said the boy; and slapped his coat pocket.

"'As bad as that?' I said; and the older boy nodded. 'It may be soft,' he replied; 'but wait till you've heard it. Sometimes I think it's some infernal thing, and the next moment, I'm just as sure that someone's playing a trick on me.'

"'Why?' I asked. 'What is to be gained?'

"'You mean,' he said, 'that people usually have some good reason for playing tricks as elaborate as this. Well, I'll tell you. There's a lady in this province, by the name of Miss Donnehue, who's going to be my wife, this day two months. She's more beautiful than they make them, and so far as I can see, I've just stuck my head into an Irish hornet's nest. There's about a score of hot young Irishmen been courting her these two years gone, and now that I'm come along and cut them out, they feel raw against me. Do you begin to understand the possibilities?'

"'Yes,' I said. 'Perhaps I do in a vague sort of way; but I don't see how all this affects the room?'

"'Like this,' he said. 'When I'd fixed it up with Miss Donnehue, I looked out for a place, and bought this little house shanty. Afterward, I told her – one evening during dinner, that I'd decided to tie up here. And then she asked me whether I wasn't afraid of the whistling room. I told her it must have been thrown in gratis, as I'd heard nothing about it. There were some of her men friends present, and I saw a smile go 'round. I found out, after a bit of questioning, that several people have bought this place during the last twenty-odd years. And it was always on the market again, after a trial.

"'Well, the chaps started to bait me a bit, and offered to take bets after dinner that I'd not stay six months in the place. I looked once or twice to Miss Donnehue, so as to be sure I was 'getting the note' of the talkee-talkee; but I could see that she didn't take it as a joke, at all. Partly, I think, because there was a bit of a sneer in the way the men were tackling me, and partly because she really believes there is something in this yarn of the Whistling Room.

"'However, after dinner, I did what I could to even things up with the others. I nailed all their bets, and screwed them down hard and safe. I guess some of them are going to be hard hit, unless I lose; which I don't mean to. Well, there you have practically the whole yarn.'

"'Not quite,' I told him. 'All that I know, is that you have bought a castle with a room in it that is in some way 'queer', and that you've been doing some betting. Also, I know that your servants have got frightened and run away. Tell me something about the whistling?'

"'Oh, that!' said Tassoc; 'that started the second night we were in. I'd had a good look 'round the room, in the daytime, as you can understand; for the talk up at Arlestrae – Miss Donnehue's place – had made me wonder a bit. But it seems just as usual as some of the other rooms in the old wing, only perhaps a bit more lonesome. But that may be only because of the talk about it, you know.

"'The whistling started about ten o'clock, on the second night, as I said. Tom and I were in the library, when we heard an awfully queer whistling, coming along the East Corridor – the room is in the East Wing, you know.

"'That's that blessed ghost!' I said to Tom, and we collared the lamps off the table, and went up to have a look. I tell you, even as we dug along the corridor, it took me a bit in the throat, it was so beastly queer. It was a sort of tune, in a way; but more as if a devil or some rotten thing were laughing at you, and going to get 'round at your back. That's how it makes you feel.

"'When we got to the door, we didn't wait; but rushed it open; and then I tell you the sound of the thing fairly hit me in the face. Tom said he got it the same way – sort of felt stunned and bewildered. We looked all 'round, and soon got so nervous, we just cleared out, and I locked the door.

"'We came down here, and had a stiff peg each. Then we got fit again, and began to think we'd been nicely had. So we took sticks, and went out into the grounds, thinking after all it must be some of these confounded Irishmen working the ghost-trick on us. But there was not a leg stirring.

"'We went back into the house, and walked over it, and then paid another visit to the room. But we simply couldn't stand it. We fairly ran out, and locked the door again. I don't know how to put it into words; but I had a feeling of being up against something that was rottenly dangerous. You know! We've carried our guns ever since.

"'Of course, we had a real turn out of the room next day, and the whole house place; and we even hunted 'round the grounds; but there was nothing queer. And now I don't know what to think; except that the sensible part of me tells me that it's some plan of these Wild Irishmen to try to take a rise out of me.'

"'Done anything since?' I asked him.

"'Yes,' he said – 'watched outside of the door of the room at nights, and chased 'round the grounds, and sounded the walls and floor of the room. We've done everything we could think of; and it's beginning to get on our nerves; so we sent for you.'

"By this, we had finished eating. As we rose from the table, Tassoc suddenly called out: 'Ssh! Hark!'

"We were instantly silent, listening. Then I heard it, an extraordinary hooning whistle, monstrous and inhuman, coming from far away through corridors to my right.

"'By G—d!' said Tassoc; 'and it's scarcely dark yet! Collar those candles, both of you, and come along.'

"In a few moments, we were all out of the door and racing up the stairs. Tassoc turned into a long corridor, and we followed, shielding our candles as we ran. The sound seemed to fill all the passage as we drew near, until I had the feeling that the whole air throbbed under the power of some wanton Immense Force – a sense of an actual taint, as you might say, of monstrosity all about us.

"Tassoc unlocked the door; then, giving it a push with his foot, jumped back, and drew his revolver. As the door flew open, the sound beat out at us, with an effect impossible to explain to one who has not heard it – with a certain, horrible personal note in it; as if in there in the darkness you could picture the room rocking and creaking in a mad, vile glee to its own filthy piping and whistling and hooning. To stand there and listen, was to be stunned by Realisation. It was as if someone showed you the mouth of a vast pit suddenly, and said: That's Hell. And you knew that they had spoken the truth. Do you get it, even a little bit?

"I stepped back a pace into the room, and held the candle over my head, and looked quickly 'round. Tassoc and his brother joined me, and the man came up at the back, and we all held our candles high. I was deafened with the shrill, piping hoon of the whistling; and then, clear in my ear, something seemed to be saying to me: 'Get out of here – quick! Quick! Quick!'

"As you chaps know, I never neglect that sort of thing. Sometimes it may be nothing but nerves; but as you will remember, it was just such a warning that saved me in the 'Grey Dog' Case, and in the 'Yellow Finger' Experiments; as well as other times. Well, I turned sharp 'round to the others: 'Out!' I said. 'For God's sake, *out* quick.' And in an instant I had them into the passage.

"There came an extraordinary yelling scream into the hideous whistling, and then, like a clap of thunder, an utter silence. I slammed the door, and locked it. Then, taking the key, I looked 'round at the others. They were pretty white, and I imagine I must have looked that way too. And there we stood a moment, silent.

"'Come down out of this, and have some whisky,' said Tassoc, at last, in a voice he tried to make ordinary; and he led the way. I was the back man, and I know we all kept looking over our shoulders. When we got downstairs, Tassoc passed the bottle 'round. He took a drink, himself, and slapped his glass down on to the table. Then sat down with a thud.

"'That's a lovely thing to have in the house with you, isn't it!' he said. And directly afterward: 'What on earth made you hustle us all out like that, Carnacki?'

"'Something seemed to be telling me to get out, quick,' I said. 'Sounds a bit silly, superstitious, I know; but when you are meddling with this sort of thing, you've got to take notice of queer fancies, and risk being laughed at.'

"I told him then about the 'Grey Dog' business, and he nodded a lot to that. 'Of course,' I said, 'this may be nothing more than those would-be rivals of yours playing some funny game; but, personally, though I'm going to keep an open mind, I feel that there is something beastly and dangerous about this thing.'

"We talked for a while longer, and then Tassoc suggested billiards, which we played in a pretty half-hearted fashion, and all the time cocking an ear to the door, as you might say, for sounds; but none came, and later, after coffee, he suggested early bed, and a thorough overhaul of the room on the morrow.

"My bedroom was in the newer part of the castle, and the door opened into the picture gallery. At the East end of the gallery was the entrance to the corridor of the East Wing; this was shut off from the gallery by two old and heavy oak doors, which looked rather odd and quaint beside the more modern doors of the various rooms.

"When I reached my room, I did not go to bed; but began to unpack my instrument trunk, of which I had retained the key. I intended to take one or two preliminary steps at once, in my investigation of the extraordinary whistling.

"Presently, when the castle had settled into quietness, I slipped out of my room, and across to the entrance of the great corridor. I opened one of the low, squat doors, and threw the beam of my pocket searchlight down the passage. It was empty, and I went through the doorway, and pushed-to the oak behind me. Then along the great passageway, throwing my light before and behind, and keeping my revolver handy.

"I had hung a 'protection belt' of garlic 'round my neck, and the smell of it seemed to fill the corridor and give me assurance; for, as you all know, it is a wonderful 'protection' against the more usual Aeiirii forms of semi-materialisation, by which I supposed the whistling might be produced; though, at that period of my investigation, I was quite prepared to find it due to some perfectly natural cause; for it is astonishing the enormous number of cases that prove to have nothing abnormal in them.

"In addition to wearing the necklet, I had plugged my ears loosely with garlic, and as I did not intend to stay more than a few minutes in the room, I hoped to be safe.

"When I reached the door, and put my hand into my pocket for the key, I had a sudden feeling of sickening funk. But I was not going to back out, if I could help it. I unlocked the door and turned the handle. Then I gave the door a sharp push with my foot, as Tassoc had done, and drew my revolver, though I did not expect to have any use for it, really.

"I shone the searchlight all 'round the room, and then stepped inside, with a disgustingly horrible feeling of walking slap into a waiting Danger. I stood a few seconds, waiting, and nothing happened, and the empty room showed bare from corner to corner. And then, you know, I realised that the room was full of an abominable silence; can you understand that? A sort of purposeful silence, just as sickening as any of the filthy noises the Things have power to make. Do you remember what I told you about that 'Silent Garden' business? Well, this room had just that same *malevolent* silence – the beastly quietness of a thing that is looking at you and not seeable itself, and thinks that it has got you. Oh, I recognised it instantly, and I whipped the top off my lantern, so as to have light over the *whole* room.

"Then I set-to, working like fury, and keeping my glance all about me. I sealed the two windows with lengths of human hair, right across, and sealed them at every frame. As I worked, a queer, scarcely perceptible tenseness stole into the air of the place, and the silence seemed, if you can understand me, to grow more solid. I knew then that I had no business there without 'full protection'; for I was practically certain that this was no mere Aeiirii development; but one of the worst forms, as the Saiitii; like that 'Grunting Man' case – you know.

"I finished the window, and hurried over to the great fireplace. This is a huge affair, and has a queer gallows-iron, I think they are called, projecting from the back of the arch. I sealed the opening with seven human hairs – the seventh crossing the six others.

"Then, just as I was making an end, a low, mocking whistle grew in the room. A cold, nervous pricking went up my spine, and 'round my forehead from the back. The hideous sound filled all the room with an extraordinary, grotesque parody of human whistling, too gigantic to be human – as if something gargantuan and monstrous made the sounds softly. As I stood there a last moment, pressing down the final seal, I had no doubt but that I had come across one of those rare and horrible cases of the *Inanimate* reproducing the functions of the *Animate*, I made a grab for my lamp, and went quickly to the door, looking over my shoulder, and listening for the thing that I expected. It came, just as I got my hand upon the handle – a squeal of incredible, malevolent anger, piercing through the low hooning of the whistling. I dashed out, slamming the door and locking it. I leant a little against the opposite wall of the corridor, feeling rather funny; for it had been a narrow squeak…. 'Theyr be noe sayfetie to be gained bye gayrds of holieness when the monyster hath pow'r to speak throe woode and stoene.' So runs the passage in the Sigsand MS., and I proved it in that

'Nodding Door' business. There is no protection against this particular form of monster, except, possibly, for a fractional period of time; for it can reproduce itself in, or take to its purpose, the very protective material which you may use, and has the power to '*forme* wythine the pentycle'; though not immediately. There is, of course, the possibility of the Unknown Last Line of the Saaamaaa Ritual being uttered; but it is too uncertain to count upon, and the danger is too hideous; and even then it has no power to protect for more than 'maybee fyve beats of the harte', as the Sigsand has it.

"Inside of the room, there was now a constant, meditative, hooning whistling; but presently this ceased, and the silence seemed worse; for there is such a sense of hidden mischief in a silence.

"After a little, I sealed the door with crossed hairs, and then cleared off down the great passage, and so to bed.

"For a long time I lay awake; but managed eventually to get some sleep. Yet, about two o'clock I was waked by the hooning whistling of the room coming to me, even through the closed doors. The sound was tremendous, and seemed to beat through the whole house with a presiding sense of terror. As if (I remember thinking) some monstrous giant had been holding mad carnival with itself at the end of that great passage.

"I got up and sat on the edge of the bed, wondering whether to go along and have a look at the seal; and suddenly there came a thump on my door, and Tassoc walked in, with his dressing gown over his pajamas.

"'I thought it would have waked you, so I came along to have a talk,' he said. '*I* can't sleep. Beautiful! Isn't it!'

"'Extraordinary!' I said, and tossed him my case.

"He lit a cigarette, and we sat and talked for about an hour; and all the time that noise went on, down at the end of the big corridor.

"Suddenly, Tassoc stood up:

"'Let's take our guns, and go and examine the brute,' he said, and turned toward the door.

"'No!' I said. 'By Jove – *no!* I can't say anything definite, yet; but I believe that room is about as dangerous as it well can be.'

"'Haunted – *really* haunted?' he asked, keenly and without any of his frequent banter.

"I told him, of course, that I could not say a definite *yes* or *no* to such a question; but that I hoped to be able to make a statement, soon. Then I gave him a little lecture on the False Re-Materialisation of the Animate-Force through the Inanimate-Inert. He began then to see the particular way in the room might be dangerous, if it were really the subject of a manifestation.

"About an hour later, the whistling ceased quite suddenly, and Tassoc went off again to bed. I went back to mine, also, and eventually got another spell of sleep.

"In the morning, I went along to the room. I found the seals on the door intact. Then I went in. The window seals and the hair were all right; but the seventh hair across the great fireplace was broken. This set me thinking. I knew that it might, very possibly, have snapped, through my having tensioned it too highly; but then, again, it might have been broken by something else. Yet, it was scarcely possible that a man, for instance, could have passed between the six unbroken hairs; for no one would ever have noticed them, entering the room that way, you see; but just walked through them, ignorant of their very existence.

"I removed the other hairs, and the seals. Then I looked up the chimney. It went up straight, and I could see blue sky at the top. It was a big, open flue, and free from any suggestion of hiding places, or corners. Yet, of course, I did not trust to any such casual examination, and after breakfast, I put on my overalls, and climbed to the very top, sounding all the way; but I found nothing.

"Then I came down, and went over the whole of the room – floor, ceiling, and walls, mapping them out in six-inch squares, and sounding with both hammer and probe. But there was nothing abnormal.

"Afterward, I made a three-weeks search of the whole castle, in the same thorough way; but found nothing. I went even further, then; for at night, when the whistling commenced, I made a microphone test. You see, if the whistling were mechanically produced, this test would have made evident to me the working of the machinery, if there were any such concealed within the walls. It certainly was an up-to-date method of examination, as you must allow.

"Of course, I did not think that any of Tassoc's rivals had fixed up any mechanical contrivance; but I thought it just possible that there had been some such thing for producing the whistling, made away back in the years, perhaps with the intention of giving the room a reputation that would ensure its being free of inquisitive folk. You see what I mean? Well, of course, it was just possible, if this were the case, that someone knew the secret of the machinery, and was utilising the knowledge to play this devil of a prank on Tassoc. The microphone test of the walls would certainly have made this known to me, as I have said; but there was nothing of the sort in the castle; so that I had practically no doubt at all now, but that it was a genuine case of what is popularly termed 'haunting'.

"All this time, every night, and sometimes most of each night, the hooning whistling of the Room was intolerable. It was as if an intelligence there knew that steps were being taken against it, and piped and hooned in a sort of mad, mocking contempt. I tell you, it was as extraordinary as it was horrible. Time after time, I went along

– tiptoeing noiselessly on stockinged feet – to the sealed door (for I always kept the Room sealed). I went at all hours of the night, and often the whistling, inside, would seem to change to a brutally malignant note, as though the half-animate monster saw me plainly through the shut door. And all the time the shrieking, hooning whistling would fill the whole corridor, so that I used to feel a precious lonely chap, messing about there with one of Hell's mysteries.

"And every morning, I would enter the room, and examine the different hairs and seals. You see, after the first week, I had stretched parallel hairs all along the walls of the room, and along the ceiling; but over the floor, which was of polished stone, I had set out little, colourless wafers, tacky-side uppermost. Each wafer was numbered, and they were arranged after a definite plan, so that I should be able to trace the exact movements of any living thing that went across the floor.

"You will see that no material being or creature could possibly have entered that room, without leaving many signs to tell me about it. But nothing was ever disturbed, and I began to think that I should have to risk an attempt to stay the night in the room, in the Electric Pentacle. Yet, mind you, I knew that it would be a crazy thing to do; but I was getting stumped, and ready to do anything.

"Once, about midnight, I did break the seal on the door, and have a quick look in; but, I tell you, the whole Room gave one mad yell, and seemed to come toward me in a great belly of shadows, as if the walls had bellied in toward me. Of course, that must have been fancy. Anyway, the yell was sufficient, and I slammed the door, and locked it, feeling a bit weak down my spine. You know the feeling.

"And then, when I had got to that state of readiness for anything, I made something of a discovery. It was about one in the morning, and

I was walking slowly 'round the castle, keeping in the soft grass. I had come under the shadow of the East Front, and far above me, I could hear the vile, hooning whistle of the Room, up in the darkness of the unlit wing. Then, suddenly, a little in front of me, I heard a man's voice, speaking low, but evidently in glee:

"'By George! You Chaps; but I wouldn't care to bring a wife home in that!' it said, in the tone of the cultured Irish.

"Someone started to reply; but there came a sharp exclamation, and then a rush, and I heard footsteps running in all directions. Evidently, the men had spotted me.

"For a few seconds, I stood there, feeling an awful ass. After all, *they* were at the bottom of the haunting! Do you see what a big fool it made me seem? I had no doubt but that they were some of Tassoc's rivals; and here I had been feeling in every bone that I had hit a real, bad, genuine Case! And then, you know, there came the memory of hundreds of details, that made me just as much in doubt again. Anyway, whether it was natural, or ab-natural, there was a great deal yet to be cleared up.

"I told Tassoc, next morning, what I had discovered, and through the whole of every night, for five nights, we kept a close watch 'round the East Wing; but there was never a sign of anyone prowling about; and all the time, almost from evening to dawn, that grotesque whistling would hoon incredibly, far above us in the darkness.

"On the morning after the fifth night, I received a wire from here, which brought me home by the next boat. I explained to Tassoc that I was simply bound to come away for a few days; but told him to keep up the watch 'round the castle. One thing I was very careful to do, and that was to make him absolutely promise never to go into the Room, between sunset and sunrise. I made it clear to him that we knew nothing definite yet, one way or the other; and if the room were what I had first thought it to be, it might be a lot better for him to die first, than enter it after dark.

"When I got here, and had finished my business, I thought you chaps would be interested; and also I wanted to get it all spread out clear in my mind; so I rung you up. I am going over again tomorrow, and when I get back, I ought to have something pretty extraordinary to tell you. By the way, there is a curious thing I forgot to tell you. I tried to get a phonographic record of the whistling; but it simply produced no impression on the wax at all. That is one of the things that has made me feel queer, I can tell you. Another extraordinary thing is that the microphone will not magnify the sound – will not even transmit it; seems to take no account of it, and acts as if it were nonexistent. I am absolutely and utterly stumped, up to the present. I am a wee bit curious to see whether any of your dear clever heads can make daylight of it. *I* cannot – not yet."

He rose to his feet.

"Goodnight, all," he said, and began to usher us out abruptly, but without offence, into the night.

A fortnight later, he dropped each of us a card, and you can imagine that I was not late this time. When we arrived, Carnacki took us straight into dinner, and when we had finished, and all made ourselves comfortable, he began again, where he had left off:

"Now just listen quietly; for I have got something pretty queer to tell you. I got back late at night, and I had to walk up to the castle, as I had not warned them that I was coming. It was bright moonlight; so that the walk was rather a pleasure, than otherwise. When I got there, the whole place was in darkness, and I thought I would take a walk 'round outside, to see whether Tassoc or his brother was keeping watch. But I could not find them anywhere, and concluded that they had got tired of it, and gone off to bed.

"As I returned across the front of the East Wing, I caught the hooning whistling of the Room, coming down strangely through the stillness of the night. It had a queer note in it, I remember – low and constant, queerly meditative. I looked up at the window, bright in the moonlight, and got a sudden thought to bring a ladder from the stable yard, and try to get a look into the Room, through the window.

"With this notion, I hunted 'round at the back of the castle, among the straggle of offices, and presently found a long, fairly light ladder; though it was heavy enough for one, goodness knows! And I thought at first that I should never get it reared. I managed at last, and let the ends rest very quietly against the wall, a little below the sill of the larger window. Then, going silently, I went up the ladder. Presently, I had my face above the sill and was looking in alone with the moonlight.

"Of course, the queer whistling sounded louder up there; but it still conveyed that peculiar sense of something whistling quietly to itself – can you understand? Though, for all the meditative lowness of the note, the horrible, gargantuan quality was distinct – a mighty parody of the human, as if I stood there and listened to the whistling from the lips of a monster with a man's soul.

"And then, you know, I saw something. The floor in the middle of the huge, empty room, was puckered upward in the centre into a strange soft-looking mound, parted at the top into an ever-changing hole, that pulsated to that great, gentle hooning. At times, as I watched, I saw the heaving of the indented mound, gap across with a queer, inward suction, as with the drawing of an enormous breath; then the thing would dilate and pout once more to the incredible melody. And suddenly, as I stared, dumb, it came to me that the thing was living. I was looking at two enormous, blackened lips, blistered and brutal, there in the pale moonlight....

"Abruptly, they bulged out to a vast, pouting mound of force and sound, stiffened and swollen, and hugely massive and clean-cut in the moon-beams. And a great sweat lay heavy on the vast upper-lip. In the same moment of time, the whistling had burst into a mad screaming note, that seemed to stun me, even where I stood, outside of the window. And then, the following moment, I was staring blankly at the solid, undisturbed floor of the room – smooth, polished stone flooring, from wall to wall; and there was an absolute silence.

"You can picture me staring into the quiet Room, and knowing what I knew. I felt like a sick, frightened kid, and wanted to slide *quietly* down the ladder, and run away. But in that very instant, I heard Tassoc's voice calling to me from within the Room, for help, *help*. My God! But I got such an awful dazed feeling; and I had a vague, bewildered notion that, after all, it was the Irishmen who had got him in there, and were taking it out of him. And then the call came again, and I burst the window, and jumped in to help him. I had a confused idea that the call had come from within the shadow of the great fireplace, and I raced across to it; but there was no one there.

"'Tassoc!' I shouted, and my voice went empty-sounding 'round the great apartment; and then, in a flash, *I knew that Tassoc had never called*. I whirled 'round, sick with fear, toward the window, and as I did so, a frightful, exultant whistling scream burst through the Room. On my left, the end wall had bellied in toward me, in a pair of gargantuan lips, black and utterly monstrous, to within a yard of my face. I fumbled for a mad instant at my revolver; not for *it*, but myself; for the danger was a thousand times worse than death. And then, suddenly, the Unknown Last Line of the Saaamaaa Ritual was whispered quite audibly in the room. Instantly, the thing happened that I have known once before. There came a sense as of dust falling continually and monotonously, and I knew that my life hung uncertain and suspended for a flash, in a brief, reeling vertigo of unseeable things. Then *that* ended, and I knew that I might live. My soul and body blended again, and life and power came to me. I dashed furiously at the window, and hurled myself out head-foremost; for I can tell you that I had stopped being afraid of death. I crashed down on to the ladder, and slithered, grabbing and grabbing; and so came some way or other alive to the bottom. And there I sat in the soft, wet grass, with the moonlight all about me; and far above, through the broken window of the Room, there was a low whistling.

"That is the chief of it. I was not hurt, and I went 'round to the front, and knocked Tassoc up. When they let me in, we had a long yarn, over some good whisky – for I was shaken to pieces – and I explained things as much as I could, I told Tassoc that the room would have to come down, and every fragment of it burned in a blast-furnace, erected within a pentacle. He nodded. There was nothing to say. Then I went to bed.

"We turned a small army on to the work, and within ten days, that lovely thing had gone up in smoke, and what was left was calcined, and clean.

"It was when the workmen were stripping the paneling, that I got hold of a sound notion of the beginnings of that beastly development. Over the great fireplace, after the great oak panels had been torn down, I found that there was let into the masonry a scrollwork of stone, with on it an old inscription, in ancient Celtic, that here in this room was burned Dian Tiansay, Jester of King Alzof, who made the Song of Foolishness upon King Ernore of the Seventh Castle.

"When I got the translation clear, I gave it to Tassoc. He was tremendously excited; for he knew the old tale, and took me down to the library to look at an old parchment that gave the story in detail. Afterward, I found that the incident was well known about the countryside; but always regarded more as a legend than as history. And no one seemed ever to have dreamt that the old East Wing of Iastrae Castle was the remains of the ancient Seventh Castle.

"From the old parchment, I gathered that there had been a pretty dirty job done, away back in the years. It seems that King Alzof and King Ernore had been enemies by birthright, as you might say truly; but that nothing more than a little raiding had occurred on either side for years, until Dian Tiansay made the Song of Foolishness upon King Ernore, and sang it before King Alzof; and so greatly was it appreciated that King Alzof gave the jester one of his ladies, to wife.

"Presently, all the people of the land had come to know the song, and so it came at last to King Ernore, who was so angered that he made war upon his old enemy, and took and burned him and his castle; but Dian Tiansay, the jester, he brought with him to his own place, and having torn his tongue out because of the song which he had made and sung, he imprisoned him in the Room in the East Wing (which was evidently used for unpleasant purposes), and the jester's wife he kept for himself, having a fancy for her prettiness.

"But one night, Dian Tiansay's wife was not to be found, and in the morning they discovered her lying dead in her husband's arms, and he sitting, whistling the Song of Foolishness, for he had no longer the power to sing it.

"Then they roasted Dian Tiansay, in the great fireplace – probably from that selfsame 'galley-iron' which I have already mentioned. And until he died, Dian Tiansay ceased not to whistle the Song of Foolishness, which he could no longer sing. But afterward, 'in that room' there was often heard at night the sound of something whistling; and there 'grew a power in that room', so that none dared to sleep in it. And presently, it would seem, the King went to another castle; for the whistling troubled him.

"There you have it all. Of course, that is only a rough rendering of the translation of the parchment. But it sounds extraordinarily quaint. Don't you think so?"

"Yes," I said, answering for the lot. "But how did the thing grow to such a tremendous manifestation?"

"One of those cases of continuity of thought producing a positive action upon the immediate surrounding material," replied Carnacki. "The development must have been going forward through centuries, to have produced such a monstrosity. It was a true instance of Saiitii manifestation, which I can best explain by likening it to a living spiritual fungus, which involves the very structure of the aether-fiber itself, and, of course, in so doing, acquires an essential control over the 'material substance' involved in it. It is impossible to make it plainer in a few words."

"What broke the seventh hair?" asked Taylor.

But Carnacki did not know. He thought it was probably nothing but being too severely tensioned. He also explained that they found out that the men who had run away had not been up to mischief; but had come over secretly, merely to hear the whistling, which, indeed, had suddenly become the talk of the whole countryside.

"One other thing," said Arkright, "have you any idea what governs the use of the Unknown Last Line of the Saaamaaa Ritual? I know, of course, that it was used by the Ab-human Priests in the Incantation of Raaaee; but what used it on your behalf, and what made it?"

"You had better read Harzan's Monograph, and my Addenda to it, on Astral and Astral Co-ordination and Interference," said Carnacki. "It is an extraordinary subject, and I can only say here that the human vibration may not be insulated from the astral (as is always believed to be the case, in interferences by the Ab-human), without immediate action being taken by those Forces which govern the spinning of the outer circle. In other words, it is being proved, time after time, that there is some inscrutable Protective Force constantly intervening between the human soul (not the body, mind you) and the Outer Monstrosities. Am I clear?"

"Yes, I think so," I replied. "And you believe that the Room had become the material expression of the ancient Jester – that his soul, rotten with hatred, had bred into a monster – eh?" I asked.

"Yes," said Carnacki, nodding, "I think you've put my thought rather neatly. It is a queer coincidence that Miss Donnehue is supposed to be descended (so I have heard since) from the same King Ernore. It makes one think some curious thoughts, doesn't it? The marriage coming on, and the Room waking to fresh life. If she had gone into that room, ever...eh? *It* had waited a long time. Sins of the fathers. Yes, I've thought of that. They're to be married next week, and I am to be best man, which is a thing I hate. And he won his bets, rather! Just think, *if* ever she had gone into that room. Pretty horrible, eh?"

He nodded his head, grimly, and we four nodded back. Then he rose and took us collectively to the door, and presently thrust us forth in friendly fashion on the Embankment and into the fresh night air.

"Goodnight," we all called back, and went to our various homes. If she had, eh? If she had? That is what I kept thinking.

The Toll-House
W.W. Jacobs

"It's all nonsense," said Jack Barnes. "Of course people have died in the house; people die in every house. As for the noises – wind in the chimney and rats in the wainscot are very convincing to a nervous man. Give me another cup of tea, Meagle."

"Lester and White are first," said Meagle, who was presiding at the tea-table of the Three Feathers Inn. "You've had two."

Lester and White finished their cups with irritating slowness, pausing between sips to sniff the aroma, and to discover the sex and dates of arrival of the 'strangers' which floated in some numbers in the beverage. Mr. Meagle served them to the brim, and then, turning to the grimly expectant Mr. Barnes, blandly requested him to ring for hot water.

"We'll try and keep your nerves in their present healthy condition," he remarked. "For my part I have a sort of half-and-half belief in the supernatural."

"All sensible people have," said Lester. "An aunt of mine saw a ghost once."

White nodded.

"I had an uncle that saw one," he said.

"It always is somebody else that sees them," said Barnes.

"Well, there is a house," said Meagle, "a large house at an absurdly low rent, and nobody will take it. It has taken toll of at least one life of every family that has lived there – however short the time – and since it has stood empty caretaker after caretaker has died there. The last caretaker died fifteen years ago."

"Exactly," said Barnes. "Long enough ago for legends to accumulate."

"I'll bet you a sovereign you won't spend the night there alone, for all your talk," said White, suddenly.

"And I," said Lester.

"No," said Barnes slowly. "I don't believe in ghosts nor in any supernatural things whatever; all the same I admit that I should not care to pass a night there alone."

"But why not?" inquired White.

"Wind in the chimney," said Meagle with a grin.

"Rats in the wainscot," chimed in Lester. "As you like," said Barnes, colouring.

"Suppose we all go," said Meagle. "Start after supper, and get there about eleven. We have been walking for ten days now without an adventure – except Barnes's discovery that ditchwater smells longest. It will be a novelty, at any rate, and, if we break the spell by all surviving, the grateful owner ought to come down handsome."

"Let's see what the landlord has to say about it first," said Lester. "There is no fun in passing a night in an ordinary empty house. Let us make sure that it is haunted."

He rang the bell, and, sending for the landlord, appealed to him in the name of our common humanity not to let them waste a night watching in a house in which spectres and hobgoblins had no part. The reply was more than reassuring, and the landlord, after describing with considerable art the exact appearance of a head which had been seen hanging out of a window in the moonlight, wound up with a polite but urgent request that they would settle his bill before they went.

"It's all very well for you young gentlemen to have your fun," he said indulgently; "but supposing as how you are all found dead in the morning, what about me? It ain't called the Toll-House for nothing, you know."

"Who died there last?" inquired Barnes, with an air of polite derision.

"A tramp," was the reply. "He went there for the sake of half a crown, and they found him next morning hanging from the balusters, dead."

"Suicide," said Barnes. "Unsound mind."

The landlord nodded. "That's what the jury brought it in," he said slowly; "but his mind was sound enough when he went in there. I'd known him, off and on, for years. I'm a poor man, but I wouldn't spend the night in that house for a hundred pounds."

He repeated this remark as they started on their expedition a few hours later. They left as the inn was closing for the night; bolts shot noisily behind them, and, as the regular customers trudged slowly homewards, they set off at a brisk pace in the direction of the house. Most of the cottages were already in darkness, and lights in others went out as they passed.

"It seems rather hard that we have got to lose a night's rest in order to convince Barnes of the existence of ghosts," said White.

"It's in a good cause," said Meagle. "A most worthy object; and something seems to tell me that we shall succeed. You didn't forget the candles, Lester?"

"I have brought two," was the reply; "all the old man could spare."

There was but little moon, and the night was cloudy. The road between high hedges was dark, and in one place, where it ran through a wood, so black that they twice stumbled in the uneven ground at the side of it.

"Fancy leaving our comfortable beds for this!" said White again. "Let me see; this desirable residential sepulchre lies to the right, doesn't it?"

"Farther on," said Meagle.

They walked on for some time in silence, broken only by White's tribute to the softness, the cleanliness, and the comfort of the bed which was receding farther and farther into the distance. Under Meagle's guidance they turned oft at last to the right, and, after a walk of a quarter of a mile, saw the gates of the house before them.

The lodge was almost hidden by overgrown shrubs and the drive was choked with rank growths. Meagle leading, they pushed through it until the dark pile of the house loomed above them.

"There is a window at the back where we can get in, so the landlord says," said Lester, as they stood before the hall door.

"Window?" said Meagle. "Nonsense. Let's do the thing properly. Where's the knocker?"

He felt for it in the darkness and gave a thundering rat-tat-tat at the door.

"Don't play the fool," said Barnes crossly.

"Ghostly servants are all asleep," said Meagle gravely, "but I'll wake them up before I've done with them. It's scandalous keeping us out here in the dark."

He plied the knocker again, and the noise volleyed in the emptiness beyond. Then with a sudden exclamation he put out his hands and stumbled forward.

"Why, it was open all the time," he said, with an odd catch in his voice. "Come on."

"I don't believe it was open," said Lester, hanging back. "Somebody is playing us a trick."

"Nonsense," said Meagle sharply. "Give me a candle. Thanks. Who's got a match?"

Barnes produced a box and struck one, and Meagle, shielding the candle with his hand, led the way forward to the foot of the stairs. "Shut the door, somebody," he said, "there's too much draught."

"It is shut," said White, glancing behind him.

Meagle fingered his chin. "Who shut it?" he inquired, looking from one to the other. "Who came in last?"

"I did," said Lester, "but I don't remember shutting it – perhaps I did, though."

Meagle, about to speak, thought better of it, and, still carefully guarding the flame, began to explore the house, with the others close behind. Shadows danced on the walls and lurked in the corners as they proceeded. At the end of the passage they found a second staircase, and ascending it slowly gained the first floor.

"Careful!" said Meagle, as they gained the landing.

He held the candle forward and showed where the balusters had broken away. Then he peered curiously into the void beneath.

"This is where the tramp hanged himself, I suppose," he said thoughtfully.

"You've got an unwholesome mind," said White, as they walked on. "This place is qutie creepy enough without your remembering that. Now let's find a comfortable room and have a little nip of whiskey apiece and a pipe. How will this do?"

He opened a door at the end of the passage and revealed a small square room. Meagle led the way with the candle, and, first melting a drop or two of tallow, stuck it on the mantelpiece. The others seated themselves on the floor and watched pleasantly as White drew from his pocket a small bottle of whiskey and a tin cup.

"H'm! I've forgotten the water," he exclaimed. "I'll soon get some," said Meagle.

He tugged violently at the bell-handle, and the rusty jangling of a bell sounded from a distant kitchen. He rang again.

"Don't play the fool," said Barnes roughly.

Meagle laughed. "I only wanted to convince you," he said kindly. "There ought to be, at any rate, one ghost in the servants' hall."

Barnes held up his hand for silence.

"Yes?" said Meagle with a grin at the other two. "Is anybody coming?"

"Suppose we drop this game and go back," said Barnes suddenly. "I don't believe in spirits, but nerves are outside anybody's command. You may laugh as you like, but it really seemed to me that I heard a door open below and steps on the stairs."

His voice was drowned in a roar of laughter.

"He is coming round," said Meagle with a smirk. "By the time I have done with him he will be a confirmed believer. Well, who will go and get some water? Will you, Barnes?"

"No," was the reply.

"If there is any it might not be safe to drink after all these years," said Lester. "We must do without it."

Meagle nodded, and taking a seat on the floor held out his hand for the cup. Pipes were lit and the clean, wholesome smell of tobacco filled the room. White produced a pack of cards; talk and laughter rang through the room and died away reluctantly in distant corridors.

"Empty rooms always delude me into the belief that I possess a deep voice," said Meagle. "Tomorrow—"

He started up with a smothered exclamation as the light went out suddenly and something struck him on the head. The others sprang to their feet. Then Meagle laughed.

"It's the candle," he exclaimed. "I didn't stick it enough."

Barnes struck a match and relighting the candle stuck it on the mantelpiece, and sitting down took up his cards again.

"What was I going to say?" said Meagle. "Oh, I know; tomorrow I—"

"Listen!" said White, laying his hand on the other's sleeve. "Upon my word I really thought I heard a laugh."

"Look here!" said Barnes. "What do you say to going back? I've had enough of this. I keep fancying that I hear things too; sounds of something moving about in the passage outside. I know it's only fancy, but it's uncomfortable."

"You go if you want to," said Meagle, "and we will play dummy. Or you might ask the tramp to take your hand for you, as you go downstairs."

Barnes shivered and exclaimed angrily. He got up and, walking to the half-closed door, listened.

"Go outside," said Meagle, winking at the other two. "I'll dare you to go down to the hall door and back by yourself."

Barnes came back and, bending forward, lit his pipe at the candle.

"I am nervous but rational," he said, blowing out a thin cloud of smoke. "My nerves tell me that there is something prowling up and down the long passage outside; my reason tells me that it is all nonsense. Where are my cards?"

He sat down again, and taking up his hand, looked through it carefully and led.

"Your play, White," he said after a pause. White made no sign.

"Why, he is asleep," said Meagle. "Wake up, old man. Wake up and play."

Lester, who was sitting next to him, took the sleeping man by the arm and shook him, gently at first and then with some roughness; but

White, with his back against the wall and his head bowed, made no sign. Meagle bawled in his ear and then turned a puzzled face to the others.

"He sleeps like the dead," he said, grimacing. "Well, there are still three of us to keep each other company."

"Yes," said Lester, nodding. "Unless—Good Lord! Suppose—"

He broke off and eyed them trembling.

"Suppose what?" inquired Meagle.

"Nothing," stammered Lester. "Let's wake him. Try him again. *White! White!*"

"It's no good," said Meagle seriously; "there's something wrong about that sleep."

"That's what I meant," said Lester; "and if he goes to sleep like that, why shouldn't—"

Meagle sprang to his feet. "Nonsense," he said roughly. "He's tired out; that's all. Still, let's take him up and clear out. You take his legs and Barnes will lead the way with the candle. Yes? Who's that?"

He looked up quickly towards the door. "Thought I heard somebody tap," he said with a shamefaced laugh. "Now, Lester, up with him. One, two— Lester! Lester!"

He sprang forward too late; Lester, with his face buried in his arms, had rolled over on the floor fast asleep, and his utmost efforts failed to awaken him.

"He – is – asleep," he stammered. "'Asleep!'"

Barnes, who had taken the candle from the mantelpiece, stood peering at the sleepers in silence and dropping tallow over the floor.

"We must get out of this," said Meagle. "Quick!" Barnes hesitated. "We can't leave them here—" he began.

"We must," said Meagle in strident tones. "If you go to sleep I shall go—Quick! Come."

He seized the other by the arm and strove to drag him to the door. Barnes shook him off, and putting the candle back on the mantelpiece, tried again to arouse the sleepers.

"It's no good," he said at last, and, turning from them, watched Meagle. "Don't you go to sleep," he said anxiously.

Meagle shook his head, and they stood for some time in uneasy silence. "May as well shut the door," said Barnes at last.

He crossed over and closed it gently. Then at a scuffling noise behind him he turned and saw Meagle in a heap on the hearthstone.

With a sharp catch in his breath he stood motionless. Inside the room the candle, fluttering in the draught, showed dimly the grotesque attitudes of the sleepers. Beyond the door there seemed to his over-wrought imagination a strange and stealthy unrest. He tried to whistle, but his lips were parched, and in a mechanical fashion he stooped, and began to pick up the cards which littered the floor.

He stopped once or twice and stood with bent head listening. The unrest outside seemed to increase; a loud creaking sounded from the stairs.

"Who is there?" he cried loudly.

The creaking ceased. He crossed to the door and flinging it open, strode out into the corridor. As he walked his fears left him suddenly.

"Come on!" he cried with a low laugh. "All of you! All of you! Show your faces – your infernal ugly faces! Don't skulk!"

He laughed again and walked on; and the heap in the fireplace put out his head tortoise fashion and listened in horror to the retreating footsteps. Not until they had become inaudible in the distance did the listeners' features relax.

"Good Lord, Lester, we've driven him mad," he said in a frightened whisper. "We must go after him."

There was no reply. Meagle sprung to his feet. "Do you hear?" he cried. "Stop your fooling now; this is serious. White! Lester! Do you hear?"

He bent and surveyed them in angry bewilderment. "All right," he said in a trembling voice. "You won't frighten me, you know."

He turned away and walked with exaggerated carelessness in the direction of the door. He even went outside and peeped through the crack, but the sleepers did not stir. He glanced into the blackness behind, and then came hastily into the room again.

He stood for a few seconds regarding them. The stillness in the house was horrible; he could not even hear them breathe. With a sudden resolution he snatched the candle from the mantelpiece and held the flame to White's finger. Then as he reeled back stupefied the footsteps again became audible.

He stood with the candle in his shaking hand listening. He heard them ascending the farther staircase, but they stopped suddenly as he went to the door. He walked a little way along the passage, and they went scurrying down the stairs and then at a jog-trot along the corridor below. He went back to the main staircase, and they ceased again.

For a time he hung over the balusters, listening and trying to pierce the blackness below; then slowly, step by step, he made his way downstairs, and, holding the candle above his head, peered about him.

"Barnes!" he called. "Where are you?" Shaking with fright, he made his way along the passage, and summoning up all his courage pushed open doors and gazed fearfully into empty rooms. Then, quite suddenly, he heard the footsteps in front of him.

He followed slowly for fear of extinguishing the candle, until they led him at last into a vast bare kitchen with damp walls and a broken floor. In front of him a door leading into an inside room had just closed. He ran towards it and flung it open, and a cold air blew out the candle. He stood aghast.

"Barnes!" he cried again. "Don't be afraid! It is I – Meagle!"

There was no answer. He stood gazing into the darkness, and all the time the idea of something close at hand watching was upon him. Then suddenly the steps broke out overhead again.

He drew back hastily, and passing through the kitchen groped his way along the narrow passages. He could now see better in the darkness, and finding himself at last at the foot of the staircase began to ascend it noiselessly. He reached the landing just in time to see a figure disappear round the angle of a wall. Still careful to make no noise, he followed the sound of the steps until they led him to the top floor, and he cornered the chase at the end of a short passage.

"Barnes!" he whispered. "Barnes!"

Something stirred in the darkness. A small circular window at the end of the passage just softened the blackness and revealed the dim outlines of a motionless figure. Meagle, in place of advancing, stood almost as still as a sudden horrible doubt took possession of him. With his eyes fixed on the shape in front he fell back slowly and, as it advanced upon him, burst into a terrible cry.

"Barnes! For God's sake! Is it you?"

The echoes of his voice left the air quivering, but the figure before him paid no heed. For a moment he tried to brace his courage up to endure its approach, then with a smothered cry he turned and fled.

The passages wound like a maze, and he threaded them blindly in a vain search for the stairs. If he could get down and open the hall door—

He caught his breath in a sob; the steps had begun again. At a lumbering trot they clattered up and down the bare passages, in and out, up and down, as though in search of him. He stood appalled, and then as they drew near entered a small room and stood behind the door as they rushed by. He came out and ran swiftly and noiselessly in the other direction, and in a moment the steps were after him. He found the long corridor and raced along it at top speed. The stairs he knew were at the end, and with the steps close behind he descended them in blind haste. The steps gained on him, and he shrank to the side to let them pass, still continuing his headlong flight. Then suddenly he seemed to slip off the earth into space.

Lester awoke in the morning to find the sunshine streaming into the room, and White sitting up and regarding with some perplexity a badly blistered finger.

"Where are the others?" inquired Lester. "Gone, I suppose," said White. "We must have been asleep."

Lester arose, and stretching his stiffened limbs, dusted his clothes with his hands, and went out into the corridor. White followed. At the noise of their approach a figure which had been lying asleep at the other end sat up and revealed the face of Barnes. "Why, I've been asleep," he said in surprise. "I don't remember coming here. How did I get here?"

"Nice place to come for a nap," said Lester, severely, as he pointed to the gap in the balusters. "Look there! Another yard and where would you have been?"

He walked carelessly to the edge and looked over. In response to his startled cry the others drew near, and all three stood gazing at the dead man below.

Lost Hearts

M.R. James

It was, as far as I can ascertain, in September of the year 1811 that a post-chaise drew up before the door of Aswarby Hall, in the Heart of Lincolnshire. The little boy who jumped out as soon as it had stopped, looked about him with the keenest curiosity during the short interval that elapsed between the ringing of the bell and the opening of the hall door. He saw a tall, square, red-brick house, built in the reign of Anne; a stone-pillared porch had been added in the purest classical style of 1790; the windows of the house were many, tall and narrow, with small panes and thick white woodwork. A pediment, pierced with a round window, crowned the front. There were wings to right and left, connected by curious glazed galleries, supported by colonnades, with the central block. These wings plainly contained the stables and offices of the house. Each was surmounted by an ornamental cupola with a gilded vane.

An evening light shone on the building, making the window-panes glow like so many fires. Away from the Hall in front stretched a flat park studded with oaks and fringed with firs, which stood out against the sky. The clock in the church-tower, buried in trees on the edge of the park, only its golden weather-cock catching the light, was striking six, and the sound came gently beating down the wind. It was altogether a pleasant impression, though tinged with the sort of melancholy appropriate to an evening in early autumn, that was conveyed to the mind of the boy who was standing in the porch waiting for the door to open to him.

The post-chaise had brought him from Warwickshire, where, some six months before, he had been left an orphan. Now, owing to the generous offer of his elderly cousin, Mr. Abney, he had come to live at Aswarby. The offer was unexpected, because all who knew anything of Mr. Abney looked upon him as a somewhat austere recluse, into whose steady-going household the advent of a small boy would import a new and, it seemed, incongruous element. The truth is that very little was known of Mr. Abney's pursuits or temper. The Professor of Greek at Cambridge had been heard to say that no one knew more of the religious beliefs of the later pagans than did the owner of Aswarby. Certainly his library contained all the then available books bearing on the Mysteries, the Orphic poems, the worship of Mithras, and the Neo-Platonists. In the marble-paved hall stood a fine group of Mithras slaying a bull, which had been imported from the Levant at great expense by the owner. He had contributed a description of it to the *Gentleman's Magazine*, and he had written a remarkable series of articles in the *Critical Museum* on the superstitions of the Romans of the Lower Empire. He was looked upon, in fine, as a man wrapped up in his books, and it was a matter of great surprise among his neighbours that he should even have heard of his cousin, Stephen Elliot, much more that he should have volunteered to make him an inmate of Aswarby Hall.

Whatever may have been expected by his neighbours, it is certain that Mr. Abney – the tall, the thin, the austere – seemed inclined to give his young cousin a kindly reception. The moment the front door was opened he darted out of his study, rubbing his hands with delight.

"How are you, my boy? – how are you? How old are you?" said he – "that is, you are not too much tired, I hope, by your journey to eat your supper?"

"No, thank you, sir," said Master Elliot; "I am pretty well."

"That's a good lad," said Mr. Abney. "And how old are you, my boy?"

It seemed a little odd that he should have asked the question twice in the first two minutes of their acquaintance.

"I'm twelve years old next birthday, sir," said Stephen.

"And when is your birthday, my dear boy? Eleventh of September, eh? That's well – that's very well. Nearly a year hence, isn't it? I like – ha, ha! – I like to get these things down in my book. Sure it's twelve? Certain?"

"Yes, quite sure, Sir."

"Well, Well! Take him to Mrs. Bunch's room, Parkes, and let him have his tea – supper – whatever it is."

"Yes, sir," answered the staid Mr. Parkes: and conducted Stephen to the lower regions.

Mrs. Bunch was the most comfortable and human person whom Stephen had as yet met in Aswarby. She made him completely at home: they were great friends in a quarter of an hour: and great friends they remained. Mrs. Bunch had been born in the neighbourhood some fifty-five years before the date of Stephen's arrival, and her residence at the Hall was of twenty years standing. Consequently, if anyone knew the ins and outs of the house and the district, Mrs. Bunch knew them; and she was by no means disinclined to communicate her information.

Certainly there were plenty of things about the Hall and the Hall gardens which Stephen, who was of an adventurous and enquiring turn, was anxious to have explained to him. Who built the temple at the end of the laurel walk? Who was the old man whose picture hung on the staircase, sitting at a table, with a skull under his hand? These and many similar points were cleared up by the resources of Mrs. Bunch's powerful intellect. There were others, however, of which the explanations furnished were less satisfactory.

One November evening Stephen was sitting by the fire in the housekeeper's room reflecting on his surroundings.

"Is Mr. Abney a good man, and will he go to heaven?" he suddenly asked, with the peculiar confidence which children possess in the ability of their elders to settle these questions, the decision of which is believed to be reserved for other tribunals.

"Good? – bless the child!" said Mrs. Bunch. "Master's as kind a soul as ever I see! Didn't I never tell you of the little boy as he took in out of the street, as you may say, this seven years back? and the little girl, two years after I first come here?"

"No. Do tell me all about them, Mrs. Bunch – now this minute!"

"Well," said Mrs. Bunch, "the little girl I don't seem to recollect so much about. I know master brought her back with him from his walk one day, and give orders to Mrs. Ellis, as was housekeeper then, as she should be took every care with. And the pore child hadn't no one belonging to her – she told me so her own self – and here she lived with us a matter of three weeks it might be; and then, whether she were somethink of a gipsy in her blood or what not, but one morning she out of her bed afore any of us had opened a eye, and neither track nor yet trace of her have I set eyes on since. Master was wonderful put about, and had all the ponds dragged; but it's my belief she was had away by them gypsies, for there was singing round the house for as much as an hour the night she went, and Parkes, he declares he heard them a-calling in the woods all that afternoon. Dear, dear! a hodd child she was, so silent in her ways and all, but I was wonderful taken up with her, so domesticated she was – surprising."

"And what about the little boy?" said Stephen.

"Ah, that poor boy!" sighed Mrs. Bunch. "He were a foreigner – Jevanny he called himself – and he come a-tweakin' his hurdy-gurdy round and about the drive one winter day, and master 'ad him in that minute, and ast all about where he came from, and how old he was, and how he made his way, and where was his relatives, and all as kind as heart could wish. But it went the same way with him. They're a hunruly lot, them foreign nations, I do suppose, and he was off one fine morning just the same as the girl. Why he went and what he done was our question for as much as a year after; for he never took his 'urdy-gurdy, and there it lays on the shelf."

The remainder of the evening was spent by Stephen in miscellaneous cross-examination of Mrs. Bunch and in efforts to extract a tune from the hurdy-gurdy.

That night he had a curious dream. At the end of the passage at the top of the house, in which his bedroom was situated, there was an old disused bathroom. It was kept locked, but the upper half of the door was glazed, and, since the muslin curtains which used to hang there had long been gone, you could look in and see the lead-lined bath affixed to the wall on the right hand, with its head towards the window. On the night of which I am speaking, Stephen Elliot found himself, as he thought, looking through the glazed door. The moon was shining through the window, and he was gazing at a figure which lay in the bath.

His description of what he saw reminds me of what I once beheld myself in the famous vaults of St. Michan's Church in Dublin, which possess the horrid property of preserving corpses from decay for centuries. A figure inexpressibly thin and pathetic, of a dusty leaden colour, enveloped in a shroud-like garment, the thin lips crooked into a faint and dreadful smile, the hands pressed tightly over the region of the heart.

As he looked upon it, a distant, almost inaudible moan seemed to issue from its lips, and the arms began to stir. The terror of the sight forced Stephen backwards, and he awoke to the fact that he was indeed standing on the cold boarded floor of the passage in the full light of the moon. With a courage which I do not think can be common among boys of his age, he went to the door of the bathroom to ascertain if the figure of his dream were really there. It was not, and he went back to bed.

Mrs. Bunch was much impressed next morning by his story, and went so far as to replace the muslin curtain over the glazed door of the bathroom. Mr. Abney, moreover, to whom he confided his experiences at breakfast, was greatly interested, and made notes of the matter in what he called 'his book'.

The spring equinox was approaching, as Mr. Abney frequently reminded his cousin, adding that this had been always considered by the ancients to be a critical time for the young: that Stephen would do well to take care of himself, and shut his bedroom window at night; and that Censorinus had some valuable remarks on the subject. Two incidents that occurred about this time made an impression upon Stephen's mind.

The first was after an unusually uneasy and oppressed night that he had passed – though he could not recall any particular dream that he had had.

The following evening Mrs. Bunch was occupying herself in mending his nightgown.

"Gracious me, Master Stephen!" she broke forth rather irritably, "how do you manage to tear your nightdress all to flinders this way? Look here, sir, what trouble you do give to poor servants that have to darn and mend after you!"

There was indeed a most destructive and apparently wanton series of slits or scorings in the garment, which would undoubtedly require a skilful needle to make good. They were confined to the left side of the chest – long, parallel slits, about six inches in length, some of them not quite piercing the texture of the linen. Stephen could only express his entire ignorance of their origin: he was sure that they were not there the night before.

"But," he said, "Mrs. Bunch, they are just the same as the scratches on the outside of my bedroom door; and I'm sure I never had anything to do with making them."

Mrs. Bunch gazed at him open-mouthed, then snatched up a candle, departed hastily from the room, and was heard making her way upstairs. In a few minutes she came down.

"Well," she said, "Master Stephen, it's a funny thing to me how them marks and scratches can 'a' come there – too high up for any cat or dog to 'ave made 'em, much less a rat; for all the world like a Chinaman's finger-nails, as my uncle in the tea-trade used to tell us of when we was girls together. I wouldn't say nothing to master, not if I was you, Master Stephen, my dear; and just turn the key of your door when you go to your bed."

"I always do, Mrs. Bunch, as soon as I've said my prayers."

"Ah, that's a good child: always say your prayers, and then no one can't hurt you."

Herewith Mrs. Bunch addressed herself to mending the injured nightgown, with intervals of meditation, until bed-time. This was on a Friday night in March, 1812.

On the following evening the usual duet of Stephen and Mrs. Bunch was augmented by the sudden arrival of Mr. Parkes, the butler, who as a rule kept himself rather to himself in the pantry. He did not see that Stephen was there: he was, moreover, flustered, and less slow of speech than was his wont.

"Master may get up his own wine, if he likes, of an evening," was his first remark. "Either I do it in the daytime or not at all, Mrs. Bunch. I don't know what it may be: very like it's the rats, or the wind got into the cellars; but I'm not as young as I was, and I can't go through with it as I have done."

"Well, Mr. Parkes, you know it is a surprising place for the rats, is the Hall."

"I'm not denying that, Mrs. Bunch; and to be sure, many a time I've heard the tale from the men in the shipyards about the rat that could speak. I never laid no confidence in that before; but tonight, if I'd demeaned myself to lay my ear to the door of the further bin, I could pretty much have heard what they was saying."

"Oh, there, Mr. Parkes, I've no patience with your fancies! Rats talking in the wine-cellar indeed!"

"Well, Mrs. Bunch, I've no wish to argue with you: all I say is, if you choose to go to the far bin, and lay your ear to the door, you may prove my words this minute."

"What nonsense you do talk, Mr. Parkes – not fit for children to listen to! Why, you'll be frightening Master Stephen there out of his wits."

"What! Master Stephen?" said Parkes, awaking to the consciousness of the boy's presence. "Master Stephen knows well enough when I'm a-playing a joke with you, Mrs. Bunch."

In fact, Stephen knew much too well to suppose that Mr. Parkes had in the first instance intended a joke. He was interested, not altogether pleasantly, in the situation; but all his questions were unsuccessful in inducing the butler to give any more detailed account of his experiences in the wine-cellar.

* * *

We have now arrived at March 24, 1812. It was a day of curious experiences for Stephen: a windy, noisy day, which filled the house and the gardens with a restless impression. As Stephen stood by the fence of the grounds, and looked out into the park, he felt as if an endless procession of unseen people were sweeping past him on the wind, borne on restlessly and aimlessly, vainly striving to stop themselves, to catch at something that might arrest their flight and bring them once again into contact with the living world of which they had formed a part. After luncheon that day Mr. Abney said:

"Stephen, my boy, do you think you could manage to come to me tonight as late as eleven o'clock in my study? I shall be busy until that time, and I wish to show you something connected with your future life which it is most important that you should know. You are not to mention this matter to Mrs. Bunch nor to anyone else in the house; and you had better go to your room at the usual time."

Here was a new excitement added to life; Stephen eagerly grasped at the opportunity of sitting up till eleven o'clock. He looked in at the library door on his way upstairs that evening, and saw a brazier, which he had often noticed in the corner of the room, moved out before the fire; an old silver-gilt cup stood on the table, filled with red wine, and some written sheets of paper lay near it. Mr. Abney was sprinkling some incense on the brazier from a round silver box as Stephen passed, but did not seem to notice his step.

The wind had fallen, and there was a still night and a full moon. At about ten o'clock Stephen was standing at the open window of his bedroom, looking out over the country. Still as the night was, the mysterious population of the distant moonlit woods was not yet lulled to rest. From time to time strange cries as of lost and despairing wanderers sounded from across the mere. They might be the notes of owls or water-birds, yet they did not quite resemble either sound. Were not they coming nearer? Now they sounded from the nearer side of the water, and in a few moments they seemed to be floating about among the shrubberies. Then they ceased; but just as Stephen was thinking of shutting the window and resuming his reading of *Robinson Crusoe*, he caught sight of two figures standing on the gravelled terrace that ran along the garden side of the Hall – the figures of a boy and girl, as it seemed; they stood side by side, looking up at the windows. Something in the form of the girl recalled irresistibly his dream of the figure in the bath. The boy inspired him with more acute fear.

Whilst the girl stood still, half smiling, with her hands clasped over her heart, the boy, a thin shape, with black hair and ragged clothing, raised his arms in the air with an appearance of menace and of unappeasable hunger and longing. The moon shone upon his almost transparent hands, and Stephen saw that the nails were fearfully long and that the light shone through them. As he stood with his arms thus raised, he disclosed a terrifying spectacle. On the left side of his chest there opened a black and gaping rent; and there fell upon Stephen's brain, rather than upon his ear, the impression of one of those hungry and desolate cries that he had heard resounding over the woods of Aswarby all that evening. In another moment this dreadful pair had moved swiftly and noiselessly over the dry grass and he saw them no more.

Inexpressibly frightened as he was, he determined to take his candle and go down to Mr. Abney's study, for the hour appointed for their meeting was near at hand. The study or library opened out of the front hall on one side, and Stephen, urged on by his terrors, did not take long in getting there. To effect an entrance was not so easy. The door was not locked, he felt sure, for the key was on the outside of it as usual. His repeated knocks produced no answer. Mr. Abney was engaged: he was speaking. What! why did he try to cry out? and why was the cry choked in his throat? Had, he, too, seen the mysterious children? But now everything was quiet, and the door yielded to Stephen's terrified and frantic pushing.

* * *

On the table in Mr. Abney's study certain papers were found which explained the situation to Stephen Elliot when he was of an age to understand them. The most important sentences were as follows:

It was a belief very strongly and generally held by the ancients – of whose wisdom in these matters I have had such experience as induces me to place confidence in their assertions – that by enacting certain processes, which to us moderns have something of a barbaric complexion, a very remarkable enlightenment of the spiritual faculties in man may be attained: that, for example, by absorbing the personalities of a certain number of his fellow-creatures, an individual may gain a complete ascendancy over those orders of spiritual beings which control the elemental forces of our universe.

It is recorded of Simon Magus that he was able to fly in the air, to become invisible, or to assume any form he pleased, by the agency of the soul of a boy whom, to use the libellous phrase employed by the author of the Clementine Recognitions, he had 'murdered'. I find it set down, moreover, with considerable detail in the writings of Hermes Trismegistus, that similar happy results may be produced by the absorption of the hearts of not less than three human beings below the age of twenty-one years. To the testing of the truth of this receipt I have devoted the greater part of the last twenty years, selecting as the corpora vilia *of my experiment such persons as could conveniently be removed without occasioning a sensible gap in society. The first step I effected by the removal of one Phoebe Stanley, a girl of gipsy extraction, on March 24, 1792. The second, by the removal of a wandering Italian lad, named Giovanni Paoli, on the night of March 23, 1805. The final 'victim' – to employ a word repugnant in the highest degree to my feelings – must be my cousin, Stephen Elliott. His day must be this March 24, 1812.*

The best means of effecting the required absorption is to remove the heart from the living subject, to reduce it to ashes, and to mingle them with about a pint of red wine, preferably port. The remains of the first two subjects, at least, it will be well to conceal: a disused bathroom or wine-cellar will be found convenient for such a purpose. Some annoyance may be experienced from the psychic portion of the subjects, which popular language dignifies with the name of ghosts. But the man of philosophic temperament – to whom alone the experiment is appropriate – will be little prone to attach importance to the feeble efforts of these beings to wreak their vengeance on him. I contemplate with the liveliest satisfaction the enlarged and emancipated existence which the experiment, if successful, will confer on me; not only placing me beyond the reach of human justice (so-called) but eliminating to a great extent the prospect of death itself.

* * *

Mr. Abney was found in his chair, his head thrown back, his face stamped with an expression of rage, fright and mortal pain. In his left side was a terrible lacerated wound, exposing the heart. There was no blood on his hands, and a long knife that lay on the table was perfectly clean. A savage wild-cat might have inflicted the injuries. The window of the study was open, and it was the opinion of the coroner that Mr. Abney had met his death by the agency of some wild creature. But Stephen Elliot's study of the papers I have quoted led him to a very different conclusion.

The Judge's House

Bram Stoker

When the time for his examination drew near Malcolm Malcolmson made up his mind to go somewhere to read by himself. He feared the attractions of the seaside, and also he feared completely rural isolation, for of old he knew its charms, and so he determined to find some unpretentious little town where there would be nothing to distract him. He refrained from asking suggestions from any of his friends, for he argued that each would recommend some place of which he had knowledge, and where he had already acquaintances. As Malcolmson wished to avoid friends he had no wish to encumber himself with the attention of friends' friends, and so he determined to look out for a place for himself. He packed a portmanteau with some clothes and all the books he required, and then took ticket for the first name on the local time-table which he did not know.

When at the end of three hours' journey he alighted at Benchurch, he felt satisfied that he had so far obliterated his tracks as to be sure of having a peaceful opportunity of pursuing his studies. He went straight to the one inn which the sleepy little place contained, and put up for the night. Benchurch was a market town, and once in three weeks was crowded to excess, but for the remainder of the twenty-one days it was as attractive as a desert. Malcolmson looked around the day after his arrival to try to find quarters more isolated than even so quiet an inn as 'The Good Traveller' afforded. There was only one place which took his fancy, and it certainly satisfied his wildest ideas regarding quiet; in fact, quiet was not the proper word to apply to it – desolation was the only term conveying any suitable idea of its isolation. It was an old rambling, heavy-built house of the Jacobean style, with heavy gables and windows, unusually small, and set higher than was customary in such houses, and was surrounded with a high brick wall massively built. Indeed, on examination, it looked more like a fortified house than an ordinary dwelling. But all these things pleased Malcolmson. "Here," he thought, "is the very spot I have been looking for, and if I can get opportunity of using it I shall be happy." His joy was increased when he realised beyond doubt that it was not at present inhabited.

From the post-office he got the name of the agent, who was rarely surprised at the application to rent a part of the old house. Mr. Carnford, the local lawyer and agent, was a genial old gentleman, and frankly confessed his delight at anyone being willing to live in the house.

"To tell you the truth," said he, "I should be only too happy, on behalf of the owners, to let anyone have the house rent free for a term of years if only to accustom the people here to see it inhabited. It has been so long empty that some kind of absurd prejudice has grown up about it, and this can be best put down by its occupation – if only," he added with a sly glance at Malcolmson, "by a scholar like yourself, who wants its quiet for a time."

Malcolmson thought it needless to ask the agent about the 'absurd prejudice'; he knew he would get more information, if he should require it, on that subject from other quarters. He paid his three months' rent, got a receipt, and the name of an old woman who would probably undertake to 'do' for him, and came away with the keys in his pocket. He then went to the landlady of the inn, who was a cheerful and most kindly person, and asked her advice as to such stores and provisions as he would be likely to require. She threw up her hands in amazement when he told her where he was going to settle himself.

"Not in the Judge's House!" she said, and grew pale as she spoke. He explained the locality of the house, saying that he did not know its name. When he had finished she answered:

"Aye, sure enough – sure enough the very place! It is the Judge's House sure enough." He asked her to tell him about the place, why so called, and what there was against it. She told him that it was so called locally because it had been many years before – how long she could not say, as she was herself from another part of the country, but she thought it must have been a hundred years or more – the abode of a judge who was held in great terror on account of his harsh sentences and his hostility to prisoners at Assizes. As to what there was against the house itself she could not tell. She had often asked, but no one could inform her; but there was a general feeling that there was *something*, and for her own part she would not take all the money in Drinkwater's Bank and stay in the house an hour by herself. Then she apologised to Malcolmson for her disturbing talk.

"It is too bad of me, sir, and you – and a young gentlemen, too – if you will pardon me saying it, going to live there all alone. If you were my boy – and you'll excuse me for saying it – you wouldn't sleep there a night, not if I had to go there myself and pull the big alarm bell that's on the roof!" The good creature was so manifestly in earnest, and was so kindly in her intentions, that Malcolmson, although amused, was touched. He told her kindly how much he appreciated her interest in him, and added:

"But, my dear Mrs. Witham, indeed you need not be concerned about me! A man who is reading for the Mathematical Tripos has too much to think of to be disturbed by any of these mysterious 'somethings', and his work is of too exact and prosaic a kind to allow of his having any corner in his mind for mysteries of any kind. Harmonical Progression, Permutations and Combinations, and Elliptic Functions have sufficient mysteries for me!" Mrs. Witham kindly undertook to see after his commissions, and he went himself to look for the old woman who had been recommended to him. When he returned to the Judge's House with her, after an interval of a couple of hours, he found Mrs. Witham herself waiting with several men and boys carrying parcels, and an upholsterer's man with a bed in a car, for she said, though tables and chairs might be all very well, a bed that hadn't been aired for mayhap fifty years was not proper for young bones to lie on. She was evidently curious to see the inside of the house; and though manifestly so afraid of the 'somethings' that at the slightest sound she clutched on to Malcolmson, whom she never left for a moment, went over the whole place.

After his examination of the house, Malcolmson decided to take up his abode in the great dining-room, which was big enough to serve for all his requirements; and Mrs. Witham, with the aid of the charwoman, Mrs. Dempster, proceeded to arrange matters. When the hampers were brought in and unpacked, Malcolmson saw that with much kind forethought she had sent from her own kitchen sufficient provisions to last for a few days. Before going she expressed all sorts of kind wishes; and at the door turned and said:

"And perhaps, sir, as the room is big and draughty it might be well to have one of those big screens put round your bed at night – though, truth to tell, I would die myself if I were to be so shut in with all kinds of – of 'things', that put their heads round the sides, or over the top, and look on me!" The image which she had called up was too much for her nerves, and she fled incontinently.

Mrs. Dempster sniffed in a superior manner as the landlady disappeared, and remarked that for her own part she wasn't afraid of all the bogies in the kingdom.

"I'll tell you what it is, sir," she said; "bogies is all kinds and sorts of things – except bogies! Rats and mice, and beetles; and creaky doors, and loose slates, and broken panes, and stiff drawer handles, that stay out when you pull them and then fall down in the middle of the night. Look at the wainscot of the room! It is old – hundreds of years old! Do you think there's no rats and beetles there! And do you imagine, sir, that you won't see none of them? Rats is bogies, I tell you, and bogies is rats; and don't you get to think anything else!"

"Mrs. Dempster," said Malcolmson gravely, making her a polite bow, "you know more than a Senior Wrangler! And let me say, that, as a mark of esteem for your indubitable soundness of head and heart, I shall, when I go, give you possession of this house, and let you stay here by yourself for the last two months of my tenancy, for four weeks will serve my purpose."

"Thank you kindly, sir!" she answered, "but I couldn't sleep away from home a night. I am in Greenhow's Charity, and if I slept a night away from my rooms I should lose all I have got to live on. The rules is very strict; and there's too many watching for a vacancy for me to run any risks in the matter. Only for that, sir, I'd gladly come here and attend on you altogether during your stay."

"My good woman," said Malcolmson hastily, "I have come here on purpose to obtain solitude; and believe me that I am grateful to the late Greenhow for having so organised his admirable charity – whatever it is – that I am perforce denied the opportunity of suffering from such a form of temptation! Saint Anthony himself could not be more rigid on the point!"

The old woman laughed harshly. "Ah, you young gentlemen," she said, "you don't fear for naught; and belike you'll get all the solitude you want here." She set to work with her cleaning; and by nightfall, when Malcolmson returned from his walk – he always had one of his books to study as he walked – he found the room swept and tidied, a fire burning in the old hearth, the lamp lit, and the table spread for supper with Mrs. Witham's excellent fare. "This is comfort, indeed," he said, as he rubbed his hands.

When he had finished his supper, and lifted the tray to the other end of the great oak dining-table, he got out his books again, put fresh wood on the fire, trimmed his lamp, and set himself down to a spell of real hard work. He went on without pause till about eleven o'clock, when he knocked off for a bit to fix his fire and lamp, and to make himself a cup of tea. He had always been a tea-drinker, and during his college life had sat late at work and had taken tea late. The rest was a great luxury to him, and he enjoyed it with a sense of delicious, voluptuous ease. The renewed fire leaped and sparkled, and threw quaint shadows through the great old room; and as he sipped his hot tea he revelled in the sense of isolation from his kind. Then it was that he began to notice for the first time what a noise the rats were making.

"Surely," he thought, "they cannot have been at it all the time I was reading. Had they been, I must have noticed it!" Presently, when the noise increased, he satisfied himself that it was really new. It was evident that at first the rats had been frightened at the presence of a stranger, and the light of fire and lamp; but that as the time went on they had grown bolder and were now disporting themselves as was their wont.

How busy they were! And hark to the strange noises! Up and down behind the old wainscot, over the ceiling and under the floor they raced, and gnawed, and scratched! Malcolmson smiled to himself as he recalled to mind the saying of Mrs. Dempster, "Bogies is rats, and rats is bogies!" The tea began to have its effect of intellectual and nervous stimulus, he saw with joy another long spell of work to be done before the night was past, and in the sense of security which it gave him, he allowed himself the luxury of a good look round the room. He took his lamp in one hand, and went all around, wondering that so quaint and beautiful an old house had been so long neglected. The carving of the oak on the panels of the wainscot was fine, and on and round the doors and windows it was beautiful and of rare merit. There were some old pictures on the walls, but they were coated so thick with dust and dirt that he could not distinguish any detail of them, though he held his lamp as high as he could over his head. Here and there as he went round he saw some crack or hole blocked for a moment by the face of a rat with its bright eyes glittering in the light, but in an instant it was gone, and a squeak and a scamper followed. The thing that most struck him, however, was the rope of the great alarm bell on the roof, which hung down in a corner of the room on the right-hand side of the fireplace. He pulled up close to the hearth a great high-backed carved oak chair, and sat down to his last cup of tea. When this was done he made up the fire, and went back to his work, sitting at the corner of the table, having the fire to his left. For a little while the rats disturbed him somewhat with their perpetual scampering, but he got accustomed to the noise as one does to the ticking of a clock or to the roar of moving water; and he became so immersed in his work that everything in the world, except the problem which he was trying to solve, passed away from him.

He suddenly looked up, his problem was still unsolved, and there was in the air that sense of the hour before the dawn, which is so dread to doubtful life. The noise of the rats had ceased. Indeed it seemed to him that it must have ceased but lately and that it was the sudden cessation which had disturbed him. The fire had fallen low, but still it threw out a deep red glow. As he looked he started in spite of his *sang froid*.

There on the great high-backed carved oak chair by the right side of the fireplace sat an enormous rat, steadily glaring at him with baleful eyes. He made a motion to it as though to hunt it away, but it did not stir. Then he made the motion of throwing something. Still it did not stir, but showed its great white teeth angrily, and its cruel eyes shone in the lamplight with an added vindictiveness.

Malcolmson felt amazed, and seizing the poker from the hearth ran at it to kill it. Before, however, he could strike it, the rat, with a squeak that sounded like the concentration of hate, jumped upon the floor, and, running up the rope of the alarm bell, disappeared in the darkness beyond the range of the green-shaded lamp. Instantly, strange to say, the noisy scampering of the rats in the wainscot began again.

By this time Malcolmson's mind was quite off the problem; and as a shrill cock-crow outside told him of the approach of morning, he went to bed and to sleep.

He slept so sound that he was not even waked by Mrs. Dempster coming in to make up his room. It was only when she had tidied up the place and got his breakfast ready and tapped on the screen which closed in his bed that he woke. He was a little tired still after his night's hard work, but a strong cup of tea soon freshened him up and, taking his book, he went out for his morning walk, bringing with him a few sandwiches lest he should not care to return till dinner time. He found a quiet walk between high elms some way outside the town, and here he spent the greater part of the day studying his Laplace. On his return he looked in to see Mrs. Witham and to thank her for her kindness. When she saw him coming through the diamond-paned bay window of her sanctum she came out to meet him and asked him in. She looked at him searchingly and shook her head as she said:

"You must not overdo it, sir. You are paler this morning than you should be. Too late hours and too hard work on the brain isn't good for any man! But tell me, sir, how did you pass the night? Well, I hope? But my heart! Sir, I was glad when Mrs. Dempster told me this morning that you were all right and sleeping sound when she went in."

"Oh, I was all right," he answered smiling, "the 'somethings' didn't worry me, as yet. Only the rats; and they had a circus, I tell you, all over the place. There was one wicked looking old devil that sat up on my own chair by the fire, and wouldn't go till I took the poker to him, and then he ran up the rope of the alarm bell and got to somewhere up the wall or the ceiling – I couldn't see where, it was so dark."

"Mercy on us," said Mrs. Witham, "an old devil, and sitting on a chair by the fireside! Take care, sir! Take care! There's many a true word spoken in jest."

"How do you mean? 'Pon my word I don't understand."

"An old devil! The old devil, perhaps. There! Sir, you needn't laugh," for Malcolmson had broken into a hearty peal. "You young folks thinks it easy to laugh at things that makes older ones shudder. Never mind, sir! Never mind! Please God, you'll laugh all the time. It's what I wish you myself!" and the good lady beamed all over in sympathy with his enjoyment, her fears gone for a moment.

"Oh, forgive me!" said Malcolmson presently. "Don't think me rude; but the idea was too much for me – that the old devil himself was on the chair last night!" And at the thought he laughed again. Then he went home to dinner.

This evening the scampering of the rats began earlier; indeed it had been going on before his arrival, and only ceased whilst his presence by its freshness disturbed them. After dinner he sat by the fire for a while and had a smoke; and then, having cleared his table, began to work as before. Tonight the rats disturbed him more than they had done on the previous night. How they scampered up and down and under and over! How they squeaked, and scratched, and gnawed! How they, getting bolder by degrees, came to the mouths of their holes and to the chinks and cracks and crannies in the wainscoting till their eyes shone like tiny lamps as the firelight rose and fell. But to him, now doubtless accustomed to them, their eyes were not wicked; only their playfulness touched him. Sometimes the boldest of them made sallies out on the floor or along the mouldings of the wainscot. Now and again as they disturbed him Malcolmson made a sound to frighten them, smiting the table with his hand or giving a fierce "Hsh, hsh", so that they fled straightway to their holes.

And so the early part of the night wore on; and despite the noise Malcolmson got more and more immersed in his work.

All at once he stopped, as on the previous night, being overcome by a sudden sense of silence. There was not the faintest sound of gnaw, or scratch, or squeak. The silence was as of the grave. He remembered the odd occurrence of the previous night, and instinctively he looked at the chair standing close by the fireside. And then a very odd sensation thrilled through him.

There, on the great old high-backed carved oak chair beside the fireplace sat the same enormous rat, steadily glaring at him with baleful eyes.

Instinctively he took the nearest thing to his hand, a book of logarithms, and flung it at it. The book was badly aimed and the rat did not stir, so again the poker performance of the previous night was repeated; and again the rat, being closely pursued, fled up the rope of the alarm bell. Strangely too, the departure of this rat was instantly followed by the renewal of the noise made by the general rat community. On this occasion, as on the previous one, Malcolmson could not see at what part of the room the rat disappeared, for the green shade of his lamp left the upper part of the room in darkness, and the fire had burned low.

On looking at his watch he found it was close on midnight; and, not sorry for the *divertissement*, he made up his fire and made himself his nightly pot of tea. He had got through a good spell of work, and thought himself entitled to a cigarette; and so he sat on the great oak chair before the fire and enjoyed it. Whilst smoking he began to think that he would like to know where the rat disappeared to, for he had certain ideas for the morrow not entirely disconnected with a rat-trap. Accordingly he lit another lamp and placed it so that it would shine well into the right-hand corner of the wall by the fireplace. Then he got all the books he had with him, and placed them handy to throw at the vermin. Finally he lifted the rope of the alarm bell and placed the end of it on the table, fixing the extreme end under the lamp. As he handled it he could not help noticing how pliable it was, especially for so strong a rope, and one not in use. "You could hang a man with it," he thought to himself. When his preparations were made he looked around, and said complacently:

"There now, my friend, I think we shall learn something of you this time!" He began his work again, and though as before somewhat disturbed at first by the noise of the rats, soon lost himself in his propositions and problems.

Again he was called to his immediate surroundings suddenly. This time it might not have been the sudden silence only which took his attention; there was a slight movement of the rope, and the lamp moved. Without stirring, he looked to see if his pile of books was within range, and then cast his eye along the rope. As he looked he saw the great rat drop from the rope on the oak arm-chair and sit there glaring at him. He raised a book in his right hand, and taking careful aim, flung it at the rat. The latter, with a quick movement, sprang aside and dodged the missile. He then took another book, and a third, and flung them one after another at the rat, but each time unsuccessfully. At last, as he stood with a book poised in his hand to throw, the rat squeaked and seemed afraid. This made Malcolmson more than ever eager to strike, and the book flew and struck the rat a resounding blow. It gave a terrified squeak, and turning on his pursuer a look of terrible malevolence, ran up the chair-back and made a great jump to the rope of the alarm bell and ran up it like lightning. The lamp rocked under the sudden strain, but it was a heavy one and did not topple over. Malcolmson kept his eyes on the rat, and saw it by the light of the second lamp leap to a moulding of the wainscot and disappear through a hole in one of the great pictures which hung on the wall, obscured and invisible through its coating of dirt and dust.

"I shall look up my friend's habitation in the morning," said the student, as he went over to collect his books. "The third picture from the fireplace; I shall not forget." He picked up the books one by one, commenting on them as he lifted them. "*Conic Sections* he does not mind, nor *Cycloidal Oscillations*, nor the *Principia*, nor *Quaternions*, nor *Thermodynamics*. Now for the book that fetched him!' Malcolmson took it up and looked at it. As he did so he started, and a sudden pallor overspread his face. He looked round uneasily and shivered slightly, as he murmured to himself:

"The Bible my mother gave me! What an odd coincidence." He sat down to work again, and the rats in the wainscot renewed their gambols. They did not disturb him, however; somehow their presence gave him a sense of companionship. But he could not attend to his work, and after striving to master the subject on which he was engaged gave it up in despair, and went to bed as the first streak of dawn stole in through the eastern window.

He slept heavily but uneasily, and dreamed much; and when Mrs. Dempster woke him late in the morning he seemed ill at ease, and for a few minutes did not seem to realise exactly where he was. His first request rather surprised the servant.

"Mrs. Dempster, when I am out today I wish you would get the steps and dust or wash those pictures – specially that one the third from the fireplace – I want to see what they are."

Late in the afternoon Malcolmson worked at his books in the shaded walk, and the cheerfulness of the previous day came back to him as the day wore on, and he found that his reading was progressing well. He had worked out to a satisfactory conclusion all the problems which had as yet baffled him, and it was in a state of jubilation that he paid a visit to Mrs. Witham at 'The Good Traveller'. He found a stranger in the cosy sitting-room with the landlady, who was introduced to him as Dr. Thornhill. She was not quite at ease, and this, combined with the doctor's plunging at once into a series of questions, made Malcolmson come to the conclusion that his presence was not an accident, so without preliminary he said:

"Dr. Thornhill, I shall with pleasure answer you any question you may choose to ask me if you will answer me one question first."

The doctor seemed surprised, but he smiled and answered at once, "Done! What is it?"

"Did Mrs. Witham ask you to come here and see me and advise me?"

Dr. Thornhill for a moment was taken aback, and Mrs. Witham got fiery red and turned away; but the doctor was a frank and ready man, and he answered at once and openly.

"She did: but she didn't intend you to know it. I suppose it was my clumsy haste that made you suspect. She told me that she did not like the idea of your being in that house all by yourself, and that she thought you took too much strong tea. In fact, she wants me to advise you if possible to give up the tea and the very late hours. I was a keen student in my time, so I suppose I may take the liberty of a college man, and without offence, advise you not quite as a stranger."

Malcolmson with a bright smile held out his hand. "Shake! As they say in America," he said. "I must thank you for your kindness and Mrs. Witham too, and your kindness deserves a return on my part. I promise to take no more strong tea – no tea at all till you let me – and I shall go to bed tonight at one o'clock at latest. Will that do?"

"Capital," said the doctor. "Now tell us all that you noticed in the old house," and so Malcolmson then and there told in minute detail all that had happened in the last two nights. He was interrupted every now and then by some exclamation from Mrs. Witham, till finally when he told of the episode of the Bible the landlady's pent-up emotions found vent in a shriek; and it was not till a stiff glass of brandy and water had been administered that she grew composed again. Dr. Thornhill listened with a face of growing gravity, and when the narrative was complete and Mrs. Witham had been restored he asked:

"The rat always went up the rope of the alarm bell?"

"Always."

"I suppose you know," said the Doctor after a pause, "what the rope is?"

"No!"

"It is," said the Doctor slowly, "the very rope which the hangman used for all the victims of the Judge's judicial rancour!" Here he was interrupted by another scream from Mrs. Witham, and steps had to be taken for her recovery. Malcolmson having looked at his watch, and found that it was close to his dinner hour, had gone home before her complete recovery.

When Mrs. Witham was herself again she almost assailed the Doctor with angry questions as to what he meant by putting such horrible ideas into the poor young man's mind. "He has quite enough there already to upset him," she added. Dr. Thornhill replied:

"My dear madam, I had a distinct purpose in it! I wanted to draw his attention to the bell rope, and to fix it there. It may be that he is in a highly overwrought state, and has been studying too much, although I am bound to say that he seems as sound and healthy a young man, mentally and bodily, as ever I saw – but then the rats – and that suggestion of the devil." The doctor shook his head and went on. "I would have offered to go and stay the first night with him but that I felt sure it would have been a cause of offence. He may get in the night some strange fright or hallucination; and if he does I want him to pull that rope. All alone as he is it will give us warning, and we may reach him in time to be of service. I shall be sitting up pretty late tonight and shall keep my ears open. Do not be alarmed if Benchurch gets a surprise before morning."

"Oh, Doctor, what do you mean? What do you mean?"

"I mean this; that possibly – nay, more probably – we shall hear the great alarm bell from the Judge's House tonight," and the Doctor made about as effective an exit as could be thought of.

When Malcolmson arrived home he found that it was a little after his usual time, and Mrs. Dempster had gone away – the rules of Greenhow's Charity were not to be neglected. He was glad to see that the place was bright and tidy with a cheerful fire and a well-trimmed lamp. The evening was colder than might have been expected in April, and a heavy wind was blowing with such rapidly-increasing strength that there was every promise of a storm during the night. For a few minutes after his entrance the noise of the rats ceased; but so soon as they became accustomed to his presence they began again. He was glad to hear them, for he felt once more the feeling of companionship in their noise, and his mind ran back to the strange fact that they only ceased to manifest themselves when that other – the great rat with the baleful eyes – came upon the scene. The reading-lamp only was lit and its green shade kept the ceiling and the upper part of the room in darkness, so that the cheerful light from the hearth spreading over the floor and shining on the white cloth laid over the end of the table was warm and cheery. Malcolmson sat down to his dinner with a good appetite and a buoyant spirit. After his dinner and a cigarette he sat steadily down to work, determined not to let anything disturb him, for he remembered his promise to the doctor, and made up his mind to make the best of the time at his disposal.

For an hour or so he worked all right, and then his thoughts began to wander from his books. The actual circumstances around him, the calls on his physical attention, and his nervous susceptibility were not to be denied. By this time the wind had become a gale, and the gale a storm. The old house, solid though it was, seemed to shake to its foundations, and the storm roared and raged through its many chimneys and its queer old gables, producing strange, unearthly sounds in the empty rooms and corridors. Even the great alarm bell on the roof must have felt the force of the wind, for the rope rose and fell slightly, as though the bell were moved a little from time to time and the limber rope fell on the oak floor with a hard and hollow sound.

As Malcolmson listened to it he bethought himself of the doctor's words, "It is the rope which the hangman used for the victims of the Judge's judicial rancour," and he went over to the corner of the fireplace and took it in his hand to look at it. There seemed a sort of deadly interest in it, and as he stood there he lost himself for a moment in speculation as to who these victims were, and the grim wish of the Judge to have such a ghastly relic ever under his eyes. As he stood there the swaying of the bell on the roof still lifted the rope now and again; but presently there came a new sensation – a sort of tremor in the rope, as though something was moving along it.

Looking up instinctively Malcolmson saw the great rat coming slowly down towards him, glaring at him steadily. He dropped the rope and started back with a muttered curse, and the rat turning ran up the rope again and disappeared, and at the same instant Malcolmson became conscious that the noise of the rats, which had ceased for a while, began again.

All this set him thinking, and it occurred to him that he had not investigated the lair of the rat or looked at the pictures, as he had intended. He lit the other lamp without the shade, and, holding it up went and stood opposite the third picture from the fireplace on the right-hand side where he had seen the rat disappear on the previous night.

At the first glance he started back so suddenly that he almost dropped the lamp, and a deadly pallor overspread his face. His knees shook, and heavy drops of sweat came on his forehead, and he trembled like an aspen. But he was young and plucky, and pulled himself together, and after the pause of a few seconds stepped forward again, raised the lamp, and examined the picture which had been dusted and washed, and now stood out clearly.

It was of a judge dressed in his robes of scarlet and ermine. His face was strong and merciless, evil, crafty, and vindictive, with a sensual mouth, hooked nose of ruddy colour, and shaped like the beak of a bird of prey. The rest of the face was of a cadaverous colour. The eyes were of peculiar brilliance and with a terribly malignant expression. As he looked at them, Malcolmson grew cold, for he saw there the very counterpart of the eyes of the great rat. The lamp almost fell from his hand, he saw the rat with its baleful eyes peering out through the hole in the corner of the picture, and noted the sudden cessation of the noise of the other rats. However, he pulled himself together, and went on with his examination of the picture.

The Judge was seated in a great high-backed carved oak chair, on the right-hand side of a great stone fireplace where, in the corner, a rope hung down from the ceiling, its end lying coiled on the floor. With a feeling of something like horror, Malcolmson recognised the scene of the room as it stood, and gazed around him in an awestruck manner as though he expected to find some strange presence behind him. Then he looked over to the corner of the fireplace – and with a loud cry he let the lamp fall from his hand.

There, in the Judge's arm-chair, with the rope hanging behind, sat the rat with the Judge's baleful eyes, now intensified and with a fiendish leer. Save for the howling of the storm without there was silence.

The fallen lamp recalled Malcolmson to himself. Fortunately it was of metal, and so the oil was not spilt. However, the practical need of attending to it settled at once his nervous apprehensions. When he had turned it out, he wiped his brow and thought for a moment.

"This will not do," he said to himself. "If I go on like this I shall become a crazy fool. This must stop! I promised the doctor I would not take tea. Faith, he was pretty right! My nerves must have been getting into a queer state. Funny I did not notice it. I never felt better in my life. However, it is all right now, and I shall not be such a fool again."

Then he mixed himself a good stiff glass of brandy and water and resolutely sat down to his work.

It was nearly an hour when he looked up from his book, disturbed by the sudden stillness. Without, the wind howled and roared louder than ever, and the rain drove in sheets against the windows, beating like hail on the glass; but within there was no sound whatever save the echo of the wind as it roared in the great chimney, and now and then a hiss as a few raindrops found their way down the chimney in a lull of the storm. The fire had fallen low and had ceased to flame, though it threw out a red glow. Malcolmson listened attentively, and presently heard a thin, squeaking noise, very faint. It came from the corner of the room where the rope hung down, and he thought it was the creaking of the rope on the floor as the swaying of the bell raised and lowered it. Looking up, however, he saw in the dim light the great rat clinging to the rope and gnawing it. The rope was already nearly gnawed through – he could see the lighter colour where the strands were laid bare. As he looked the job was completed, and the severed end of the rope fell clattering on the oaken floor, whilst for an instant the great rat remained like a knob or tassel at the end of the rope, which now began to sway to and fro. Malcolmson felt for a moment another pang of terror as he thought that now the possibility of calling the outer world to his assistance was cut off, but an intense anger took its place, and seizing the book he was reading he hurled it at the rat. The blow was well aimed, but before the missile could reach him the rat dropped off and struck the floor with a soft thud. Malcolmson instantly rushed over towards him, but it darted away and disappeared in the darkness of the shadows of the room. Malcolmson felt that his work was over for the night, and determined then and there to vary the monotony of the proceedings by a hunt for the rat, and took off the green shade of the lamp so as to insure a wider spreading light. As he did so the gloom of the upper part of the room was relieved, and in the new flood of light, great by comparison with the previous darkness, the pictures on the wall stood out boldly. From where he stood, Malcolmson saw right opposite to him the third picture on the wall from the right of the fireplace. He rubbed his eyes in surprise, and then a great fear began to come upon him.

In the centre of the picture was a great irregular patch of brown canvas, as fresh as when it was stretched on the frame. The background was as before, with chair and chimney-corner and rope, but the figure of the Judge had disappeared.

Malcolmson, almost in a chill of horror, turned slowly round, and then he began to shake and tremble like a man in a palsy. His strength seemed to have left him, and he was incapable of action or movement, hardly even of thought. He could only see and hear.

There, on the great high-backed carved oak chair sat the Judge in his robes of scarlet and ermine, with his baleful eyes glaring vindictively, and a smile of triumph on the resolute, cruel mouth, as he lifted with his hands a *black cap*. Malcolmson felt as if the blood was running from his heart, as one does in moments of prolonged suspense. There was a singing in his ears. Without, he could hear the roar and howl of the tempest, and through it, swept on the storm, came the striking of midnight by the great chimes in the market place. He stood for a space of time that seemed to him endless still as a statue, and with wide-open, horror-struck eyes, breathless. As the clock struck, so the smile of triumph on the Judge's face intensified, and at the last stroke of midnight he placed the black cap on his head.

Slowly and deliberately the Judge rose from his chair and picked up the piece of the rope of the alarm bell which lay on the floor, drew it through his hands as if he enjoyed its touch, and then deliberately began to knot one end of it, fashioning it into a noose. This he tightened and tested with his foot, pulling hard at it till he was satisfied and then making a running noose of it, which he held in his hand. Then he began to move along the table on the opposite side to Malcolmson keeping his eyes on him until he had passed him, when with a quick movement he stood in front of the door. Malcolmson then began to feel that he was trapped, and tried to think of what he should do. There was some fascination in the Judge's eyes, which he never took off him, and he had, perforce, to look. He saw the Judge approach – still keeping between him and the door – and raise the noose and throw it towards him as if to entangle him. With a great effort he made a quick movement to one side, and saw the rope fall beside him, and heard it strike the oaken floor. Again the Judge raised the noose and tried to ensnare him, ever keeping his baleful eyes fixed on him, and each time by a mighty effort the student just managed to evade it. So this went on for many times, the Judge seeming never discouraged nor discomposed at failure, but playing as a cat does with a mouse. At last in despair, which had reached its climax, Malcolmson cast a quick glance round him. The lamp seemed to have blazed up, and there was a fairly good light in the room. At the many rat-holes and in the chinks and crannies of the wainscot he saw the rats' eyes; and this aspect, that was purely physical, gave him a gleam of comfort. He looked around and saw that the rope of the great alarm bell was laden with rats. Every inch of it was covered with them, and more and more were pouring through the small circular hole in the ceiling whence it emerged, so that with their weight the bell was beginning to sway.

Hark! It had swayed till the clapper had touched the bell. The sound was but a tiny one, but the bell was only beginning to sway, and it would increase.

At the sound the Judge, who had been keeping his eyes fixed on Malcolmson, looked up, and a scowl of diabolical anger overspread his face. His eyes fairly glowed like hot coals, and he stamped his foot with a sound that seemed to make the house shake. A dreadful peal of thunder broke overhead as he raised the rope again, whilst the rats kept running up and down the rope as though working against time. This time, instead of throwing it, he drew close to his victim, and held open the noose as he approached. As he came closer there seemed something paralysing in his very presence, and Malcolmson stood rigid as a corpse. He felt the Judge's icy fingers touch his throat as he adjusted the rope. The noose tightened – tightened. Then the Judge, taking the rigid form of the student in his arms, carried him over and placed him standing in the oak chair, and stepping up beside him, put his hand up and caught the end of the swaying rope of the alarm bell. As he raised his hand the rats fled squeaking, and disappeared through the hole in the ceiling. Taking the end of the noose which was round Malcolmson's neck he tied it to the hanging-bell rope, and then descending pulled away the chair.

* * *

When the alarm bell of the Judge's House began to sound a crowd soon assembled. Lights and torches of various kinds appeared, and soon a silent crowd was hurrying to the spot. They knocked loudly at the door, but there was no reply. Then they burst in the door, and poured into the great dining-room, the doctor at the head.

There at the end of the rope of the great alarm bell hung the body of the student, and on the face of the Judge in the picture was a malignant smile.

The Red Room

H.G. Wells

"I can assure you," said I, "that it will take a very tangible ghost to frighten me." And I stood up before the fire with my glass in my hand.

"It is your own choosing," said the man with the withered arm, and glanced at me askance.

"Eight-and-twenty years," said I, "I have lived, and never a ghost have I seen as yet."

The old woman sat staring hard into the fire, her pale eyes wide open. "Ay," she broke in; "and eight-and-twenty years you have lived and never seen the likes of this house, I reckon. There's a many things to see, when one's still but eight-and-twenty." She swayed her head slowly from side to side. "A many things to see and sorrow for."

I half suspected the old people were trying to enhance the spiritual terrors of their house by their droning insistence. I put down my empty glass on the table and looked about the room, and caught a glimpse of myself, abbreviated and broadened to an impossible sturdiness, in the queer old mirror at the end of the room. "Well," I said, "if I see anything tonight, I shall be so much the wiser. For I come to the business with an open mind."

"It's your own choosing," said the man with the withered arm once more.

I heard the sound of a stick and a shambling step on the flags in the passage outside, and the door creaked on its hinges as a second old man entered, more bent, more wrinkled, more aged even than the first. He supported himself by a single crutch, his eyes were covered by a shade, and his lower lip, half averted, hung pale and pink from his decaying yellow teeth. He made straight for an arm-chair on the opposite side of the table, sat down clumsily, and began to cough. The man with the withered arm gave this new-comer a short glance of positive dislike; the old woman took no notice of his arrival, but remained with her eyes fixed steadily on the fire.

"I said – it's your own choosing," said the man with the withered arm, when the coughing had ceased for a while.

"It's my own choosing," I answered.

The man with the shade became aware of my presence for the first time, and threw his head back for a moment and sideways, to see me. I caught a momentary glimpse of his eyes, small and bright and inflamed. Then he began to cough and splutter again.

"Why don't you drink?" said the man with the withered arm, pushing the beer towards him. The man with the shade poured out a glassful with a shaky hand that splashed half as much again on the deal table. A monstrous shadow of him crouched upon the wall and mocked his action as he poured and drank. I must confess I had scarce expected these grotesque custodians. There is to my mind something inhuman in senility, something crouching and atavistic; the human qualities seem to drop from old people insensibly day by day. The three of them made me feel uncomfortable, with their gaunt silences, their bent carriage, their evident unfriendliness to me and to one another.

"If," said I, "you will show me to this haunted room of yours, I will make myself comfortable there."

The old man with the cough jerked his head back so suddenly that it startled me, and shot another glance of his red eyes at me from under the shade; but no one answered me. I waited a minute, glancing from one to the other.

"If," I said a little louder, "if you will show me to this haunted room of yours, I will relieve you from the task of entertaining me."

"There's a candle on the slab outside the door," said the man with the withered arm, looking at my feet as he addressed me. "But if you go to the red room tonight—"

("This night of all nights!" said the old woman.)

"You go alone."

"Very well," I answered. "And which way do I go?"

"You go along the passage for a bit," said he, "until you come to a door, and through that is a spiral staircase, and half-way up that is a landing and another door covered with baize. Go through that and down the long corridor to the end, and the red room is on your left up the steps."

"Have I got that right?" I said, and repeated his directions. He corrected me in one particular.

"And are you really going?" said the man with the shade, looking at me again for the third time, with that queer, unnatural tilting of the face.

("This night of all nights!" said the old woman.)

"It is what I came for," I said, and moved towards the door. As I did so, the old man with the shade rose and staggered round the table, so as to be closer to the others and to the fire. At the door I turned and looked at them, and saw they were all close together, dark against the firelight, staring at me over their shoulders, with an intent expression on their ancient faces.

"Good-night," I said, setting the door open.

"It's your own choosing," said the man with the withered arm.

I left the door wide open until the candle was well alight, and then I shut them in and walked down the chilly, echoing passage.

I must confess that the oddness of these three old pensioners in whose charge her ladyship had left the castle, and the deep-toned, old-fashioned furniture of the housekeeper's room in which they foregathered, affected me in spite of my efforts to keep myself at a matter-of-fact phase. They seemed to belong to another age, an older age, an age when things spiritual were different from this of ours, less certain; an age when omens and witches were credible, and ghosts beyond denying. Their very existence was spectral; the cut of their clothing, fashions born in dead brains. The ornaments and conveniences of the room about them were ghostly – the thoughts of vanished men, which still haunted rather than participated in the world of today. But with an effort I sent such thoughts to the right-about. The long, draughty subterranean passage was chilly and dusty, and my candle flared and made the shadows cower and quiver. The echoes rang up and down the spiral staircase, and a shadow came sweeping up after me, and one fled before me into the darkness overhead. I came to the landing and stopped there for a moment, listening to a rustling that I fancied I heard; then, satisfied of the absolute silence, I pushed open the baize-covered door and stood in the corridor.

The effect was scarcely what I expected, for the moonlight, coming in by the great window on the grand staircase, picked out everything in vivid black shadow or silvery illumination. Everything was in its place: the house might have been deserted on the yesterday instead of eighteen months ago. There were candles in the sockets of the sconces, and whatever dust had gathered on the carpets or upon the polished flooring was distributed so evenly as to be invisible in the moonlight. I was about to advance, and stopped abruptly. A bronze group stood upon the landing, hidden from me by the corner of the wall, but its shadow fell with marvellous distinctness upon the white panelling, and gave me the impression of someone crouching to waylay me. I stood rigid for half a minute perhaps. Then, with my hand in the pocket that held my revolver, I advanced, only to discover a Ganymede and Eagle glistening in the moonlight. That incident for a time restored my nerve, and a porcelain Chinaman on a buhl table, whose head rocked silently as I passed him, scarcely startled me.

The door to the red room and the steps up to it were in a shadowy corner. I moved my candle from side to side, in order to see clearly the nature of the recess in which I stood before opening the door. Here it was, thought I, that my predecessor was found, and the memory of that story gave me a sudden twinge of apprehension. I glanced over my shoulder at the Ganymede in the moonlight, and opened the door of the red room rather hastily, with my face half turned to the pallid silence of the landing.

I entered, closed the door behind me at once, turned the key I found in the lock within, and stood with the candle held aloft, surveying the scene of my vigil, the great red room of Lorraine Castle, in which the young duke had died. Or, rather, in which he had begun his dying, for he had opened the door and fallen headlong down the steps I had just ascended. That had been the end of his vigil, of his gallant attempt to conquer the ghostly tradition of the place, and never, I thought, had apoplexy better served the ends of superstition. And there were other and older stories that clung to the room, back to the half-credible beginning of it all, the tale of a timid wife and the tragic end that came to her husband's jest of frightening her. And looking around that large sombre room, with its shadowy window bays, its recesses and alcoves, one could well understand the legends that had sprouted in its black corners, its germinating darkness. My candle was a little tongue of light in its vastness, that failed to pierce the opposite end of the room, and left an ocean of mystery and suggestion beyond its island of light.

I resolved to make a systematic examination of the place at once, and dispel the fanciful suggestions of its obscurity before they obtained a hold upon me. After satisfying myself of the fastening of the door, I began to walk about the room, peering round each article of furniture, tucking up the valances of the bed, and opening its curtains wide. I pulled up the blinds and examined the fastenings of the several windows before closing the shutters, leant forward and looked up the blackness of the wide chimney, and tapped the dark oak panelling for any secret opening. There were two big mirrors in the room, each with a pair of sconces bearing candles, and on the mantelshelf, too, were more candles in china candlesticks. All these I lit one after the other. The fire was laid, an unexpected consideration from the old housekeeper, – and I lit it, to keep down any disposition to shiver, and when it was burning well, I stood round with my back to it and regarded the room again.

I had pulled up a chintz-covered arm-chair and a table, to form a kind of barricade before me, and on this lay my revolver ready to hand. My precise examination had done me good, but I still found the remoter darkness of the place, and its perfect stillness, too stimulating for the imagination. The echoing of the stir and crackling of the fire was no sort of comfort to me. The shadow in the alcove at the end in particular, had that undefinable quality of a presence, that odd suggestion of a lurking, living thing, that comes so easily in silence and solitude. At last, to reassure myself, I walked with a candle into it, and satisfied myself that there was nothing tangible there. I stood that candle upon the floor of the alcove, and left it in that position.

By this time I was in a state of considerable nervous tension, although to my reason there was no adequate cause for the condition. My mind, however, was perfectly clear. I postulated quite unreservedly that nothing supernatural could happen, and to pass the time I began to string some rhymes together, Ingoldsby fashion, of the original legend of the place. A few I spoke aloud, but the echoes were not pleasant. For the same reason I also abandoned, after a time, a conversation with myself upon the impossibility of ghosts and haunting. My mind reverted to the three old and distorted people downstairs, and I tried to keep it upon that topic. The sombre reds and blacks of the room troubled, me; even with seven candles the place was merely dim. The one in the alcove flared in a draught, and the fire-flickering kept the shadows and penumbra perpetually shifting and stirring. Casting about for a remedy, I recalled the candles I had seen in the passage, and, with a slight effort, walked out into the moonlight, carrying a candle and leaving the door open, and presently returned with as many as ten.

These I put in various knick-knacks of china with which the room was sparsely adorned, lit and placed where the shadows had lain deepest, some on the floor, some in the window recesses, until at last my seventeen candles were so arranged that not an inch of the room but had the direct light of at least one of them. It occurred to me that when the ghost came, I could warn him not to trip over them. The room was now quite brightly illuminated. There was something very cheery and reassuring in these little streaming flames, and snuffing them gave me an occupation, and afforded a helpful sense of the passage of time. Even with that, however, the brooding expectation of the vigil weighed heavily upon me. It was after midnight that the candle in the alcove suddenly went out, and the black shadow sprang back to its place there. I did not see the candle go out; I simply turned and saw that the darkness was there, as one might start and see the unexpected presence of a stranger. "By Jove!" said I aloud; "That draught's a strong one!" and, taking the matches from the table, I walked across the room in a leisurely manner, to relight the corner again. My first match would not strike, and as I succeeded with the second, something seemed to blink on the wall before me. I turned my head involuntarily, and saw that the two candles on the little table by the fireplace were extinguished. I rose at once to my feet.

"Odd!" I said. "Did I do that myself in a flash of absent-mindedness?"

I walked back, relit one, and as I did so, I saw the candle in the right sconce of one of the mirrors wink and go right out, and almost immediately its companion followed it. There was no mistake about it. The flame vanished, as if the wicks had been suddenly nipped between a finger and a thumb, leaving the wick neither glowing nor smoking, but black. While I stood gaping, the candle at the foot of the bed went out, and the shadows seemed to take another step towards me.

"This won't do!" said I, and first one and then another candle on the mantelshelf followed.

"What's up?" I cried, with a queer high note getting into my voice somehow. At that the candle on the wardrobe went out, and the one I had relit in the alcove followed.

"Steady on!" I said. "These candles are wanted," speaking with a half-hysterical facetiousness, and scratching away at a match the while for the mantel candlesticks. My hands trembled so much that twice I missed the rough paper of the matchbox. As the mantel emerged from darkness again, two candles in the remoter end of the window were eclipsed. But with the same match I also relit the larger mirror candles, and those on the floor near the doorway, so that for the moment I seemed to gain on the extinctions. But then in a volley there vanished four lights at once in different corners of the room, and I struck another match in quivering haste, and stood hesitating whither to take it.

As I stood undecided, an invisible hand seemed to sweep out the two candles on the table. With a cry of terror, I dashed at the alcove, then into the corner, and then into the window, relighting three, as two more vanished by the fireplace; then, perceiving a better way, I dropped the matches on the iron-bound deed-box in the corner, and caught up the bedroom candlestick. With this I avoided the delay of striking matches; but for all that the steady process of extinction went on, and the shadows I feared and fought against returned, and crept in upon me, first a step gained on this side of me and then on that. It was like a ragged storm-cloud sweeping out the stars. Now and then one returned for a minute, and was lost again. I was now almost frantic with the horror of the coming darkness, and my self-possession deserted me. I leaped panting and dishevelled from candle to candle, in a vain struggle against that remorseless advance.

I bruised myself on the thigh against the table, I sent a chair headlong, I stumbled and fell and whisked the cloth from the table in my fall. My candle rolled away from me, and I snatched another as I rose. Abruptly this was blown out, as I swung it off the table by the wind of my sudden movement, and immediately the two remaining candles followed. But there was light still in the room, a red light that staved off the shadows from me. The fire! Of course I could still thrust my candle between the bars and relight it!

I turned to where the flames were still dancing between the glowing coals, and splashing red reflections upon the furniture, made two steps towards the grate, and incontinently the flames dwindled and vanished, the glow vanished, the reflections rushed together and vanished, and as I thrust the candle between the bars darkness closed upon me like the shutting of an eye, wrapped about me in a stifling embrace, sealed my vision, and crushed the last vestiges of reason from my brain. The candle fell from my hand. I flung out my arms in a vain effort to thrust that ponderous blackness away from me, and, lifting up my voice, screamed with all my might – once, twice, thrice. Then I think I must have staggered to my feet. I know I thought suddenly of the moonlit corridor, and, with my head bowed and my arms over my face, made a run for the door.

But I had forgotten the exact position of the door, and struck myself heavily against the corner of the bed. I staggered back, turned, and was either struck or struck myself against some other bulky furniture. I have a vague memory of battering myself thus, to and fro in the darkness, of a cramped struggle, and of my own wild crying as I darted to and fro, of a heavy blow at last upon my forehead, a horrible sensation of falling that lasted an age, of my last frantic effort to keep my footing, and then I remember no more.

I opened my eyes in daylight. My head was roughly bandaged, and the man with the withered arm was watching my face. I looked about me, trying to remember what had happened, and for a space I could not recollect. I rolled my eyes into the corner, and saw the old woman, no longer abstracted, pouring out some drops of medicine from a little blue phial into a glass. "Where am I?" I asked; "I seem to remember you, and yet I cannot remember who you are."

They told me then, and I heard of the haunted Red Room as one who hears a tale. "We found you at dawn," said he, "and there was blood on your forehead and lips."

It was very slowly I recovered my memory of my experience. "You believe now," said the old man, "that the room is haunted?" He spoke no longer as one who greets an intruder, but as one who grieves for a broken friend.

"Yes," said I; "the room is haunted."

"And you have seen it. And we, who have lived here all our lives, have never set eyes upon it. Because we have never dared ...Tell us, is it truly the old earl who—"

"No," said I; "it is not."

"I told you so," said the old lady, with the glass in her hand. "It is his poor young countess who was frightened—"

"It is not," I said. "There is neither ghost of earl nor ghost of countess in that room, there is no ghost there at all; but worse, far worse—"

"Well?" they said.

"The worst of all the things that haunt poor mortal man," said I; "and that is, in all its nakedness – Fear that will not have light nor sound, that will not bear with reason, that deafens and darkens and overwhelms. It followed me through the corridor, it fought against me in the room—"

I stopped abruptly. There was an interval of silence. My hand went up to my bandages.

Then the man with the shade sighed and spoke. "That is it," said he. "I knew that was it. A power of darkness. To put such a curse upon a woman! It lurks there always. You can feel it even in the daytime, even of a bright summer's day, in the hangings, in the curtains, keeping behind you however you face about. In the dusk it creeps along the corridor and follows you, so that you dare not turn. There is Fear in that room of hers – black Fear, and there will be – so long as this house of sin endures."

Mr. Jones
Edith Wharton

Chapter I

Lady Jane Lynke was unlike other people: when she heard that she had inherited Bells, the beautiful old place which had belonged to the Lynkes of Thudeney for something like six hundred years, the fancy took her to go and see it unannounced. She was staying at a friend's nearby, in Kent, and the next morning she borrowed a motor and slipped away alone to Thudeney-Blazes, the adjacent village.

It was a lustrous motionless day. Autumn bloom lay on the Sussex downs, on the heavy trees of the weald, on streams moving indolently, far off across the marshes. Farther still, Dungeness, a fitful streak, floated on an immaterial sky which was perhaps, after all, only sky.

In the softness Thudeney-Blazes slept: a few aged houses bowed about a duck-pond, a silvery spire, orchards thick with dew. Did Thudeney-Blazes ever wake?

Lady Jane left the motor to the care of the geese on a miniature common, pushed open a white gate into a field (the griffoned portals being padlocked), and struck across the park toward a group of carved chimney stacks. No one seemed aware of her.

In a dip of the land, the long low house, its ripe brick masonry overhanging a moat deeply sunk about its roots, resembled an aged cedar spreading immemorial red branches. Lady Jane held her breath and gazed.

A silence distilled from years of solitude lay on lawns and gardens. No one had lived at Bells since the last Lord Thudeney, then a penniless younger son, had forsaken it sixty years before to seek his fortune in Canada. And before that, he and his widowed mother, distant poor relations, were housed in one of the lodges, and the great place, even in their day, had been as mute and solitary as the family vault.

Lady Jane, daughter of another branch, to which an earldom and considerable possessions had accrued, had never seen Bells, hardly heard its name. A succession of deaths, and the whim of an old man she had never known, now made her heir to all this beauty; and as she stood and looked she was glad she had come to it from so far, from impressions so remote and different. "It would be dreadful to be used to it – to be thinking already about the state of the roof, or the cost of a heating system."

Till this her thirty-fifth year, Lady Jane had led an active, independent and decided life. One of several daughters, moderately but sufficiently provided for, she had gone early from home, lived in London lodgings, travelled in tropic lands, spent studious summers in Spain and Italy, and written two or three brisk business-like little books about cities usually dealt with sentimentally. And now, just back from a summer in the south of France, she stood ankle deep in wet bracken, and gazed at Bells lying there under a September sun that looked like moonlight.

"I shall never leave it!" she ejaculated, her heart swelling as if she had taken the vow to a lover.

She ran down the last slope of the park and entered the faded formality of gardens with clipped yews as ornate as architecture, and holly hedges as solid as walls. Adjoining the house rose a low deep-buttressed chapel. Its door was ajar, and she thought this of good augury: her forebears were waiting for her. In the porch she remarked fly-blown notices of services, an umbrella stand, a dishevelled door-mat: no doubt the chapel served as the village church. The thought gave her a sense of warmth and neighbourliness. Across the damp flags of the chancel, monuments and brasses showed through a traceried screen. She examined them curiously. Some hailed her with vocal memories, others whispered out of the remote and the unknown: it was a shame to know so little about her own family. But neither Crofts nor Lynkes had ever greatly distinguished themselves; they had gathered substance simply by holding on to what they had, and slowly accumulating privileges and acres. "Mostly by clever marriages," Lady Jane thought with a faint contempt.

At that moment her eyes lit on one of the less ornate monuments: a plain sarcophagus of gray marble niched in the wall and surmounted by the bust of a young man with a fine arrogant head, a Byronic throat and tossed-back curls.

'Peregrine Vincent Theobald Lynke, Baron Clouds, fifteenth Viscount Thudeney of Bells, Lord of the Manors of Thudeney, Thudeney-Blazes, Upper Lynke, Lynke-Linnet—' so it ran, with the usual tedious enumeration of honours, titles, court and county offices, ending with; 'Born on May 1st, 1790, perished of the plague at Aleppo in 1828.' And underneath, in small cramped characters, as if crowded as an afterthought into an insufficient space: 'Also His Wife'.

That was all. No name, dates, honours, epithets, for the Viscountess Thudeney. Did she too die of the plague at Aleppo? Or did the 'also' imply her actual presence in the sarcophagus which her husband's pride had no doubt prepared for his own last sleep, little guessing that some Syrian drain was to receive him? Lady Jane racked her memory in vain. All she knew was that the death without issue of this Lord Thudeney had caused the property to revert to the Croft-Lynkes, and so, in the end, brought her to the chancel step where, shyly, she knelt a moment, vowing to the dead to carry on their trust.

She passed on to the entrance court, and stood at last at the door of her new home, a blunt tweed figure in heavy mud-stained shoes. She felt as intrusive as a tripper, and her hand hesitated on the doorbell. "I ought to have brought someone with me," she thought; an odd admission on the part of a young woman who, when she was doing her books of travel, had prided herself on forcing single-handed the most closely guarded doors. But those other places, as she looked back, seemed easy and accessible compared to Bells.

She rang, and a tinkle answered, carried on by a flurried echo which seemed to ask what in the world was happening. Lady Jane, through the nearest window, caught the spectral vista of a long room with shrouded furniture. She could not see its farther end, but she had the feeling that someone stationed there might very well be seeing her.

"Just at first," she thought, "I shall have to invite people here – to take the chill off."

She rang again, and the tinkle again prolonged itself; but no one came.

At last she reflected that the caretakers probably lived at the back of the house, and pushing open a door in the courtyard wall she worked her way around to what seemed a stable-yard. Against the purple brick sprawled a neglected magnolia, bearing one late flower as big as a planet. Lady Jane rang at a door marked 'Service'. This bell, though also languid, had a wakefuller sound, as if it were more used to being rung, and still knew what was likely to follow; and after a delay during which Lady Jane again had the sense of being peered at – from above, through a lowered blind – a bolt shot, and a woman looked out. She was youngish, unhealthy, respectable and frightened; and she blinked at Lady Jane like someone waking out of sleep.

"Oh," said Lady Jane – "do you think I might visit the house?"

"The house?"

"I'm staying near here – I'm interested in old houses. Mightn't I take a look?"

The young woman drew back. "The house isn't shown."

"Oh, but not to – not to—" Jane weighed the case. "You see," she explained, "I know some of the family: the Northumberland branch."

"You're related, madam?"

"Well – distantly, yes." It was exactly what she had not meant to say; but there seemed no other way.

The woman twisted her apron strings in perplexity.

"Come, you know," Lady Jane urged, producing half-a-crown. The woman turned pale.

"I couldn't, madam; not without asking." It was clear that she was sorely tempted.

"Well, ask, won't you?" Lady Jane pressed the tip into a hesitating hand. The young woman shut the door and vanished. She was away so long that the visitor concluded her half-crown had been pocketed, and there was an end; and she began to be angry with herself, which was more often her habit than to be so with others.

"Well, for a fool, Jane, you're a complete one," she grumbled.

A returning footstep, listless, reluctant – the tread of one who was not going to let her in. It began to be rather comic.

The door opened, and the young woman said in her dull sing-song: "Mr. Jones says that no one is allowed to visit the house."

She and Lady Jane looked at each other for a moment, and Lady Jane read the apprehension in the other's eyes.

"Mr. Jones? Oh? – Yes; of course, keep it…" She waved away the woman's hand.

"Thank you, madam." The door closed again, and Lady Jane stood and gazed up at the inexorable face of her old home.

Chapter II

"But you didn't get in? You actually came back without so much as a peep?"

Her story was received, that evening at dinner, with mingled mirth and incredulity.

"But, my dear! You mean to say you asked to see the house, and they wouldn't let you? *Who* wouldn't?" Lady Jane's hostess insisted.

"Mr. Jones."

"Mr. Jones?"

"He said no one was allowed to visit it."

"Who on earth is Mr. Jones?"

"The caretaker, I suppose. I didn't see him."

"Didn't see him either? But I never heard such nonsense! Why in the world didn't you insist?"

"Yes; why didn't you?" they all chorused; and she could only answer, a little lamely: "I think I was afraid."

"Afraid? *You*, darling?" There was fresh hilarity. "Of Mr. Jones?"

"I suppose so." She joined in the laugh, yet she knew it was true: she had been afraid.

Edward Stramer, the novelist, an old friend of her family, had been listening with an air of abstraction, his eyes on his empty coffee cup. Suddenly, as the mistress of the house pushed back her chair, he looked across the table at Lady Jane. "It's odd: I've just remembered something. Once, when I was a youngster, I tried to see Bells; over thirty years ago it must have been." He glanced at his host. "Your mother drove me over. And we were not let in."

There was a certain flatness in this conclusion, and someone remarked that Bells had always been known as harder to get into than any house thereabouts.

"Yes," said Stramer; "but the point is that we were refused in exactly the same words. Mr. Jones said no one was allowed to visit the house."

"Ah – he was in possession already? Thirty years ago? Unsociable fellow, Jones. Well, Jane, you've got a good watch-dog."

They moved to the drawing room, and the talk drifted to other topics. But Stramer came and sat down beside Lady Jane. "It is queer, though, that at such a distance of time we should have been given exactly the same answer."

She glanced up at him curiously. "Yes; and you didn't try to force your way in either?"

"Oh no: it was not possible."

"So I felt," she agreed.

"Well, next week, my dear, I hope we shall see it all, in spite of Mr. Jones," their hostess intervened, catching their last words as she moved toward the piano.

"I wonder if we shall see Mr. Jones," said Stramer.

Chapter III

Bells was not nearly as large as it looked; like many old houses it was very narrow, and but one storey high, with servant's rooms in the low attics, and much space wasted in crooked passages and superfluous stairs. If she closed the great saloon, Jane thought, she might live there comfortably with the small staff which was the most she could afford. It was a relief to find the place less important than she had feared.

For already, in that first hour of arrival, she had decided to give up everything else for Bells. Her previous plans and ambitions – except such as might fit in with living there – had fallen from her like a discarded garment, and things she had hardly thought about, or had shrugged away with the hasty subversiveness of youth, were already laying quiet hands on her; all the lives from which her life had issued, with what they bore of example or admonishment. The very shabbiness of the house moved her more than splendours, made it, after its long abandonment, seem full of the careless daily coming and going of people long dead, people to whom it had not been a museum, or a page of history, but cradle, nursery, home, and sometimes, no doubt, a prison. If those marble lips in the chapel could speak! If she could hear some of their comments on the old house which had spread its silent shelter over their sins and sorrows, their follies and submissions! A long tale, to which she was about to add another chapter, subdued and humdrum beside some of those earlier annals, yet probably freer and more varied than the unchronicled lives of the great-aunts and great-grandmothers buried there so completely that they must hardly have known when they passed from their beds to their graves. "Piled up like dead leaves,"

Jane thought, "layers and layers of them, to preserve something forever budding underneath."

Well, all these piled-up lives had at least preserved the old house in its integrity; and that was worthwhile. She was satisfied to carry on such a trust.

She sat in the garden looking up at those rosy walls, iridescent with damp and age. She decided which windows should be hers, which rooms given to the friends from Kent who were motoring over, Stramer among them, for a modest house-warming; then she got up and went in.

The hour had come for domestic questions; for she had arrived alone, unsupported even by the old family housemaid her mother had offered her. She preferred to start afresh, convinced that her small household could be staffed from the neighbourhood. Mrs. Clemm, the rosy-cheeked old person who had curtsied her across the threshold, would doubtless know.

Mrs. Clemm, summoned to the library, curtsied again. She wore black silk, gathered and spreading as to skirt, flat and perpendicular as to bodice. On her glossy false front was a black lace cap with ribbons which had faded from violet to ash-colour, and a heavy watch-chain descended from the lava brooch under her crochet collar. Her small round face rested on the collar like a red apple on a white plate: neat, smooth, circular, with a pursed-up mouth, eyes like black seeds, and round ruddy cheeks with the skin so taut that one had to look close to see that it was as wrinkled as a piece of old crackly.

Mrs. Clemm was sure there would be no trouble about servants. She herself could do a little cooking: though her hand might be a bit out. But there was her niece to help; and she was quite of her ladyship's opinion, that there was no need to get in strangers. They were mostly a poor lot; and besides, they might not take to Bells. There were persons who didn't. Mrs. Clemm smiled a sharp little smile, like the scratch of a pin, as she added that she hoped her ladyship wouldn't be one of them.

As for under-servants…well, a boy, perhaps? She had a great-nephew she might send for. But about women – under-housemaids – if her ladyship thought they couldn't manage as they were; well, she really didn't know. Thudeney-Blazes? Oh, she didn't think so…. There was more dead than living at Thudeney-Blazes…everyone was leaving there…or in the church-yard…one house after another being shut… death was everywhere, wasn't it, my lady? Mrs. Clemm said it with another of her short sharp smiles, which provoked the appearance of a frosty dimple.

"But my niece Georgiana is a hard worker, my lady; her that let you in the other day…"

"That didn't," Lady Jane corrected.

"Oh, my lady, it was too unfortunate. If only your ladyship had have said…poor Georgiana had ought to have seen; but she never *did* have her wits about her, not for answering the door."

"But she was only obeying orders. She went to ask Mr. Jones."

Mrs. Clemm was silent. Her small hands, wrinkled and resolute, fumbled with the folds of her apron, and her quick eyes made the circuit of the room and then came back to Lady Jane's.

"Just so, my lady; but, as I told her, she'd ought to have known—"

"And who is Mr. Jones?"

Mrs. Clemm's smile snapped out again, deprecating, respectful. "Well, my lady, he's more dead than living, too…if I may say so," was her surprising answer.

"Is he? I'm sorry to hear that; but who is he?"

"Well, my lady, he's…he's my great-uncle, as it were…my grandmother's own brother, as you might say."

"Ah; I see." Lady Jane considered her with growing curiosity. "He must have reached a great age, then."

"Yes, my lady; he has that. Though I'm not," Mrs. Clemm added, the dimple showing, "as old myself as your ladyship might suppose. Living at Bells all these years has been ageing to me; it would be to anybody."

"I suppose so. And yet," Lady Jane continued, "Mr. Jones has survived; has stood it well – as you certainly have?"

"Oh. Not as well as I have," Mrs. Clemm interjected, as if resentful of the comparison.

"At any rate, he still mounts guard; mounts it as well as he did thirty years ago."

"Thirty years ago?" Mrs. Clemm echoed, her hands dropping from her apron to her sides.

"Wasn't he here thirty years ago?"

"Oh, yes, my lady; certainly; he's never once been away that I know of."

"What a wonderful record! And what exactly are his duties?"

Mrs. Clemm paused again, her hands still motionless in the folds of her skirt. Lady Jane noticed that the fingers were tightly clenched, as if to check an involuntary gesture.

"He began as pantry-boy; then footman; then butler, my lady; but it's hard to say, isn't it, what an old servant's duties are, when he's stayed on in the same house so many years?"

"Yes; and that house always empty."

"Just so, my lady. Everything came to depend on him; one thing after another. His late lordship thought the world of him."

"His late lordship? But he was never here! He spent all his life in Canada."

Mrs. Clemm seemed slightly disconcerted. "Certainly, my lady." (Her voice said: "Who are you, to set me right as to the chronicles of Bells?") "But by letter, my lady; I can show you the letters. And there was his lordship before, the sixteenth Viscount. He *did* come here once."

"Ah, did he?" Lady Jane was embarrassed to find how little she knew of them all. She rose from her seat. "They were lucky, all these absentees, to have someone to watch over their interests so faithfully. I should like to see Mr. Jones – to thank him. Will you take me to him now?"

"Now?" Mrs. Clemm moved back a step or two; Lady Jane fancied her cheeks paled a little under their ruddy varnish. "Oh, not today, my lady."

"Why? Isn't he well enough?"

"Not nearly. He's between life and death, as it were," Mrs. Clemm repeated, as if the phrase were the nearest approach she could find to a definition of Mr. Jones's state.

"He wouldn't even know who I was?"

Mrs. Clemm considered a moment. "I don't say *that*, my lady;" her tone implied that to do so might appear disrespectful. "He'd know you, my lady; but you wouldn't know *him*." She broke off and added hastily: "I mean, for what he is: he's in no state for you to see him."

"He's so very ill? Poor man! And is everything possible being done?"

"Oh, everything; and more too, my lady. But perhaps," Mrs. Clemm suggested, with a clink of keys, "this would be a good time for your ladyship to take a look about the house. If your ladyship has no objection, I should like to begin with the linen."

Chapter IV

"And Mr. Jones?" Stramer queried, a few days later, as they sat, Lady Jane and the party from Kent, about an improvised tea-table in a recess of one of the great holly-hedges.

The day was as hushed and warm as that on which she had first come to Bells, and Lady Jane looked up with a smile of ownership at the old walls which seemed to smile back, the windows which now looked at her with friendly eyes.

"Mr. Jones? Who's Mr. Jones?" the others asked; only Stramer recalled their former talk.

Lady Jane hesitated. "Mr. Jones is my invisible guardian; or rather, the guardian of Bells."

They remembered then. "Invisible? You don't mean to say you haven't seen him yet?"

"Not yet; perhaps I never shall. He's very old – and very ill, I'm afraid."

"And he still rules here?"

"Oh, absolutely. The fact is," Lady Jane added "I believe he's the only person left who really knows all about Bells."

"Jane, my *dear*! That big shrub over there against the wall! I verily believe it's Templetonia retusa. It *is*! Did anyone ever hear of it standing an English winter?" Gardeners all, they dashed towards the shrub in its sheltered angle. "I shall certainly try it on a south wall at Dipway," cried the hostess from Kent.

Tea over, they moved on to inspect the house. The short autumn day was drawing to a close; but the party had been able to come only for an afternoon, instead of staying over the week-end, and having lingered so long in the gardens they had only time, indoors, to puzzle out what they could through the shadows. Perhaps, Lady

Jane thought, it was the best hour to see a house like Bells, so long abandoned, and not yet warmed into new life.

The fire she had had lit in the saloon sent its radiance to meet them, giving the great room an air of expectancy and welcome. The portraits, the Italian cabinets, the shabby armchairs and rugs, all looked as if life had but lately left them; and Lady Jane said to herself: "Perhaps Mrs. Clemm is right in advising me to live here and close the blue parlour."

"My dear, what a fine room! Pity it faces north. Of course you'll have to shut it in winter. It would cost a fortune to heat."

Lady Jane hesitated. "I don't know: I *had* meant to. But there seems to be no other..."

"No other? In all this house?" They laughed; and one of the visitors, going ahead and crossing a panelled anteroom, cried out: "But here! A delicious room; windows south – yes, and west. The warmest of the house. This is perfect."

They followed, and the blue room echoed with exclamations. "Those charming curtains with the parrots...and the blue of that petit point fire-screen! But, Jane, of course you must live here. Look at this citron-wood desk!"

Lady Jane stood on the threshold. "It seems that the chimney smokes hopelessly."

"Hopelessly? Nonsense! Have you consulted anybody? I'll send you a wonderful man..."

"Besides, if you put in one of those one-pipe heaters..... At Dipway..."

Stramer was looking over Lady Jane's shoulder. "What does Mr. Jones say about it?"

"He says no one has ever been able to use this room; not for ages. It was the housekeeper who told me. She's his great-niece, and seems simply to transmit his oracles."

Stramer shrugged. "Well, he's lived at Bells longer than you have. Perhaps he's right."

"How absurd!" one of the ladies cried. "The housekeeper and Mr. Jones probably spend their evenings here, and don't want to be disturbed. Look – ashes on the hearth! What did I tell you?"

Lady Jane echoed the laugh as they turned away. They had still to see the library, damp and dilapidated, the panelled dining room, the breakfast parlour, and such bedrooms as had any old furniture left; not many, for the late lords of Bells, at one time or another, had evidently sold most of its removable treasures.

When the visitors came down their motors were waiting. A lamp had been placed in the hall, but the rooms beyond were lit only by the broad clear band of western sky showing through uncurtained casements. On the doorstep one of the ladies exclaimed that she had lost her handbag – no, she remembered; she had laid it on the desk in the blue room. Which way was the blue room?

"I'll get it," Jane said, turning back. She heard Stramer following. He asked if he should bring the lamp.

"Oh, no; I can see."

She crossed the threshold of the blue room, guided by the light from its western window; then she stopped. Someone was in the room already; she felt rather than saw another presence. Stramer, behind her, paused also; he did not speak or move. What she saw, or thought she saw, was simply an old man with bent shoulders turning away from the citron-wood desk. Almost before she had received the impression there was no one there; only the slightest stir of the needlework curtain over the farther door. She heard no step or other sound.

"There's the bag," she said, as if the act of speaking, and saying something obvious were a relief.

In the hall her glance crossed Stramer's, but failed to find there the reflection of what her own had registered.

He shook hands, smiling. "Well, goodbye. I commit you to Mr. Jones's care; only don't let him say that *you're* not shown to visitors."

She smiled: "Come back and try," and then shivered a little as the lights of the last motor vanished beyond the great black hedges.

Chapter V

Lady Jane had exulted in her resolve to keep Bells to herself till she and the old house should have had time to make friends. But after a few days she recalled the uneasy felling which had come over her as she stood on the threshold after her first tentative ring. Yes; she had been right in thinking she would have to have people about her to take the chill off. The house was too old, too mysterious, too much withdrawn into its own secret past, for her poor little present to fit into it without uneasiness.

But it was not a time of year when, among Lady Jane's friends, it was easy to find people free. Her own family were all in the north, and impossible to dislodge. One of her sisters, when invited, simply sent her back a list of shooting-dates; and her mother wrote: "Why not come to us? What can you have to do all alone in that empty house at this time of year? Next summer we're all coming."

Having tried one or two friends with the same result, Lady Jane bethought her of Stramer. He was finishing a novel, she knew, and at such times he liked to settle down somewhere in the country where he could be sure of not being disturbed. Bells was a perfect asylum, and though it was probable that some other friend had anticipated her, and provided the requisite seclusion, Lady Jane decided to invite him. "Do bring your work and stay till it's finished – and don't be in a hurry to finish. I promise that no one shall bother you—" and she added, half-nervously: "Not even Mr. Jones." As she wrote she felt an absurd impulse to blot the words out. "He might not like it," she thought; and the 'he' did not refer to Stramer.

Was the solitude already making her superstitious? She thrust the letter into an envelope, and carried it herself to the post-office at Thudeney-Blazes. Two days later a wire from Stramer announced his arrival.

He came on a cold stormy afternoon, just before dinner, and as they went up to dress Lady Jane called after him: "We shall sit in the blue parlour this evening." The housemaid Georgiana was crossing the passage with hot water for the visitor. She stopped and cast a vacant glance at Lady Jane. The latter met it, and said carelessly: "You hear Georgiana? The fire in the blue parlour."

While Lady Jane was dressing she heard a knock, and saw Mrs. Clemm's round face just inside the door, like a red apple on a garden wall.

"Is there anything wrong about the saloon, my lady? Georgiana understood—"

"That I want the fire in the blue parlour. Yes. What's wrong with the saloon is that one freezes there."

"But the chimney smokes in the blue parlour."

"Well, we'll give it a trial, and if it does I'll send for someone to arrange it."

"Nothing can be done, my lady. Everything has been tried, and—"

Lady Jane swung about suddenly. She had heard Stramer singing a cheerful hunting-song in a cracked voice, in his dressing room at the other end of the corridor.

"That will do, Mrs. Clemm. I want the fire in the blue parlour."

"Yes, my lady." The door closed on the housekeeper.

"So you decided on the saloon after all?" Stramer said, as Lady Jane led the way there after their brief repast.

"Yes, I hope you won't be frozen. Mr. Jones swears that the chimney in the blue parlour isn't safe; so, until I can fetch the mason over from Strawbridge—"

"Oh, I see." Stramer drew up to the blaze in the great fireplace. "We're very well off here; though heating this room is going to be ruinous. Meanwhile, I note that Mr. Jones still rules."

Lady Jane gave a slight laugh.

"Tell me," Stramer continued, as she bent over the mixing of the Turkish coffee, "what is there about him? I'm getting curious."

Lady Jane laughed again, and heard the embarrassment in her laugh. "So am I."

"Why – you don't mean to say you haven't seen him yet?"

"No. He's still too ill."

"What's the matter with him? What does the doctor say?"

"He won't see the doctor."

"But, look here – if things take a worse turn – I don't know; but mightn't you be held to have been negligent?"

"What can I do? Mrs. Clemm says he has a doctor who treats him by correspondence. I don't see that I can interfere."

"Isn't there someone beside Mrs. Clemm whom you can consult?"

She considered: certainly, as yet, she had not made much effort to get into relation with her neighbours. "I expected the vicar to call. But I've enquired: there's no vicar any longer at Thudeney-Blazes. A curate comes from Strawbridge every other Sunday. And the one who comes now is new: nobody about the place seems to know him."

"But I thought the chapel here was in use? It looked so when you showed it to us the other day."

"I thought so too. It used to be the parish church of Lynke-Linnet and Lower-Lynke; but it seems that was years ago. The parishioners objected to coming so far; and there weren't enough of them. Mrs. Clemm says that nearly everybody has died off or left. It's the same at Thudeney-Blazes."

Stramer glanced about the great room, with its circle of warmth and light by the hearth, and the sullen shadows huddled at its farther end, as if hungrily listening. "With this emptiness at the centre, life was bound to cease gradually on the outskirts."

Lady Jane followed his glance. "Yes; it's all wrong. I must try to wake the place up."

"Why not open it to the public? Have a visitors' day?"

She thought a moment. In itself the suggestion was distasteful; she could imagine few things that would bore her more. Yet to do so might be a duty, a first step toward reestablishing relations between the lifeless house and its neighbourhood. Secretly, she felt that even the coming and going of indifferent unknown people would help to take the chill from those rooms, to brush from their walls the dust of too-heavy memories.

"Who's that?" asked Stramer. Lady Jane started in spite of herself, and glanced over her shoulder; but he was only looking past her at a portrait which a dart of flame from the hearth had momentarily called from its obscurity.

"That's a Lady Thudeney." She got up and went toward the picture with a lamp. "Might be an Opie, don't you think? It's a strange face, under the smirk of the period."

Stramer took the lamp and held it up. The portrait was that of a young woman in a short-waisted muslin gown caught beneath the breast by a cameo. Between clusters of beribboned curls a long fair oval looked out dumbly, inexpressively, in a stare of frozen beauty. "It's as if the house had been too empty even then," Lady Jane murmured. "I wonder which she was? Oh, I know: it must be 'Also His Wife'."

Stramer stared.

"It's the only name on her monument. The wife of Peregrine Vincent Theobald, who perished of the plague at Aleppo in 1828. Perhaps she was very fond of him, and this was painted when she was an inconsolable widow."

"They didn't dress like that as late as 1828." Stramer holding the lamp closer, deciphered the inscription on the border of the lady's India scarf; "Juliana, Viscountess Thudeney, 1818". "She must have been inconsolable before his death, then."

Lady Jane smiled. "Let's hope she grew less so after it."

Stramer passed the lamp across the canvas. "Do you see where she was painted? In the blue parlour. Look: the old panelling; and she's leaning on the citron-wood desk. They evidently used the room in winter then." The lamp paused on the background of the picture: a window framing snow-laden paths and hedges in icy perspective.

"Curious," Stramer said – "and rather melancholy: to be painted against that wintry desolation. I wish you could find out more about her. Have you dipped into your archives?"

"No. Mr. Jones—"

"He won't allow that either?"

"Yes; but he's lost the key of the muniment-room. Mrs. Clemm has been trying to get a locksmith."

"Surely the neighbourhood can still produce one?"

"There *was* one at Thudeney-Blazes; but he died the week before I came."

"Of course!"

"Of course?"

"Well, in Mrs. Clemm's hands keys get lost, chimneys smoke, locksmiths die..." Stramer stood, light in hand, looking down the shadowy length of the saloon. "I say, let's go and see what's happening now in the blue parlour."

Lady Jane laughed: a laugh seemed easy with another voice nearby to echo it. "Let's—"

She followed him out of the saloon, across the hall in which a single candle burned on a far-off table, and past the stairway yawning like a black funnel above them. In the doorway of the blue parlour Stramer paused. "Now, then, Mr. Jones!"

It was stupid, but Lady Jane's heart gave a jerk: she hoped the challenge would not evoke the shadowy figure she had half seen that other day.

"Lord, it's cold!" Stramer stood looking about him. "Those ashes are still on the hearth. Well, it's all very queer." He crossed over to the citron-wood desk. "There's where she sat for her picture – and in this very armchair – look!"

"Oh, don't!" Lady Jane exclaimed. The words slipped out unawares.

"Don't – what?"

"Try those drawers—" she wanted to reply; for his hand was stretched toward the desk.

"I'm frozen; I think I'm starting a cold. Do come away," she grumbled, backing toward the door.

Stramer lighted her out without comment. As the lamplight slid along the walls Lady Jane fancied that the needle-work curtain over the farther door stirred as it had that other day. But it may have been the wind rising outside…

The saloon seemed like home when they got back to it.

Chapter VI

"There *is* no Mr. Jones!"

Stramer proclaimed it triumphantly when they met the next morning. Lady Jane had motored off early to Strawbridge in quest of a mason and a locksmith. The quest had taken longer than she had expected, for everybody in Strawbridge was busy on jobs nearer by, and unaccustomed to the idea of going to Bells, with which the town seemed to have had no communication within living memory. The younger workmen did not even know where the place was, and the best Lady Jane could do was to coax a locksmith's apprentice to come with her, on the understanding that he would be driven back to the nearest station as soon as his job was over. As for the mason, he had merely taken note of her request, and promised half-heartedly to send somebody when he could. "Rather off our beat, though."

She returned, discouraged and somewhat weary, as Stramer was coming downstairs after his morning's work.

"No Mr. Jones?" she echoed.

"Not a trace! I've been trying the old Glamis experiment – situating his room by its window. Luckily the house is smaller…"

Lady Jane smiled. "Is this what you call locking yourself up with your work?"

"I can't work: that's the trouble. Not till this is settled. Bells is a fidgety place."

"Yes," she agreed.

"Well, I wasn't going to be beaten; so I went to try to find the head gardener."

"But there isn't—"

"No. Mrs. Clemm told me. The head gardener died last year. That woman positively glows with life whenever she announces a death. Have you noticed?"

Yes: Lady Jane had.

"Well – I said to myself that if there wasn't a head gardener there must be an underling; at least one. I'd seen somebody in the distance, raking leaves, and I ran him down. Of course he'd never seen Mr. Jones."

"You mean that poor old half-blind Jacob? He couldn't see anybody."

"Perhaps not. At any rate, he told me that Mr. Jones wouldn't let the leaves be buried for leaf-mould – I forget why. Mr. Jones's authority extends even to the gardens."

"Yet you say he doesn't exist!"

"Wait. Jacob is half-blind, but he's been here for years, and knows more about the place than you'd think. I got him talking about the house, and I pointed to one window after another, and he told me each time whose the room was, or had been. But he couldn't situate Mr. Jones."

"I beg your ladyship's pardon—" Mrs. Clemm was on the threshold, cheeks shining, skirt rustling, her eyes like drills. "The locksmith your ladyship brought back; I understand it was for the lock of the muniment-room—"

"Well?"

"He's lost one of his tools, and can't do anything without it. So he's gone. The butcher's boy gave him a lift back."

Lady Jane caught Stramer's faint chuckle. She stood and stared at Mrs. Clemm, and Mrs. Clemm stared back, deferential but unflinching.

"Gone? Very well; I'll motor after him."

"Oh, my lady, it's too late. The butcher's boy had his motor-cycle…. Besides, what could he do?"

"Break the lock," exclaimed Lady Jane, exasperated.

"Oh, my lady—" Mrs. Clemm's intonation marked the most respectful incredulity. She waited another moment, and then withdrew, while Lady Jane and Stramer considered each other.

"But this is absurd," Lady Jane declared when they had lunched, waited on, as usual, by the flustered Georgiana. "I'll break in that door myself, if I have to. – Be careful please, Georgiana," she added; "I was speaking of doors, not dishes." For Georgiana had let fall with a crash the dish she was removing from the table. She gathered up the pieces in her tremulous fingers, and vanished. Jane and Stramer returned to the saloon.

"Queer!" the novelist commented.

"Yes." Lady Jane, facing the door, started slightly. Mrs. Clemm was there again; but this time subdued, unrustling, bathed in that odd pallor which enclosed but seemed unable to penetrate the solid crimson of her cheeks.

"I beg pardon, my lady. The key is found." Her hand, as she held it out, trembled like Georgiana's.

Chapter VII

"It's not here," Stramer announced a couple of hours later.

"What isn't?" Lady Jane queried, looking up from a heap of disordered papers. Her eyes blinked at him through the fog of yellow dust raised by her manipulations.

"The clue. I've got all the 1800 to 1840 papers here; and there's a gap."

She moved over to the table above which he was bending. "A gap?"

"A big one. Nothing between 1815 and 1835. No mention of Peregrine or Juliana."

They looked at each other across the tossed papers, and suddenly Stramer exclaimed: "Someone has been here before us – just lately."

Lady Jane stared, incredulous, and then followed the direction of his downward pointing hand.

"Do you wear flat heelless shoes?" he questioned.

"And of that size? Even my feet are too small to fit into those footprints. Luckily there wasn't time to sweep the floor!"

Lady Jane felt a slight chill, a chill of a different and more inward quality than the shock of stuffy coldness which had met them as they entered the unaired attic set apart for the storing of the Thudeney archives.

"But how absurd! Of course when Mrs. Clemm found we were coming up she came – or sent someone – to open the shutters."

"That's not Mrs. Clemm's foot, or the other woman's. She must have sent a man – an old man with a shaky uncertain step. Look how it wanders."

"Mr. Jones, then!" said Lady Jane, half impatiently.

"Mr. Jones. And he got what he wanted, and put it – where?"

"Ah, *that*—! I'm freezing, you know; let's give this up for the present." She rose, and Stramer followed her without protest; the muniment-room was really untenable.

"I must catalogue all this stuff someday, I suppose," Lady Jane continued, as they went down the stairs. "But meanwhile, what do you say to a good tramp, to get the dust out of our lungs?"

He agreed, and turned back to his room to get some letters he wanted to post at Thudeney-Blazes.

Lady Jane went down alone. It was a fine afternoon, and the sun, which had made the dust-clouds of the muniment-room so dazzling, sent a long shaft through the west window of the blue parlour, and across the floor of the hall.

Certainly Georgiana kept the oak floors remarkably well; considering how much else she had to do, it was surp—

Lady Jane stopped as if an unseen hand had jerked her violently back. On the smooth parquet before her she had caught the trace of dusty footprints – the prints of broad-soled heelless shoes – making for the blue parlour and crossing its threshold. She stood still with the same inward shiver that she had felt upstairs; then, avoiding the footprints, she too stole very softly toward the blue parlour, pushed the door wider, and saw, in the long dazzle of autumn light, as if translucid, edged with the glitter, an old man at the desk.

"Mr. Jones!"

A step came up behind her: Mrs. Clemm with the post-bag. "You called, my lady?"

"I...yes..."

When she turned back to the desk there was no one there.

She faced about on the housekeeper. "Who was that?"

"Where, my lady?"

Lady Jane, without answering, moved toward the needlework curtain, in which she had detected the same faint tremor as before. "Where does that door go to – behind the curtain?"

"Nowhere, my lady. I mean; there is no door."

Mrs. Clemm had followed; her step sounded quick and assured. She lifted up the curtain with a firm hand. Behind it was a rectangle of roughly plastered wall, where an opening had visibly been bricked up.

"When was that done?"

"The wall built up? I couldn't say. I've never known it otherwise," replied the housekeeper.

The two women stood for an instant measuring each other with level eyes; then the housekeeper's were slowly lowered, and she let the curtain fall from her hand. "There are a great many things in old houses that nobody knows about," she said.

"There shall be as few as possible in mine," said Lady Jane.

"My lady!" The housekeeper stepped quickly in front of her. "My lady, what are you doing?" she gasped.

Lady Jane had turned back to the desk at which she had just seen – or fancied she had seen – the bending figure of Mr. Jones.

"I am going to look through these drawers," she said.

The housekeeper still stood in pale immobility between her and the desk. "No, my lady – no. You won't do that."

"Because—?"

Mrs. Clemm crumpled up her black silk apron with a despairing gesture. "Because – if you *will* have it – that's where Mr. Jones keeps his private papers. I know he'd oughtn't to…"

"Ah – then it was Mr. Jones I saw here?"

The housekeeper's arms sank to her sides and her mouth hung open on an unspoken word. "You *saw* him." The question came out in a confused whisper; and before Lady Jane could answer, Mrs. Clemm's arms rose again, stretched before her face as if to fend off a blaze of intolerable light, or some forbidden sight she had long since disciplined herself not to see. Thus screening her eyes she hurried across the hall to the door of the servant's wing.

Lady Jane stood for a moment looking after her; then, with a slightly shaking hand, she opened the desk and hurriedly took out from it all the papers – a small bundle – that it contained. With them she passed back into the saloon.

As she entered it her eye was caught by the portrait of the melancholy lady in the short-waisted gown, whom she and Stramer had christened 'Also His Wife'. The lady's eyes, usually so empty of all awareness save of her own frozen beauty, seemed suddenly waking to an anguished participation in the scene.

"Fudge!" muttered Lady Jane, shaking off the spectral suggestion as she turned to meet Stramer on the threshold.

Chapter VIII

The missing papers were all there. Stramer and she spread them out hurriedly on a table and at once proceeded to gloat over their find. Not a particularly important one, indeed; in the long history of the Lynkes and Crofts it took up hardly more space than the little handful of documents did, in actual bulk, among the stacks of the muniment room. But the fact that these papers filled a gap in the chronicles of the house, and situated the sad-faced beauty as veritably the wife of the Peregrine Vincent Theobald Lynke who had 'perished of the plague at Aleppo in 1828' – this was a discovery sufficiently exciting to whet amateur appetites, and to put out of Lady Jane's mind the strange incident which had attended the opening of the cabinet.

For a while she and Stramer sat silently and methodically going through their respective piles of correspondence; but presently Lady Jane, after glancing over one of the yellowing pages, uttered a startled exclamation.

"How strange! Mr. Jones again – always Mr. Jones!"

Stramer looked up from the papers he was sorting. "You too? I've got a lot of letters here addressed to a Mr. Jones by Peregrine Vincent, who seems to have been always disporting himself abroad, and chronically in want of money. Gambling debts, apparently…ah and women…a dirty record altogether…"

"Yes? My letter is not written to a Mr. Jones; but it's about one. Listen." Lady Jane began to read. "'Bells, February 20th, 1826…' (It's from poor 'Also His Wife' to her husband.) 'My dear Lord, Acknowledging as I ever do the burden of the sad impediment which denies me the happiness of being more frequently in your company, I yet fail to conceive how anything in my state obliges that close seclusion in which Mr. Jones persists – and by your express orders, so he declares – in confining me. Surely, my lord, had you found it possible to spend more time with me since the day of our marriage, you would yourself have seen it to be unnecessary to put this restraint upon me. It is true, alas, that my unhappy infirmity denies me the happiness to speak with you, or to hear the accents of the voice I should love above all others could it but reach me; but, my dear husband, I would have you consider that my mind is in no way affected by this obstacle, but goes out to you, as my heart does, in a perpetual eagerness of attention, and that to sit in this great house alone, day after day, month after month, deprived of your company, and debarred also from any intercourse but that of the servants you have chosen to put about me, is a fate more cruel than I deserve and more painful than I can bear. I have entreated Mr. Jones, since he seems all-powerful with you, to represent this to you, and to transmit this my last request – for should I fail I am resolved to make no other – that you should consent to my making the acquaintance of a few of your friends and neighbours, among whom I cannot but think there must be some kind hearts that would take pity on my unhappy situation, and afford me such companionship as would give me more courage to bear your continual absence…"

Lady Jane folded up the letter. "Deaf and dumb – ah, poor creature! That explains the look—"

"And this explains the marriage," Stramer continued, unfolding a stiff parchment document. "Here are the Viscountess Thudeney's marriage settlements. She appears to have been a Miss Portallo, daughter of Obadiah Portallo Esquire, of Purflew Castle, Caermarthenshire, and Bombay House, Twickenham, East India merchant, senior member of the banking house of Portallo and Prest – and so on and so on. And the figures run up into hundreds of thousands."

"It's rather ghastly – putting the two things together. All the millions and – imprisonment in the blue parlour. I suppose her Viscount had to have the money, and was ashamed to have it known how he had got it…" Lady Jane shivered. "Think of it – day after day, winter after winter, year after year...speechless, soundless, alone...under Mr. Jones's guardianship. Let me see: what year were they married?"

"In 1817."

"And only a year later that portrait was painted. And she had the frozen look already."

Stramer mused: "Yes; it's grim enough. But the strangest figure in the whole case is still – Mr. Jones."

"Mr. Jones – yes. Her keeper," Lady Jane mused "I suppose he must have been this one's ancestor. The office seems to have been hereditary at Bells."

"Well – I don't know."

Stramer's voice was so odd that Lady Jane looked up at him with a stare of surprise. "What if it were the same one?" suggested Stramer with a queer smile.

"The same?" Lady Jane laughed. "You're not good at figures are you? If poor Lady Thudeney's Mr. Jones were alive now he'd be—"

"I didn't say ours was alive now," said Stramer.

"Oh – why, what...?" she faltered.

But Stramer did not answer; his eyes had been arrested by the precipitate opening of the door behind his hostess, and the entry of Georgiana, a livid, dishevelled Georgiana, more than usually bereft of her faculties, and gasping out something inarticulate.

"Oh, my lady – it's my aunt – she won't answer me," Georgiana stammered in a voice of terror.

Lady Jane uttered an impatient exclamation. "Answer you? Why – what do you want her to answer?"

"Only whether she's alive, my lady," said Georgiana with streaming eyes.

Lady Jane continued to look at her severely. "Alive? Alive? Why on earth shouldn't she be?"

"She might as well be dead – by the way she just lies there."

"Your aunt dead? I saw her alive enough in the blue parlour half an hour ago," Lady Jane returned. She was growing rather blasé with regard to Georgiana's panics; but suddenly she felt this to be of a different nature from any of the others. "Where is it your aunt's lying?"

"In her own bedroom, on her bed," the other wailed, "and won't say why."

Lady Jane got to her feet, pushing aside the heaped-up papers, and hastening to the door with Stramer in her wake.

As they went up the stairs she realised that she had seen the housekeeper's bedroom only once, on the day of her first obligatory round of inspection, when she had taken possession of Bells. She did not even remember very clearly where it was, but followed Georgiana down the passage and through a door which communicated, rather surprisingly, with a narrow walled-in staircase that was unfamiliar to her. At its top she and Stramer found themselves on a small landing upon which two doors opened. Through the confusion of her mind Lady Jane noticed that these rooms, with their special staircase leading down to what had always been called his lordship's suite, must obviously have been occupied by his lordship's confidential servants. In one of them, presumably, had been lodged the original Mr. Jones, the Mr. Jones of the yellow letters, the letters purloined by Lady Jane. As she crossed the threshold, Lady Jane remembered the housekeeper's attempt to prevent her touching the contents of the desk.

Mrs. Clemm's room, like herself, was neat, glossy and extremely cold. Only Mrs. Clemm herself was no longer like Mrs. Clemm. The red-apple glaze had barely faded from her cheeks, and not a lock was disarranged in the unnatural lustre of her false front; even her cap ribbons hung symmetrically along either cheek. But death had happened to her, and had made her into someone else. At first glance it was impossible to say if the unspeakable horror in her wide-open eyes were only the reflection of that change, or of the agent by whom it had come. Lady Jane, shuddering, paused a moment while Stramer went up to the bed.

"Her hand is warm still – but no pulse." He glanced about the room. "A glass anywhere?" The cowering Georgiana took a hand-glass from the neat chest of drawers, and Stramer held it over the housekeeper's drawn-back lip…

"She's dead," he pronounced.

"Oh, poor thing! But how—?" Lady Jane drew near, and was kneeling down, taking the inanimate hand in hers, when Stramer touched her on the arm, then silently raised a finger of warning. Georgiana was crouching in the farther corner of the room, her face buried in her lifted arms.

"Look here," Stramer whispered. He pointed to Mrs. Clemm's throat, and Lady Jane, bending over, distinctly saw a circle of red marks on it – the marks of recent bruises. She looked again into the awful eyes.

"She's been strangled," Stramer whispered.

Lady Jane, with a shiver of fear, drew down the housekeeper's lids. Goergiana, her face hidden, was still sobbing convulsively in the corner. There seemed, in the air of the cold orderly room, something that forbade wonderment and silenced conjecture. Lady

Jane and Stramer stood and looked at each other without speaking. At length Stramer crossed over to Georgiana, and touched her on the shoulder. She appeared unaware of the touch, and he grasped her shoulder and shook it. "Where is Mr. Jones?" he asked.

The girl looked up, her face blurred and distorted with weeping, her eyes dilated as if with the vision of some latent terror. "Oh, sir, she's not really dead, is she?"

Stramer repeated his question in a loud authoritative tone; and slowly she echoed it in a scarce-heard whisper. "Mr. Jones—?"

"Get up, my girl, and send him here to us at once, or tell us where to find him."

Georgiana, moved by the old habit of obedience, struggled to her feet and stood unsteadily, her heaving shoulders braced against the wall. Stramer asked her sharply if she had not heard what he had said.

"Oh, poor thing, she's so upset—" Lady Jane intervened compassionately. "Tell me, Georgiana: where shall we find Mr. Jones?"

The girl turned to her with eyes as fixed as the dead woman's. "You won't find him anywhere," she slowly said.

"Why not?"

"Because he's not here."

"Not here? Where is he, then?" Stramer broke in.

Georgiana did not seem to notice the interruption. She continued to stare at Lady Jane with Mrs. Clemm's awful eyes. "He's in his grave in the church-yard – these years and years he is. Long before ever I was born...my aunt hadn't ever seen him herself, not since she was a tiny child.... That's the terror of it...that's why she always had to do what he told her to...because you couldn't ever answer him back…" Her horrified gaze turned from Lady Jane to the stony face and fast-glazing pupils of the dead woman. "You hadn't ought to have meddled with his papers, my lady…. That's what he's punished her for…. When it came to those papers he wouldn't ever listen to human reason…he wouldn't…" Then, flinging her arms above her head, Georgiana straightened herself to her full height before falling in a swoon at Stramer's feet.

Biographies
& Sources

E.F. Benson

How Fear Departed from the Long Gallery

(Originally published in *The Windsor Magazine*, December 1911, then the collection *The Room in the Tower and Other Stories*, 1912)

Edward Frederic ('E.F.') Benson (1867–1940) was born at Wellington College in Berkshire, England, where his father, the future Archbishop of Canterbury Edward White Benson, was headmaster. Benson is widely known for being a writer of reminiscences, fiction, satirical novels, biographies and autobiographical studies. His first published novel, *Dodo*, initiated his success, followed by a series of comic novels such as *Queen Lucia* and *Trouble for Lucia*. Later in life, Benson moved to Rye where he was elected mayor. It was here that he was inspired to write several macabre ghost story and supernatural collections and novels, including *Paying Guests* and *Mrs. Ames*.

Algernon Blackwood

The Decoy

(Originally published in *The Wolves of God and Other Fey Stories*, 1921)

Algernon Henry Blackwood (1869–1951) was a writer who crafted his tales with extraordinary vision. Born in Kent but working at numerous careers in America and Canada in his youth, he eventually settled back in England in his thirties. He wrote many novels and short stories, including 'The Willows', which was rated by Lovecraft as one of his favourite stories. Blackwood is credited by many scholars as a real master of imagery who wrote at a consistently high standard.

Dick Donovan

A Night of Horror

(Originally published in *Tales of Terror*, 1899)

Dick Donovan (1843–1934) was the pseudonym of J.E. Preston Muddock. Born near Southampton, England, Muddock became a journalist and travelled the globe. 'Dick Donovan' was the name of Muddock's fictional Glasgow detective – a character who so rivalled the popularity of Sherlock Holmes that Muddock later chose Donovan as his own pen name. This technique of using a fictional detective as a pseudonym was used later by Ellery Queen and Nick Carter. He was incredibly prolific in crime and horror genres in particular, and some theorise that the origin of the term 'Dick' to mean an American private detective may be linked back to him.

H.D. Everett

A Water Witch

(Originally published in *The Death-Mask and Other Ghosts*, 1920)

Born in Gillingham, Kent, Henrietta Dorothy Everett (1851–1923) married a Staffordshire solicitor in 1869 and only turned to writing in her forties. Publishing under the pen name Theo Douglas, she produced over twenty books, including several novels as well as an abundance of short stories. Whilst these included a number of historical romances, she really made her reputation with her tales of mystery and the supernatural, which were to be recommended by H.P. Lovecraft and M.R. James.

Hester Fox

Introduction

Hester Fox is a full-time writer and mother, with a background in museum work and historical archaeology. She is the author of such novels as *The Witch of Willow Hall*, *A Lullaby for Witches*, and *The Last Heir to Blackwood Library*. When she is not writing, you can find Hester exploring old cemeteries, browsing used bookshops, or curled up with a book and a pastry. Hester lives in Massachusetts with her husband and their children.

Mary E. Wilkins Freeman

The Lost Ghost

(Originally published in *The Wind in the Rose-Bush and Other Stories of the Supernatural*, Doubleday, Page & Company, 1903)

The American author Mary Eleanor Wilkins Freeman (1852–1930) was born in Randolph, Massachusetts. Most of Freeman's works were influenced by her strict childhood, as her parents were orthodox Congregationalists and harboured strong religious views. While working as a secretary for the author Oliver Wendell Holmes, Sr., she was inspired to write herself. Supernatural topics kept catching her attention, and she began to write many short stories with a combination of supernatural and domestic realism, her most famous being 'A New England Nun'. She wrote a number of ghost tales, which were turned into famous ghost story collections after her death.

William Hope Hodgson

The Whistling Room

(Originally published in *The Idler*, 1910)

William Hope Hodgson (1877–1918) was born in Essex, England, but moved several times with his family, including living for some time in County Galway, Ireland – a setting that would later inspire *The House on the Borderland*. Hodgson made several unsuccessful attempts to run away to sea, until his uncle secured him some work in the Merchant Marine. This association with the ocean would unfold later in his many sea stories. After some initial rejections of his writing, Hodgson managed to become a full-time writer of both novels and short stories, which form a fantastic legacy of adventure, mystery and horror fiction.

W.W. Jacobs

The Toll-House

(Originally published in *Sailors' Knots*, 1909)

William Wymark ('W.W.') Jacobs (1863–1943) was born in London, England, and he is known for his deeply humorous and horrifying works. Drawing upon his childhood experiences, Jacobs wrote many works reflecting on his father's profession as a dockhand and wharf manager. His first volume of stories, *Many Cargoes,* was a great success and gave Jacobs the courage to publish other stories such as 'The Monkey's Paw' and 'The Toll-House'. Jacobs used realistic experiences as well as a combination of superstition, terror, exotic adventure and humour in each one of his famous tales.

M.R. James

Lost Hearts

(Originally published in *Pall Mall Magazine*, 1895)

Montague Rhodes James (1862–1936), whose works are regarded as being at the forefront of the ghost story genre, was born in Kent, England. James dispensed with the traditional, predictable techniques of ghost story construction, instead using realistic contemporary settings for his works. He was also a British medieval scholar, so his stories tended to incorporate antiquarian elements. His stories often reflect his childhood in Suffolk and his talented acting career, which both seem to have assisted in the build-up of tension and horror in his works.

Bram Stoker

The Judge's House

(Originally published in *Illustrated Sporting and Dramatic Life's* Christmas annual *Holly Leaves*, 1891)

Abraham 'Bram' Stoker (1847–1912) was born in Dublin, Ireland. Often ill during his childhood, he spent a lot of time in bed listening to his mother's grim stories, sparking his imagination. Striking up a friendship as an adult with the actor Henry Irving, Stoker eventually came to work and live in London, meeting notable authors such as Arthur Conan Doyle and Oscar Wilde. Stoker wrote several stories based on supernatural horror, such as the gothic masterpiece *Dracula* which has left an enduring and powerful impact on the genre, creating one of the most iconic figures that horror fiction has ever seen.

H.G. Wells

The Red Room

(Originally published in *The Idler,* 1896)

Herbert George Wells (1866–1946) was born in Kent, England. Novelist, journalist, social reformer and historian, Wells is one of the greatest ever science fiction writers and, along with Jules Verne, is sometimes referred to as a 'founding father' of the genre.

With Aldous Huxley and, later, George Orwell, he defined the adventurous, social concern of early speculative fiction where the human condition was played out on a greater stage. Wells created over 50 novels, including his famous works *The Time Machine*, *The Invisible Man*, *The Island of Dr. Moreau* and *The War of the Worlds*, as well as a fantastic array of gothic short stories.

Edith Wharton

Mr. Jones

(Originally published in *Certain People*, 1930)

Edith Wharton (1862–1937), the Pulitzer Prize-winning writer of *The Age of Innocence,* was born in New York. As well as her talent as an American novelist, Wharton was also known for her short stories and designer career. Wharton was born into a controlled New York society where women were discouraged from achieving anything beyond a proper marriage. Defeating the norms, Wharton not only grew to become one of America's greatest writers, she grew to become a very self-rewarding woman. Writing numerous ghost stories and murderous tales such as 'The Lady's Maid's Bell', 'The Eyes' and 'Afterward', Wharton is widely known for the ghost tours that now take place at her old home, The Mount.

A Selection of Fantastic Reads

A range of Gothic novels, horror, crime, mystery, fantasy, adventure, dystopia, utopia, science fiction, myth, folklore and more: available and forthcoming from Flame Tree 451

Categories: Bio = Biographical, BL = Black Literature, C = Crime,
F = Fantasy, FL = Feminist Literature, G = Gothic, H = Horror, L = Literary,
M = Mystery, MF = Myth & Folklore, P = Political, SF = Science Fiction,
TH = Thriller. Organized by year of first publication.

1764	*The Castle of Otranto*, Horace Walpole	G
1786	*The History of the Caliph Vathek*, William Beckford	G
1768	*Barford Abbey*, Susannah Minifie Gunning	G
1783	*The Recess Or, a Tale of Other Times*, Sophia Lee	G
1791	*Tancred: A Tale of Ancient Times*, Joseph Fox	G
1872	*In a Glass Darkly*, Sheridan Le Fanu	C, M
1794	*Caleb Williams*, William Godwin	C, M
1794	*The Banished Man*, Charlotte Smith	G
1794	*The Mysteries of Udolpho*, Ann Radcliffe	G
1795	*The Abbey of Clugny*, Mary Meeke	G
1796	*The Monk*, Matthew Lewis	G
1798	*Wieland*, Charles Brockden Brown	G
1799	*St. Leon*, William Godwin	H, M
1799	*Ormond, or The Secret Witness*, Charles Brockden Brown	H, M
1801	*The Magus,* Francis Barrett	H, M
1807	*The Demon of Sicily*, Edward Montague	G
1811	*Undine*, Friedrich de la Motte Fouqué	G
1814	*Sintram and His Companions*, Friedrich de la Motte Fouqué	G
1818	*Northanger Abbey*, Jane Austen	G
1818	*Frankenstein*, Mary Shelley	H, G
1820	*Melmoth the Wanderer*, Charles Maturin	G
1826	*The Last Man*, Mary Shelley	SF

1828	*Pelham*, Edward Bulwer-Lytton	C, M
1831	*Short Stories & Poetry*, Edgar Allan Poe (to 1949)	C, M
1838	*The Amber Witch*, Wilhelm Meinhold	H, M
1842	*Zanoni*, Edward Bulwer-Lytton	H, M
1845	*Varney the Vampyre*, Thomas Preskett Prest	H, M
1846	*Wagner, the Wehr-wolf*, George W.M. Reynolds	H, M
1847	*Wuthering Heights*, Emily Brontë	G
1850	*The Scarlet Letter*, Nathaniel Hawthorne	H, M
1851	*The House of the Seven Gables*, Nathaniel Hawthorne	H, M
1852	*Bleak House*, Charles Dickens	C, M
1853	*Twelve Years a Slave*, Solomon Northup	Bio, BL
1859	*The Woman in White*, Wilkie Collins	C, M
1859	*Blake, or the Huts of America*, Martin R. Delany	BL
1860	*The Marble Faun*, Nathaniel Hawthorne	H, M
1861	*East Lynne*, Ellen Wood	C, M
1861	*Elsie Venner*, Oliver Wendell Holmes	H, M
1862	*A Strange Story*, Edward Bulwer-Lytton	H, M
1862	*Lady Audley's Secret*, Mary Elizabeth Braddon	C, M
1864	*Journey to the Centre of the Earth*, Jules Verne	SF
1868	*The Huge Hunter*, Edward Sylvester Ellis	SF
1868	*The Moonstone*, Wilkie Collins	C, M
1870	*Twenty Thousand Leagues Under the Sea*, Jules Verne	SF
1872	*Erewhon*, Samuel Butler	SF
1874	*The Temptation of St. Anthony*, Gustave Flaubert	H, M
1874	*The Expressman and the Detective*, Allan Pinkerton	C, M

1876	*The Man-Wolf and Other Tales*, Erckmann-Chatrian	H, M
1878	*The Haunted Hotel*, Wilkie Collins	C, M
1878	*The Leavenworth Case*, Anna Katharine Green	C, M
1886	*The Mystery of a Hansom Cab*, Fergus Hume	C, M
1886	*Robur the Conqueror*, Jules Verne	SF
1886	*The Strange Case of Dr Jekyll & Mr Hyde*, R.L. Stevenson	SF
1887	*She*, H. Rider Haggard	F
1887	*A Study in Scarlet*, Arthur Conan Doyle	C, M
1890	*The Sign of Four*, Arthur Conan Doyle	C, M
1891	*The Picture of Dorian Gray*, Oscar Wilde	G
1892	*The Big Bow Mystery*, Israel Zangwill	C, M
1894	*Martin Hewitt, Investigator*, Arthur Morrison	C, M
1895	*The Time Machine*, H.G. Wells	SF
1895	*The Three Imposters*, Arthur Machen	H, M
1897	*The Beetle*, Richard Marsh	G
1897	*The Invisible Man*, H.G. Wells	SF
1897	*Dracula*, Bram Stoker	H
1898	*The War of the Worlds*, H.G. Wells	SF
1898	*The Turn of the Screw*, Henry James	H, M
1899	*Imperium in Imperio*, Sutton E. Griggs	BL, SF
1899	*The Awakening*, Kate Chopin	FL
1899	*The Conjure Woman*, Charles W. Chesnutt	H
1902	*The Hound of the Baskervilles*, Arthur Conan Doyle	C, M
1902	*Of One Blood: Or, The Hidden Self*, Pauline Hopkins	FL, BL
1903	*The Jewel of Seven Stars*, Bram Stoker	H, M

1904	*Master of the World*, Jules Verne	SF
1905	*A Thief in the Night*, E.W. Hornung	C, M
1906	*The Empty House & Other Ghost Stories*, Algernon Blackwood	G
1906	*The House of Souls*, Arthur Machen	H, M
1907	*Lord of the World*, R.H. Benson	SF
1907	*The Red Thumb Mark*, R. Austin Freeman	C, M
1907	*The Boats of the 'Glen Carrig'*, William Hope Hodgson	H, M
1907	*The Exploits of Arsène Lupin*, Maurice Leblanc	C, M
1907	*The Mystery of the Yellow Room*, Gaston Leroux	C, M
1908	*The Mystery of the Four Fingers*, Fred M. White	SF
1908	*The Ghost Kings*, H. Rider Haggard	F
1908	*The Circular Staircase*, Mary Roberts Rinehart	C, M
1908	*The House on the Borderland*, William Hope Hodgson	H, M
1909	*The Ghost Pirates*, William Hope Hodgson	H, M
1909	*Jimbo: A Fantasy*, Algernon Blackwood	G
1909	*The Necromancers*, R.H. Benson	SF
1909	*Black Magic*, Marjorie Bowen	H, M
1910	*The Return*, Walter de la Mare	H, M
1911	*The Lair of the White Worm*, Bram Stoker	H
1911	*The Innocence of Father Brown*, G.K. Chesterton	C, M
1911	*The Centaur*, Algernon Blackwood	G
1912	*Tarzan of the Apes*, Edgar Rice Burroughs	F
1912	*The Lost World*, Arthur Conan Doyle	SF
1913	*The Return of Tarzan*, Edgar Rice Burroughs	F
1913	*Trent's Last Case*, E.C. Bentley	C, M

1913	*The Poison Belt*, Arthur Conan Doyle	SF
1915	*The Valley of Fear*, Arthur Conan Doyle	C, M
1915	*Herland*, Charlotte Perkins Gilman	SF, FL
1915	*The Thirty-Nine Steps*, John Buchan	TH
1917	*John Carter: A Princess of Mars*, Edgar Rice Burroughs	F
1917	*The Terror*, Arthur Machen	H, M
1917	*The Job*, Sinclair Lewis	L
1917	*The Sturdy Oak*, Ed. Elizabeth Jordan	FL
1918	*When I Was a Witch & Other Stories,* Charlotte Perkins Gilman	FL
1918	*Brood of the Witch-Queen*, Sax Rohmer	H, M
1918	*The Land That Time Forgot*, Edgar Rice Burroughs	F
1918	*The Citadel of Fear*, Gertrude Barrows Bennett (as Francis Stevens)	FL, TH
1919	*John Carter: A Warlord of Mars*, Edgar Rice Burroughs	F
1919	*The Door of the Unreal*, Gerald Biss	H
1919	*The Moon Pool*, Abraham Merritt	SF
1919	*The Three Eyes*, Maurice Leblanc	SF
1920	*A Voyage to Arcturus*, David Lindsay	SF
1920	*The Metal Monster*, Abraham Merritt	SF
1920	*Darkwater*, W.E.B. Du Bois	BL
1922	*The Undying Monster*, Jessie Douglas Kerruish	H
1925	*The Avenger*, Edgar Wallace	C
1925	*The Red Hawk*, Edgar Rice Burroughs	SF
1926	*The Moon Maid*, Edgar Rice Burroughs	SF
1927	*Witch Wood,* John Buchan	H, M
1927	*The Colour Out of Space*, H.P. Lovecraft	SF

1927	*The Dark Chamber*, Leonard Lanson Cline	H, M
1928	*When the World Screamed*, Arthur Conan Doyle	F
1928	*The Skylark of Space*, E.E. Smith	SF
1930	*Last and First Men*, Olaf Stapledon	SF
1930	*Belshazzar*, H. Rider Haggard	F
1934	*The Murder Monster*, Brant House (Emile C. Tepperman)	H
1934	*The People of the Black Circle*, Robert E. Howard	F
1935	*Odd John*, Olaf Stapledon	SF
1935	*The Hour of the Dragon*, Robert E. Howard	F
1935	*Short Stories Selection 1*, Robert E. Howard	F
1935	*Short Stories Selection 2*, Robert E. Howard	F
1936	*The War-Makers*, Nick Carter	C, M
1937	*Star Maker*, Olaf Stapledon	SF
1936	*Red Nails*, Robert E. Howard	F
1936	*The Shadow Out of Time*, H.P. Lovecraft	SF
1936	*At the Mountains of Madness*, H.P. Lovecraft	SF
1938	*Power*, C.K.M. Scanlon writing in *G-Men*	C, M
1939	*Almuric*, Robert E. Howard	SF
1940	*The Ghost Strikes Back*, George Chance	SF
1937	*The Road to Wigan Pier*, George Orwell	P, Bio
1938	*Homage to Catalonia*, George Orwell	P, Bio
1945	*Animal Farm*, George Orwell	P, F
1949	*Nineteen Eighty-Four*, George Orwell	P, F
1953	*The Black Star Passes*, John W. Campbell	SF
1959	*The Galaxy Primes*, E.E. Smith	SF

New Collections of Ancient Myths, Folklore and Early Literature

2014	*Celtic Myths*, J.K. Jackson (ed.)	MF
2014	*Greek & Roman Myths*, J.K. Jackson (ed.)	MF
2014	*Native American Myths*, J.K. Jackson (ed.)	MF
2014	*Norse Myths*, J.K. Jackson (ed.)	MF
2018	*Chinese Myths*, J.K. Jackson (ed.)	MF
2018	*Egyptian Myths*, J.K. Jackson (ed.)	MF
2018	*Indian Myths*, J.K. Jackson (ed.)	MF
2018	*Myths of Babylon*, J.K. Jackson (ed.)	MF
2019	*African Myths*, J.K. Jackson (ed.)	MF
2019	*Aztec Myths*, J.K. Jackson (ed.)	MF
2019	*Japanese Myths*, J.K. Jackson (ed.)	MF
2020	*Arthurian Myths*, J.K. Jackson (ed.)	MF
2020	*Irish Fairy Tales*, J.K. Jackson (ed.)	MF
2020	*Polynesian Myths*, J.K. Jackson (ed.)	MF
2020	*Scottish Myths*, J.K. Jackson (ed.)	MF
2021	*Viking Folktales*, J.K. Jackson (ed.)	MF
2021	*West African Folktales*, J.K. Jackson (ed.)	MF
2022	*East African Folktales*, J.K. Jackson (ed.)	MF
2022	*Persian Myths*, J.K. Jackson (ed.)	MF
2022	*The Tale of Beowulf*, Dr Victoria Symons (Intro.)	MF
2022	*The Four Branches of the Mabinogi*, Shân Morgain (Intro.)	MF
2023	*Slavic Myths*, Ema Lakinska (Intro.)	MF
2023	*Turkish Folktales*, Nathan Young (Intro.)	MF
2023	*Gawain and the Green Knight*, Alan Lupack (Intro.)	MF

2023	*Hungarian Folktales*, Boglárka Klitsie-Szabad (Intro.)	MF
2023	*Korean Folktales*, Dr Perry Miller (Intro.)	MF
2023	*Southern African Folktales*, Prof. Enongene Mirabeau Sone (Intro.)	MF

New Collections of Ancient, Folkloric and Classic Ghost Stories

2022	*American Ghost Stories*, Brett Riley (Intro.)	H, G
2022	*Irish Ghost Stories*, Maura McHugh (Intro.)	H, G
2022	*Scottish Ghost Stories*, Helen McClory (Intro.)	H, G
2022	*Victorian Ghost Stories*, Reggie Oliver (Intro.)	H, G
2023	*Ancient Ghost Stories*, Camilla Grudova (Intro.)	H, G
2023	*Haunted House Stories*, Hester Fox (Intro.)	H, G
2023	*Indian Ghost Stories*, Dr Mithuraaj Dusiya (Intro.)	H, G
2023	*Japanese Ghost Stories*, Hiroko Yoda (Intro.)	H, G

A TASTE FOR THE FANTASTIC

FLAME TREE offers several series with stories from the distant past to the far future, covering the entire range of imaginative literature and great works that shaped our world.

From the fireside tradition of oral storytelling, early written versions of mythology (such as Norse, African, Egyptian and Aztec) emerge in the majestic works of literature of the Middle Ages (Dante, Chaucer, Boccaccio), the Early Modern period (Shakespeare, Milton, Cervantes) and the classic speculative tales by way of Shelley, Stoker, Lovecraft and H.G. Wells.

You'll find too, early Feminist adventure fiction, and the foundations of Black proto-science fiction literature from the 1900s.

Our short story collections also gather new tales by modern writers to bring together the sensibilities of humankind from the past, the present and the future.

Find us in all good bookshops, and at *flametreepublishing.com*